Alaska Twilight

OTHER NOVELS BY COLLEEN COBLE INCLUDE

THE ROCK HARBOR SERIES
Without a Trace
Beyond a Doubt
Into the Deep
Cry in the Night

THE ALOHA REEF SERIES
Distant Echoes
Black Sands
Dangerous Depths

Alaska Twilight
Fire Dancer
Midnight Sea
Abomination
Anathema

THE LONESTAR NOVELS
Lonestar Sanctuary
Lonestar Secrets
Lonestar Homecoming
Lonestar Angel (coming October 2011)

THE MERCY FALLS SERIES
The Lightkeeper's Daughter
The Lightkeeper's Bride
The Lightkeeper's Ball

Alaska Twilight

COLLEEN COBLE

THOMAS NELSON
Since 1798

NASHVILLE   DALLAS   MEXICO CITY   RIO DE JANEIRO

Published in Nashville, Tennessee, by Thomas Nelson. Thomas Nelson is a registered trademark of Thomas Nelson, Inc.

Thomas Nelson, Inc., titles may be purchased in bulk for educational, business, fund-raising, or sales promotional use. For information, please e-mail SpecialMarkets@ThomasNelson.com.

Scripture quotation is from The New King James Version®, copyright 1979, 1980, 1982 by Thomas Nelson, Inc., Publishers.

Publisher's Note: This novel is a work of fiction. Names, characters, places, and incidents are either products of the author's imagination or used fictitiously. All characters are fictional, and any similarity to people living or dead is purely coincidental.

ISBN 978-1-4041-7418-4 (SE)

Library of Congress Cataloging-in-Publication Data

Coble, Colleen.
  Alaska twilight / Colleen Coble.
      p. cm.
  ISBN 978-1-59554-083-6
  1. Alaska—Fiction. I. Title.
  PS3553.O2285A79 2006
  813'.54—dc22   2005023316

Printed in the United States of America
11 12 13 14 15 BTY 6 5 4 3 2 1

For my friend and editor Ami McConnell,
who has taught me so much about the craft of writing

Prologue

$\mathcal{T}$he tang of wood smoke and the scent of salt from Cook Inlet mixed as the breeze rolled in from the Gulf of Alaska. He sniffed appreciatively, then moved forward through wet leaves. He carried the can of kerosene toward the small cabin. A sound alerted him, and he shrank behind a spruce tree as the girl came hurrying down the path with her fishing pole slung over her shoulder. Her blond braids flying in the wind, she hurtled past within two feet of where he stood. As soon as she rounded the bend to the lake, he tightened his grip on the can and stepped onto the path again.

At least the girl was out of the way. She was an innocent in all this, and the fact she would be spared salved his conscience. He peered into the cabin window and saw the couple still asleep in bed. He narrowed his eyes and began to splash kerosene onto the weathered logs. The stink of the chemical opened his sinuses, and he stifled a cough.

The early morning chill pierced his shirt. He shook the last drops from his can, then set it down and drew out the box of matches. He pulled one out and struck it. As it flared to life, he stared at the flicker of flame. Did he have the courage to do what must be done? Even if he didn't, the consequences would be dire. With sudden decision, he threw it into the pool of kerosene and watched it ignite. When the wall began to blaze, he positioned himself by the front door with his rifle in case the couple managed to escape the flames. He needn't have feared though. The smoke overcame them before they could stumble from bed.

He collected the can and turned to leave, and his gaze connected with a woman's. Leigh stood on a hillside in the woods, her green eyes wide. On any other day she would have smiled at him. Today, she backed away. His sense of regret was keen as he advanced toward her to explain.

One

*S*talwart, Alaska. Population 301. Haley Walsh laid down her itinerary and looked down from the small plane in which she flew to see its shadow moving over the treetops—a forest of spruce, birch, and alder. Snow melted in puddles and revealed muddy land springing to new life in the lengthening days. Then the shadow caressed Stalwart, a tiny collection of cabins and storefronts. Even though it was April, the temperature wasn't more than forty degrees in this Land of the Midnight Sun, though she'd heard tomorrow would be warmer.

"It says here that Alaska has ten million lakes and a hundred thousand glaciers," Haley's grandmother said. At seventy years of age, Augusta Walsh's blue eyes sparkled with warm liveliness and curiosity. Most people guessed her age to be in the fifties, and her blond pageboy made her look like an older Doris Day, a resemblance she generally played to the hilt. "There are immense areas that have never had a human footprint, and thousands of mountains that have never been climbed."

Augusta's awed pronouncements just served to deepen Haley's fear. She swallowed hard and tried not to look down at the vast wilderness that yawned below her. The plane dipped, the lake below grew closer, and then the tiny craft touched the water. The plane glided to a stop beside a rickety pier that jutted into the water like an accusing finger.

"Let's go, go, go," Kipp Nowak bellowed. Everyone in the plane jumped at the sound of his foghorn voice, but he either didn't notice or didn't care. Only five feet five, his voice was the only large thing about him. Bruno Magli boots encased his small, slender feet, and his dark hair had been spiked into a careless style that would have suited a twenty-year-old but just deepened the lines around his blue eyes. He looked better on film than in real life.

Haley had watched his documentaries on TV for years. His antics with bears in Yellowstone had captured the American imagination for nearly a decade. Now she was going to take pictures of his next adventure herself. He'd maintained his adventurer's image by picking them up in Anchorage and piloting them out here himself. She settled back against the seat and pulled her camera, a Nikon f/5, up to her face. She adjusted the aperture to compensate for the glare of the glass, then snapped a few shots at the wilderness outside the plane. The familiar whir and click of the camera made her feel less out of her element, though her hands were still clammy.

"That's it, boys and girls. Your last glimpse of civilization for now." Kipp rubbed his hands together. "For the next few weeks, bears will be your companions. I've been here for a month with

Tank Lassiter to get the lay of the land as the bears emerged from their dens. Now that the wildflowers are ready to bloom, it's time to shoot. There are a couple of bears I'm eager to show you yet today."

No one said anything. They all knew better than to get Kipp started on his hobbyhorse. Haley shivered. Was she strong enough for this? Staring out the window at a wilderness that seemed to go on forever, she struggled not to give in to her doubts. She lifted her chin, then moved to get out of the plane.

Haley had consulted several Web sites before purchasing Seven jeans, a long-sleeved Rebecca Beeson T-shirt, and a Timberland wool shirt and jacket. The layered outfit was supposed to keep her comfortable no matter what the weather might do. She wore rubber Wellington boots, and though they weren't as stylish as she would have liked, they would keep her feet dry. She wore a pair of thin wool socks over her regular socks as well, because a local in Anchorage told her the temperature might well drop to the teens tonight. She liked fashion, but she knew better than to let it dictate her choices totally. Functionality was key in Alaska. She remembered that much.

"I thought we'd land in town," Augusta said. She looked around the clearing. "This is nowhere."

Kipp swung open his door. "We have plenty of supplies, so I didn't want to waste time in town. It's to our north, and the bears are to our south. This area is sheltered, and our plane can float here with no problem. We're in a good central location." He got out of the plane and moored it to the dock.

The rest of the crew began to clamber out of the plane. Haley rubbed slick palms against her jeans. She turned her head and felt the blood drain from her face, leaving her vision swimming. The barren trees were still devoid of leaves, and the starkness struck her with an ominous sense of lifelessness. She clawed at her camera and brought it up to her eyes. *Adjust the aperture, focus, center the photo.* The familiar tasks gave her perspective. The camera whirred as she snapped too many pictures to count. The action gained her enough emotional distance to ease her ragged breathing.

Augusta touched her hand. "Don't look at it yet," she whispered.

Easier said than done. Her hands shaking, Haley lowered the camera. "I'll be okay in a minute. It just caught me by surprise."

Augusta cupped Haley's face in her hands and looked deep into her eyes. "I'm so proud of you. You're brave enough to face it now."

She was in her Doris Day encouragement mode. Haley was in no mood for it. "I'm not being brave," she said. "I want my movies, my friends, the malls, and especially my powdered donuts. This is not my idea of a good time. I'm only here because my shrink said this would help bring closure, so I'm going to see it through. If I reconnect with Chloe, maybe the nightmares will stop."

Augusta's brilliant smile faded, and she dropped her hands. "God would help you more than ten shrinks."

They'd been over this a thousand times. Haley decided not to make it one thousand and one. She began to gather up her belongings. She slung her knapsack of photographic equipment over her shoulder, then grabbed her single suitcase and the carrier that held her dapple dachshund, Oscar.

Oscar yelped at the sudden movement and began to bark to be let out. Haley soothed the dog. She was thankful when Augusta grabbed her suitcase and exited onto the weathered pier without saying another word. Haley followed. Uneven ground was difficult for her to navigate, and the mud didn't help as she struggled to exit the plane.

She found her balance, though, and took in the scene. The lake was a surreal blue, as blue as Augusta's eyes. Haley stared at the amazing sight and the stand of spruce on the other side. Such a wild, untamed place. She shivered again. The lake and river drained into Cook Inlet to their south, and this airy forest with new moss and sprouting ferns appeared to be the end of the world. She opened the carrier and let Oscar out to do his business. The miniature dachshund dashed out and went to nose a patch of green breaking through a dwindling patch of snow.

Haley listened. The sound of rushing water and the chatter of birds overhead roared louder than any freeway noise. It pressed down on her like a heavy blanket. Vaguely familiar scents assaulted her as well—the last vestiges of melting snow, mud, wet moss, and the decay of last year's vegetation. It might appeal to some people, but for her, it just drove home the truth that she didn't belong here. She'd rather smell other humans and hear the sounds of civilization. She hurried to join the others among the litter of suitcases and boxes of supplies at the end of the dock.

"Ah, it's good to be back," said the producer-cameraman, Denny Saumik. "I grew up in Alaska, you know." His voice held a trace of Alaskan accent, an almost toneless quality. It looked like someone had put a bowl on his black hair, then cut it with jagged scissors. The small, smile-shaped scar above his left eye made him look like he was on the verge of asking a question at any moment. A tiny bear carved from some kind of bone hung from a rawhide string around his neck.

She hadn't known what to make of Denny at first. He never shut up. Her ears still rang from listening to him all the way from the Anchorage airport. But he was friendly and had immediately made her feel part of the team.

She dared to invite more conversation. "When were you here last?"

"About two months ago. My base is here, but I'm gone much of the year. I pop back now and again."

Haley nodded, then turned to look again at the pristine wilderness, though staring at the place made her feel like a no-see-um caught on flypaper. No place could be this beautiful—and remote. Rugged, snow-covered mountains looked as though they held up a blue sky that stretched to eternity and back. Water gurgled over rocks, a festive marching band of sound as spring thaw began its parade across the land. Timber crowded along the edge of the water and reflected in the broad pool.

It was the familiar place of nightmares.

Kipp clapped his hands. "Leave the stuff here for now, and we'll get camp set up later. The bears should be out feeding, so bring your cameras and come with me." He paused long enough for Denny to pull out his digital video camera and fit Kipp with a wireless mic. "Better leave the dog here."

Haley nodded and put Oscar back in his carrier, much to his

displeasure. She gave him his rubber hot-dog-and-bun toy for solace. Some people were touched in the head, and Haley was beginning to think she was one of them to have even agreed to come along. She met Augusta's gaze as they followed Denny and Kipp to the river. The roar of the rapids grew louder until the foursome stood on the steep bank looking down onto crystal water rushing over a small waterfall.

"There they are!" Kipp pointed out two forms standing along the shore.

Haley had missed the animals at first. She took a step back. She hadn't expected them to be so _big_. They were only ten feet away, and both turned at the sound of Kipp's voice. Haley said, "One of them is yellowish. I thought brown bears were brown."

Kipp ignored her comment. "Hello, bears, I'm back." Kipp approached them confidently.

Denny kept the camera running but answered Haley's question. "Brown bears range in color from white to blond to brown to black, and all the shades in between. The tips are lighter in color. That's what give them the grizzled effect." He stepped closer to Kipp.

Kipp spoke in a soft, confident voice. "I'm just going to watch you catch fish for a while. You're doing a great job."

The closest bear, the smaller of the two and the only one she'd really call brown, swung its head around and regarded him curiously, then waded into the rushing water. It ducked its head under the stream and came up with a fish in its mouth, then carried it to the shore. It sat down and held the wiggling fish in its paws and began to eat it.

"Good catch," Kipp said, approaching still closer.

Haley wanted to shout at him to stay back, but so far neither of the bears seemed to mind his presence. They were too intent on their breakfast, ignoring both the humans and each other. She finally recovered her wits enough to begin snapping pictures. Augusta sat on the riverbank and began jotting notes for the coffee-table book she had come along to write.

The smaller bear finished its meal. It settled against a tree and began to scratch its back against the rough bark. Haley watched in fascination. The other bear finally caught a fish and lumbered to shore with it. It sat down with its back to them and began to bat the fish around as if it were a toy.

"Bears are the brothers of my soul," Kipp was saying into the camera. "We have no need to fear them. They are benign creatures who wish to live in harmony and peace with us."

She would have laughed at that before today, but watching these bears, she thought he might be right. These two animals showed no signs of aggression. When the bears ambled to a berry patch and began to strip the brambles of fruit, Kipp picked some berries for himself.

"That's a wrap for tonight. Let's get camp set up," Kipp finally said. He strode back to their things, then led the group to a clearing.

"How many adventures have you gone on with Kipp?" Haley asked Denny.

"This will be the fourth. He's quite a ham. The more outrageous the stunt, the more the crowd loves it."

"Has he ever gotten hurt? Every time I watch the show, I hold my breath. Remember that show where he walked up to the buffalo in Yellowstone and jumped on its back? The thing bucked him off and turned to gore him. I thought he'd end up in the hospital at least."

"That one was a close call," Denny admitted. "He had a few stitches. The park rangers weren't happy, and I had to do some talking to get us back into the park to do another show."

"Why does he live on the edge like that?"

"He really believes in letting people know how important it is to connect with animals, for us to realize our spirits are connected and that we aren't so very different."

"Do you really believe that?" Augusta asked.

Haley slanted a don't-get-started glance toward Augusta. She'd heard that too-quiet tone before.

Denny gave a decisive nod. "My people believe everything has a spirit: the wind, the trees, the animals. We believe that animals, like humans, have souls that can think, feel, and interact. Animal spirits are no different from human spirits. We are all one, and sickness and bad fortune come when we disrespect the spirits of the forest or the animals."

Augusta gave her head a gentle shake. "Denny, there is only one God. Man is a custodian of the earth and its creatures. Sometimes we don't do a very good job, but we are the only one created in God's image. It distresses me when I hear us lumped in with every other creature on earth. God loves all his creation, but we're God's beloved children. We're special."

Denny dropped his gaze. "We'd better get moving." Haley sighed. Leave it to her grandmother to offend and alienate the team before they even got started. She had three months of this to look forward to.

They gathered up the luggage. Haley let Oscar out of his carrier to walk, then got her walking stick out of her pack and unfolded it. Denny eyed it but didn't say anything as they started off. She panted as she stumbled over rough ground with her burden. The stick saved her from a fall more than once.

From the corner of her eye, she caught a glimpse of the heavy forest and averted her gaze, looking instead toward the lake. She wouldn't look at the forbidding tree line, not yet. They passed Augusta, who paused to take in the scenery, and when she caught up with them moments later, Haley heard her sniffling.

Haley stopped and turned. "Are you okay?"

Mist and memories illuminated Augusta's blue eyes. "I'm fine, darling. It's just hard to be here and know your father won't come striding through the trees with that booming laugh of his."

Haley remembered that laugh. She nodded and moved to catch up with the rest of the group. She staggered several times on the uneven ground, and her thigh began to ache in spite of the walking stick. This was going to be harder than she anticipated.

The ground was beginning to green up. Oscar was distracted by every blade of grass. When Kipp stopped, Haley tossed her burdens on the ground, then dug out her book on Alaska's vegetation. "That's bog star," she said, pointing to a plant growing in a small clump with small, nearly heart-shaped yellowish-green leaves at the base. "And I think that's dwarf dogwood."

Kipp flipped his tent out onto the ground and began to put it together. "We might get some company tonight. This is a fairly well-traveled fishing trail for Natives on their way to Cook Inlet. You'll get a good taste of some of the characters who inhabit the land around here."

Haley wanted to tell him this area wasn't new to her, but it was none of his business. She itched to begin her photographic journey into the past. She watched him a minute, then pulled out her own tent. She had no idea how to put one of these things together. The instructions would surely be clear enough that she could figure it out.

A man stepped into the clearing. "Howdy, you folks must be new."

The man's suspenders curved up over a big belly covered in a wool shirt. The mud that caked his boots was a good inch thick. Twigs and spruce needles stuck out of his gray beard, but the hazel eyes above his bulbous nose twinkled with goodwill. A string of traps dangled from his right shoulder. He looked familiar.

Denny stood. "Hey, Mort. I wondered if we might run into you out here." He turned to the rest. "This is Mort Winters, the best trapper this side of the Kuskokwim Mountains." He stepped out and shook the trapper's hand. "We're here to shoot bear, but only with film. Any luck finding that lost gold mine yet?" He grinned.

Mort Winters. Haley's tight grip on her emotions began to slip. She hadn't thought of Mort in twenty years. He was older now, with new lines around his eyes. The Alaskan winters had deposited age spots on his forehead and cheeks.

"No gold mine yet, but I'm still looking."

"What gold mine?" Kipp demanded.

Denny jumped in with an explanation. "Legend has it that a Russian miner from Kenai found a rich lode. He had all the gold bagged up and ready to take to town, but hit his head and lost his memory. He never found the mine again."

"If he lost his memory, how did he know there was a gold mine?" Kipp asked, chuckling.

"Ah, that's part of the big mystery." Denny's smile widened.

Mort's hazel eyes glanced around the group, then locked on Augusta. "Augusta Walsh," he said softly.

"Hello, Mort," Augusta said. The tartness in her voice could have spiced a cherry pie. "Still chasing an empty dream, I see."

"You're still as beautiful as ever." His eyes drank her in, then shifted sideways to Haley. His gaze flickered. "Haley? My little Lucy is all grown up."

Haley had forgotten about that. He used to read *The Lion, the Witch and the Wardrobe* to her when she was little. She was Lucy, and Chloe was Susan. She barely remembered the story anymore. "It's been twenty years, Mort. I'm surprised you recognized me."

"You look just like your mother."

"Thank you." Haley knew he meant it as a compliment, but it meant nothing to her. His gaze flickered back to Augusta, and Haley could see the hunger in his eyes. He'd never been willing to give up his search for gold for Augusta. Augusta wouldn't take second place to ambition when she held love for God and family to be of highest importance. She'd spoken of Mort the night Haley graduated from college, then never again. The Walsh women were nothing if not single-minded. At least they had that in common.

Mort cleared his throat. "Looks like you need some help with your tent." He dropped his own gear and got to work. He had their tent up in five minutes. Haley watched how he did it and thought she might manage next time. "Thanks, Mort." She crawled inside and rolled out her sleeping bag, then did the same with Augusta's before stepping back outside. She looked at the sky. Though it was nearly ten at night, the sun was just now starting to set.

Mort shifted from one foot to the other. He glanced at Augusta, but she didn't look at him. "I'd better be moseying back to my cabin. I'll be seeing you around." He nodded at them, then picked up his traps and vanished into the forest.

"Let's turn in. We can explore tomorrow," Kipp said. He disappeared through the small opening.

Haley glanced back at her grandmother. Augusta smiled and lifted the flap of the tent. "Let's get some sleep, darling. You look done in."

Augusta still looked fresh. Haley ducked into the tent. The flimsy walls offered no real protection, but it hid the looming forest and calmed her. She examined the tent fabric. "My book says not to touch the sides of the tent. If it rains, the oils on your hands will make the water leak through."

"I know, Haley. I'm not a complete idiot out here." Her grandmother patted her on the shoulder.

Haley stared at the sleeping bag—a top-of-the-line Western Mountaineering—with disfavor. She had thought they would be able to go to their cabin the first night. And there was no bathroom out here. Would she dare go out in the middle of the night if she needed to use the toilet? And could she even sleep on hard ground? She was used to a pillow-top mattress.

Her grandmother opened her sleeping bag, sat down and pulled off her boots, then scooted inside. "Sleep well, darling."

"Aren't you even going to talk about Mort?"

"What's to talk about? What might have been was a lifetime ago. He's not a Christian, and our lifestyles are too dissimilar. It would never have worked. I see that even more clearly now. God saved me from a terrible mistake twenty years ago." Her serene voice held no disappointment.

Haley studied Augusta's face. "You're serious."

"Completely. I have the Lord, you, my work. What more could I want? I've had a full and happy life, Haley. Now get some sleep and quit worrying."

Easier said than done. Haley looked around. At least the tent had a floor. She unzipped her satchel and pulled out a copy of *Primitive Wilderness Living and Survival Skills*. She opened the cover and looked at the table of contents. Chapter 1 was on brain-tan buckskin. Ick. She glanced through the chapters. They covered everything from making fires to building structures. Not that she planned to need such skills, but she intended to be prepared.

Augusta propped herself on one elbow. "I figured you would bring a how-to of some kind with you. What do you need to know? Maybe I already know it."

"Nothing yet. I just want to be prepared." Haley closed the book with a snap that made Oscar look at her. She took off her boots, then released her prosthesis and rubbed the stump of leg that ended just below the knee. The skin looked good, much to her surprise. She'd expected it to be red and chapped. It felt good to be free again.

She slipped into her sleeping bag. Oscar burrowed next to her, his warm little body a comfort even though he was wiggling. "Night, Augusta."

"You're a brave girl, Haley," her grandmother said softly. "Where do you want to start your tribute to Chloe?"

"Kipp says we'll be shooting the bears during early morning, late afternoon, and evening hours. That will leave me midday free to go to the cabin and to town to see the old haunts. I thought I'd start at the cabin." She wet her lips.

"I'll go with you the first time. It will be hard." Augusta studied her granddaughter's face.

"Hard, nothing. I have this as a reminder every day of my life that I killed my sister." She slapped the prosthesis lying beside her.

Augusta's face softened. "It was an accident, Haley. I hate it when you say that."

Haley shrugged. "My parents blamed me until the day they died, Augusta. They sent me away and never forgave me for something I did when I was eight years old. Now *that* was hard, but it made me stronger. I learned that I don't need approval from anyone. I can stand on my own."

"But you never really engage life, Haley," her grandmother said softly. "You observe it from there behind the lens of your camera. That's not strength. It's a twilight kind of existence that turns away from the light of truth."

Haley turned her back to her grandmother. "I'm tired, Augusta. Good night."

Augusta didn't answer for a long moment, then she finally sighed. "Good night, darling."

Haley shifted numerous times on the hard ground. Strange sounds echoed through her tent. She was used to horns blaring and tires rolling on concrete. At least these noises were all harmless.

Two

*H*aley blinked, not sure what had awakened her. The quality of twilight had changed to a strange golden haze from the full moon. She tossed in her sleeping bag, then sat up and rubbed her eyes. Her bladder was uncomfortably full, and she knew she was going to have to go out. Her muscles clenched at the thought. Could she awaken Augusta and ask her to go along? She rejected the thought as soon as it came. Her grandmother needed her rest. Haley had to do this on her own.

She glanced at the soft illumination of her watch. Three in the morning. She reached into her backpack and grabbed the biodegradable toilet paper she'd brought. Feeling along the bottom of the pack, she found the small shovel. Her hand touched her camera, and she grabbed it too. She never felt whole without the camera around her neck.

She pulled on her prosthesis, then her boots, and then crawled to the tent opening and thrust back the flap. Her warm breath fogged the frigid air as she peered out. The odd light from the full moon cast everything in a strange yellow hue. An owl hooted overhead, a mournful sound that brought an involuntary shudder. She stepped outside and nearly slipped on the ice that had formed over the puddles in the path. Skirting the other tents, she shuffled toward the woods.

Her book had forewarned her of everything except how disorienting it was to be out here in the middle of the night with strange sounds coming at her from all directions. The darkness made every bush loom in strange shapes. She managed not to scream when a porcupine lumbered from under a bush to investigate the sound of ice crackling under the tread of her boots. Every sound seemed amplified. She told herself she was a big girl now, not an eight-year-old.

When she finished, she gathered up her things and turned to go back. The moonlight glittered on the lake in a halo. She tilted her head and observed the effect. This was why she was here. She brought her camera to her face and began snapping shots. The whir of the camera released the tension in her shoulders. She stepped into the clearing and kept snapping pictures. She stopped and listened. She heard . . . people talking. At this hour? She instinctively turned and snapped a few more pictures. In the distance near the woods she saw two figures, but they were too far off to make out any features. The two men—at least she thought they were men—seemed to be arguing. Kipp and Denny? She stepped back and lost her footing in the loose shale. Their acrimonious voices fell silent when they turned at the clatter of rock and saw her. She hurried back to her tent. It was none of her business if those two chose to argue.

Haley and Augusta packed up their things, and the group traipsed along the trail to where they'd been told the cabin would be available. It was halfway between last night's campsite and their real destination by the river. The path—if you could call the faint muddy impression a path—meandered through Sitka spruce rainforest and through meadows where the wild-flowers were beginning to poke up through the last of the snow cover. Haley remembered how the long spring days once made her think she could almost watch the foliage grow. She consulted her book often as a pastime and identified fireweed, larkspur, and lowbush cranberry. It took nearly two hours to cover two miles before finally arriving at the clearing where their cabin sat. She caught teasing glimpses of the blue water through a break of white spruce, and she could hear the gentle sound of the surf on Cook Inlet.

Haley stopped in the clearing to catch her breath and look around. She eyed the stark cabin. The four-room structure seemed to be in good repair. The weathered logs looked freshly chinked. Kipp stepped to the door of the cabin and flung it open. "Here we are. The rest of the crew has been filming the area as the snow melted and the ice floes broke up. We've gotten some good coverage of snowmelt and some opening den scenes. I've given them a week off, and they're going to Anchorage for a little R and R. They'll meet back up with us in Stalwart next week."

Haley and the rest of the team crowded in behind him to take a look at their base. The common room was small—barely fifteen feet square—and it held several small camp chairs, an assortment of kerosene heaters and lanterns, a couple of coolers, and boxes of supplies. In the tiny kitchen, a small camping stove stood on a rough wooden table, and a stack of unwashed metal plates teetered on the counter. Kipp obviously hadn't cleaned up after himself. Haley exchanged a knowing glance with Denny.

Haley and Augusta explored the rest of the cabin. The first bedroom was hardly larger than a closet and contained only two cots and a wooden table, which held a cracked washbowl and pitcher. It was a wonder someone hadn't broken in and stolen the meager furnishings.

"Nice," Augusta murmured, a wry twist to her lips. She stepped into the room and dropped her satchel on the dirt floor. "We'll take this one."

Haley glanced into Augusta's face and noticed the dark circles under her eyes. "Are you okay?"

"Of course. I'm just tired like everyone else. How about you? Are you going to hold up all right? This isn't exactly Scottsdale."

"It's only for twelve weeks. I can stand it." In spite of her brave words, she wondered how she could get along without Nordstrom and Ann Taylor for a whole summer. No concerts or plays, no fine dining or museums. A dismal lump settled in her stomach.

Her grandmother smiled. "At least the sales will be starting when we get home."

"You read my mind." Haley forced a cheerful tone into her voice. "Which cot do you want?"

Augusta shuddered. "Neither looks comfortable. Or clean."

"You can put your sleeping bag on top."

Augusta studied her face. "You're taking this well."

"You haven't got my bill yet." She grinned and turned back to the common room, then went to find Kipp. "When do we meet with Tank Lassiter?" she asked.

Glaze spiked Kipp's hair, and every strand had been carefully placed for maximum casual effect. She supposed someone in the public eye had to think about those things. Kipp's gaze skittered away. Even after only two days in his company, Haley was beginning to realize he only imparted as much information to his team as he deemed necessary.

He waved his hand. "Let's get this stuff put away, then we can worry about Lassiter."

"I don't like the sound of that. Is he a problem?" She picked up a box of canned goods and walked to the cupboard with it. Numerous scars and wounds gouged the pine cabinets. She opened the doors and shoved items inside. The stink of dirt and mildew began to give her a headache.

Kipp still didn't answer her. A gust of wind blew in, and she realized the door was open. The cabin suddenly seemed darker. Haley turned to see a big man blocking the doorway. His shoulders spanned the breadth of the door. Shaggy black hair fell across his broad forehead and looked as though it needed a trim. He wore jeans tucked into hiking boots and a red and black wool shirt. Paul Bunyan, transplanted from Minnesota to Alaska. His scowl was as dark as the shadow he cast across the room.

Oscar yipped at him once, then scooted behind her. The dog peeked past her pants leg at the big man. When the man's gaze raked her, Haley took a step backward and nearly stumbled over her dog. She wouldn't want to get on this guy's bad side.

"Good morning, Tank. The team was just asking about you." Kipp held out his hand with a winning smile.

This was Tank Lassiter, the famous wildlife biologist? He looked like he'd be more comfortable hewing trees than documenting the bear population. His hands were as big as bear paws, and she wondered what size shoe he wore. *At least a fifteen,* she thought, eyeing his boots. Maybe his name was a nickname and not his real name. He looked like a tank. Dangerous and impervious to hurt.

Tank's dark brows lowered over piercing blue eyes, and he looked even more ferocious. "You lied to me, Nowak." He threw the paper in his hand to the floor. "You said you were here studying the effect of global warming on the bears' hibernation patterns. Now I find that's not it at all. You're here to do a documentary—see the great Kipp Nowak hand-feeding the bears? See how strong and brave he is? See how bears aren't dangerous?"

Kipp didn't wince at his derisive tone. "I *am* here to study the effects of global warming as well. I saw no need to tell you the full scope until I was ready."

"You mean until you went around my back and got the cooperation of my superiors," Tank said. "You'll have tourists thinking they can waltz in here and pet the bears."

"Your boss at the Alaska Department of Fish and Game has given me permission to stay as long as I want and to film as many bears as I want." His victory smile flashed. "I'll need your services for the next twelve weeks."

Tank curled his big paws into fists at his side, and his jaw hardened. "So I've been told. But I'll not have any bears put in jeopardy by any of your stunts. I went to the Anchorage library and watched some of your videos. You're not a scientist; you're a menace. You won't pull any of those shenanigans with my bears. No touching or feeding the bears here. Is that understood?"

Kipp smiled. "You're blowing this all out of proportion, Tank. No one is going to get hurt. Not us or the bears. We're all going to have a fun summer. You'll see. For a big man, you've got a lot of fear. Let go of it and see how free you are."

Tank's mouth dangled open; then he seemed to realize it. He snapped it shut without a word, spun on his heel, and stomped out.

Kipp followed him as far as the doorway. "I'll be over later today. You're to give us your full cooperation," he called. He shut the door with obvious satisfaction. "He'll cooperate now." He glanced around the room. "Let's go looking for wildlife this afternoon. Maybe a wolf or an eagle."

The last thing Haley wanted to do was to watch him gloat. "Maybe later. This place needs cleaning before I can sleep here."

Kipp frowned. "I'll be back in a while. Anyone want to go with me?"

"I'll tag along. I might get some ideas for the text." Augusta grabbed a notebook and followed him.

"I like your grandmother," Denny said. "How many books has she written?"

"Nearly fifty. Her travelogues, some biographies, and her famous zoo books."

"She's a cool lady."

"She can be demanding. She likes things to run her own way." Haley opened the box marked *Cleaning Supplies* and lifted out a bottle of Mr. Clean. The burly man on the front reminded her of Tank Lassiter minus the mop of wild hair. "Did you know we were going to run into objections from Lassiter?"

"Nope. Kipp likes surprises." Denny grabbed a roll of paper towels and glass cleaner. "I call dibs on the windows."

"Bless you," Haley said. If he was trying to get on her good side, he was succeeding.

Denny went toward the hand pump at the sink. "We need some water to prime this. You got a bottle anywhere?"

"Probably somewhere." They'd had one of these growing up, but Haley didn't remember it looking so much like an alien creature. Or some kind of torture device. She shuddered.

Denny gave the pump a few experimental pushes. "It sure takes me back. We lived in a shack with a sod roof. Had a pump like this."

She looked at him again. Really looked. "Do you ever miss that life?"

He shrugged. "It was a lot simpler. We wore caribou clothing—over our Levi's of course—and ate what we killed. There was no endless cycle of materialism. I should show you my seal carvings sometime. But in the end it wasn't enough for me. I love what I create on film."

She hadn't seen his work yet. "I'm sure it's very good." She looked at the pump. "So you know how to prime this thing?"

"Sure. Get me some water."

Haley nodded and went to the bedroom, where she found

Augusta's water bottle. She returned to the kitchen with it. Denny took it and poured the rest of the water into the pump. "Now try it."

After a few attempts, cold water began gushing out. It looked like rusty mud and smelled like nails. Haley recoiled. Where she came from, water was clear and summoned by the twist of a tap.

"We're in business," Denny said.

"You don't seriously propose we drink that." Haley hefted the handle again. More water gushed out, but this time it was a little clearer.

"If we pump it a few more times, it will clear up." Denny took over, and the water soon looked more normal. He held Augusta's empty plastic bottle under the flow and filled it, then handed it to Haley. "See how it tastes."

"I'm no guinea pig. You try it."

"Well water is good. You'll like it."

Haley grimaced and took the bottle. It looked okay. She took a cautious sip, then spit it into the sink. "It tastes like rust mixed with rotten eggs."

"Well water has minerals in it. Think of it as a One-A-Day vitamin." Denny pumped the handle and quickly cupped his hands under the flow before it stopped. He bent his head and slurped at the water in his palms. "Delicious. You'll get used to it."

Never. Haley would endure it, but she wouldn't like it. She set the bottle of water down.

Denny grabbed a battered pan and pumped water into it. "Now we heat this so I can clean. You want to do it?"

"Do I look like Suzy Homemaker?" She smiled to take the sting out of her words. "This looks like a propane gas stove. You might see if it works." She found an old broom and swept the floor, then scooped the debris onto a piece of cardboard. She and Denny worked steadily. The menial labor helped Haley keep from thinking about the burned cabin, but she knew she was going to have to face it sooner or later. Preferably later.

Two hours later her stomach growled, and she realized it was lunchtime. The cabin looked good though. "I think I'll have a cup of soup." Denny had cobwebs and dust in his hair. Haley didn't want to look too closely in case the cobwebs were occupied.

"Sounds great," he said. "Should we fix something for Kipp and Augusta?"

"You can if you want. I didn't come along to be a personal maid and cook. My job is to chronicle Kipp's contact with the bears." And make her peace with Chloe in the hope that the nightmares would cease.

Tank Lassiter wanted to break something, but he always made every effort not to let his strength get out of hand. Throwing a chair through his cabin window would scare his daughter. Five-year-old Brooke sat coloring at the rustic kitchen table. Sunlight dappled her hair as she bent over the book with an absorption that made him smile. She'd be six in four months.

Tank panted as he did two more lunges with his weights. Perspiration dripped down his back and face. The muscles in his legs bulged with the strain. He set his weights down and grabbed a towel to wipe his face.

"Hard day?" His sister, Libby Lassiter, sat cross-legged on the braided blue and yellow rug that covered the center of the hard plank floor. She was restringing the cello across her lap. "You haven't said two words since you came charging in here like a bull moose and went straight to your weights." The aroma of beef stew—a trifle burned—hung in the air. He grabbed a towel and wiped the sweat from his face.

"I'm going to have to babysit an idiot who thinks bears are cuddly animals that can be tamed. I met him a few weeks ago, but he didn't tell me what he was *really* here for. I just found out he'll be here all summer to make a documentary that shows how safe bears are. We'll have tourists being mauled next year, you mark my words. I don't have time for this. I need to be tagging bears and working on my own research. Have you ever heard of Kipp Nowak?"

Libby's eyes widened. "*The* Kipp Nowak? Have you been living in a cave? Oh, I forgot, you have." She giggled. "My dear obtuse brother, Kipp Nowak is a crazier version of Steve Irwin, only with bears. I can't believe you've never watched him. He's a wild man. Totally fearless. And the bears never hurt him. He's yummy."

Tank snorted. "He's at least fifty—way too old for you." He gave her a thoughtful look. "Speaking of yummy, maybe his viewers would relish the sight of a bear eating him. Maybe I could arrange that." She made a face just like he thought she would, and he grinned at her.

"Twenty years isn't too much of a spread," she said loftily. "He might be looking for someone to help him stay young."

Libby's grin told her brother she was being deliberately annoying to coax him out of his mood. "I'll be glad to introduce you," he said.

"Is he by himself?"

He shook his head. "A young woman was there with a camera around her neck. I imagine the man is the producer. Maybe a cameraman. I don't know what the older lady does. He didn't introduce them. Either way, it's the usual hodgepodge of weekend nature lovers."

Libby looked suddenly eager. "Maybe I'll take them some cookies. It's been awfully boring around here lately. You don't talk much, and sometimes I get hungry to do more than answer Brooke's constant barrage of questions."

"Cookies? Or hockey pucks?" He grinned. She stuck her tongue out at him.

When Leigh died a year ago, Libby gave up her cellist seat with the Philadelphia Orchestra and came to help him raise Brooke without a murmur. Libby deserved fun and happiness, but it was a major effort to get to town several times a month for supplies. His gaze swept the cabin. These five rooms with their handmade furnishings were a small domain after the excitement of a big city.

Tank's smile faded. "I'm sorry, sis," he said.

"Don't look so guilty. I love being here with you and Brooke. But sometimes it's nice to meet new people. People who aren't covered by fur and hibernate, I mean." Her grin widened.

"You need to get married and have some kids of your own." He winced inwardly at his faux pas. It was a touchy subject. Her fiancé had not been happy when she came up here. He broke off the engagement.

She looked away. "There's time for that later. I'm not ready to settle down yet." She stood and looked out the window. "Hey, Chet is here."

"Brooke, Grandpa's here," Tank said.

"Gramps?" His daughter dropped her crayon and slipped down from her chair. She ran toward the door and tugged at the doorknob. He joined her and opened the door.

Trooper Chet Gillespie lumbered toward the steps like a genial moose. Dressed in his blue uniform, his belly hung over his gun and holster. His smile broadened when he saw his granddaughter. "Hi, munchkin. Come give your old Gramps a hug." He stopped and caught Brooke when she launched herself into his arms.

She wrapped chubby arms around his neck and kissed his cheek. "You're not old, Gramps. You're vintage. Aunt Libby says vintage means classy and worthy instead of old and decrepit."

Chet laughed. "Vintage, huh? I'll go for that. You're too precocious, Brooke." He nodded at Tank. "What a week."

"Trouble in town?" Tank stepped back to allow his father-in-law to enter with Brooke in his arms.

"Just busy. The town is swarming with search-and-rescue workers and their dogs in for a training exercise. They'll be in town for several weeks. And a couple of youngsters broke into the mine by the Walsh archeology dig. Said they were looking for the lost gold." He grinned.

"The boys should talk to Mort. He'd tell them he's already combed every inch of land out here." Alaska was steeped in legend—some of it true, but much of it not. The legend of the lost Russian gold mine was one of the myths that wouldn't die, in spite of the lack of proof.

Chet grinned but didn't look at Tank.

Tank's senses went on alert. He took Brooke from Chet's arms. "Hey, sweetheart, why don't you and Aunt Libby go get me and Grandpa some coffee and cookies? Grandpa looks hungry."

Libby frowned, then looked from Tank to Chet. "I could do with a cookie myself. How about you, Brooke?"

"Mommy said sweets are bad for my teeth. But I'll get you one." Brooke took her aunt's hand, and Libby guided her to the kitchen where they couldn't overhear.

Chet wore a pained expression. "She looks so much like Leigh. I was afraid she'd forget about her."

"If anything, she talks about her mom even more now. I don't think this is a social call, Chet. What's up?"

Chet slowly reached into the pocket of his jacket and brought out an envelope. It looked official, and Tank's gut tightened. He didn't need any more blows. Losing his wife a year ago had grieved him enough for a lifetime.

Chet extended the envelope, but Tank didn't reach out to take it. "I'm sorry, Tank," Chet said. He laid it on the table. "Marley is suing you for custody of Brooke."

"What?" While Tank hadn't known what to expect from the official-looking document, this possibility had never crossed his mind. He balled up his fists. "Can't you stop her? And what lawyer would take a case like this? She doesn't stand a chance."

Chet pressed his lips together so hard they turned white. "I tried to talk her out of this, but she was beyond listening. She and Leigh were so close—twins usually are—and losing her seems to have changed Marley in ways I can't do anything about. If her mother were still alive, maybe she could get through to her. Her lawyer is a sorority friend from college. She's always catered to Marley."

Tank couldn't seem to get his mind around it. "It's not like I neglect Brooke or anything." His sister-in-law had been vocal in her opinion that it was dangerous for Brooke to be raised out here. He and Leigh used to roll their eyes at Marley's overprotectiveness.

"She blames the wilderness for killing Leigh and doesn't want the same thing to happen to Brooke."

There was more Chet wasn't telling him. Tank could feel it. "What else?"

Chet sighed and rubbed his forehead. "She intends to move outside once she has custody. To New York."

"She can't do that! I'm Brooke's father. She needs to be with me." He remembered the moment he first held Brooke. Her small face was red, and her mouth was screwed up into a little bow. A tuft of dark fuzz stuck out from the top of the yellow quilt Leigh's mother had made. She'd been as light as a handful of cottonwood seeds when the midwife placed Brooke in his arms, and a wave of protective love had nearly choked him. His daughter was totally dependent on him and Libby. Now Brooke was all he had left. They were a family. What was Marley thinking?

"I'll have to talk her into dropping the case. She can't take Brooke away from me." He would be lost without his daughter. She was the glue that held him together. He wanted his daughter to grow up to love God and have more original thoughts than new shoes and designer handbags. Marley had no interest in spiritual things.

Chet's head wagged like he was trying to clear it. "Good luck. She seems set on her course."

Tank had never gotten along well with Marley. She thought him too far beneath her sister. Her dreams for Leigh hadn't included living in a cabin with no electricity and only a hand pump for water. Her attitude had added to Leigh's discontent with their marriage once the stars wore off. Maybe he even blamed Marley a bit for Leigh's death. His wife's dissatisfaction had caused the restlessness that drove her to the lake.

He'd rather face a mother bear than his sister-in-law's contempt, but it had to be done. "Do you know where she is? I'll go talk to her now," he told Chet.

"You can't. She flew to Seattle this morning. She won't be back in Anchorage until next week. In the meantime, you'd better find a lawyer." He shuffled and looked away. "For more than just the custody thing."

"What do you mean?"

"She's got connections at the department. She talked Ed Bixby into taking another look at Leigh's death. Sorry, buddy." He blinked moist eyes.

The Alaska Department of Public Safety was Alaska's primary law enforcement and public safety organization. It comprised four divisions: the Division of Alaska State Troopers, the Division of Fire Prevention, the Division of Statewide Services, and the Division of Administrative Services. In towns too small for a police department or in rural areas, the Alaska State Troopers held jurisdiction, and unlike most states, there was no sheriff's department. Tank had thought the DPS probe was behind him. Trooper Ed Bixby, sent to Stalwart from Anchorage to investigate Leigh's death, had been loud and vocal in his opinion that Tank murdered Leigh, but most people knew it for the sour grapes it was: Leigh had broken off her engagement to Ed when Tank moved to Stalwart. Bixby took a post in Anchorage shortly after. He'd managed to get her body exhumed two months ago for an autopsy, though the results weren't back yet. With Marley pushing him, he was apt to get louder still.

"When is Ed coming?"

"Probably tomorrow. He'll be wanting to take a fresh statement from you."

"I have nothing to hide."

"You don't have to defend yourself to me."

Was Chet's staunch assurance too hearty? Tank examined his father-in-law's face and found nothing but unswerving faith. Tank wished he could be as certain that he was blameless in the unhappiness that led to Leigh's death. "Marley's attorney will be formidable. Even though she's an old school chum, Marley doesn't settle for second best. I'll have to run up to Anchorage and see who I can find."

"I'd recommend Garth Jagger. He's pretty good. Young and full of passion."

Tank took a notepad off the counter and jotted down the name. "Thanks. I'll give him a call." Could this day get any worse? He had to babysit Pretty Boy Nowak, and now this. But no one was taking his baby girl from him. If he had to disappear into the bush, that's what he'd do.

Chet nodded. "Check with the office. We probably have his number on file." He hesitated. "You haven't seen Joe around, have you?"

Dr. Joe Wooten was the town doctor. Tank shook his head. "Not since I stopped by the office last week and asked him about the sleeping pills Libby found under the area rug. Why?" Libby had found a brown, unmarked packet of pills under the large rug when she was moving the bedroom furniture. Dr. Wooten had identified them as a common sleeping pill. It raised questions among them all that maybe Leigh killed herself, that she deliberately took sleeping pills and then walked into the water. He didn't want to believe that. Neither did Chet.

Chet frowned. "His wife says he's been gone for two days. She expected him back from a fishing trip late last night. He never showed up. What did he say about the pills?"

Tank shrugged. "That he never gave them to Leigh, and that he didn't believe she was in a state of mind to hurt herself. He suggested maybe they dropped out of her mom's purse one day when she was here." Queenie had died of a heart attack while taking a bath three months before Leigh died.

"Yeah, that's probably it. Queenie took them occasionally when she had trouble sleeping. Well, if you see the doc, tell him his wife is gunning for him." Chet grinned.

Tank nodded, only half listening. He could hear a commotion outside—birds squawking, the sound of metal falling. He went to the door and threw it open. A brown bear nosed the bear-proof trash bin at the end of the driveway. Tank recognized the notch on the bear's ear. Miki. He hadn't seen the bear he'd raised from a cub since last fall. Miki's fur was mottled and scruffy from hibernation, and he was thin. Tank was tempted to find the bear some food, but that wasn't the best thing for Miki. This was the bear's second summer on his own, and he needed to learn to be wild.

He grabbed an old garbage-can lid he kept handy to scare the bears off and banged on it with his fist. "Get out of here, Miki!"

Miki's head swung around. Black flies hung around the bear's head, but he didn't seem to notice. He lumbered toward Tank as if the noise didn't bother him. Tank backed away. Miki had never shown any sign of viciousness, but he was still a wild animal. Tank had been careful not to try to domesticate the bear, but Miki was a lovable beast. The bear continued on, and Tank gave up the fight and stepped into the cabin.

"He still doesn't get it that he's a bear and you're a man," Chet observed. "I hope it doesn't get him in trouble at the park. The first time he charges a tourist, the rangers will shoot him."

It was Tank's big worry. He had to find some way to help the young bear forget his human contact. If it could be done. Most bear biologists recommended destroying orphaned brown-bear cubs because of the danger they posed to humans after being inured to contact with them. He'd disregarded that order and bottle-fed Miki after his mother was shot by poachers, but was it the right decision? Tank watched out the window as Miki nosed around the front door, then ambled back toward the woods and the lake. Good. Maybe he'd see fishing was a better way to get food than to raid the garbage can. He'd better follow, staying downwind of Miki.

He opened the door. "Eat some cookies with Brooke. I'll be right back." He pulled the door shut behind him and moved downwind of the bear. He kept Miki in sight as the bear made a beeline for the lake. Traveling this route took him within sight of the cabin where the four visitors were staying. Seeing Kipp and the older lady wandering the partially thawed meadow angered Tank again. He didn't know how he was going to get rid of them.

He skirted the clearing and walked for about fifteen minutes. A movement caught his eye, and he saw the pretty young photographer walking toward the burned cabin at the edge of the lake. She had her head down and was watching where she put her walking stick instead of looking where she was going. That kind of behavior could get her killed in this land. He changed course to intercept her.

Three

Several birds called from the evergreen trees to Haley's left. She thumbed through her wildlife book. Killdeer. She craned her neck and looked up at the birds, then fumbled in her pack for powdered-sugar donuts and nibbled on two of them before throwing the birds some crumbs. The powdery sweetness melted on her tongue. The birds chattered and flew down to eat the bits of donut. She looked around for her dog, but he'd vanished under the tree boughs.

Haley looked around. She'd always heard things were smaller in reality than children perceived them to be, but that was wrong. To her, reality was larger. The trees were bigger, darker. The sky was bluer and wider. She didn't remember the spruce having such a sharp scent or the air having such an edge.

Where had Oscar gone? "Come on, Oscar. Stay with me." Oscar raced out of the trees, then threw himself onto the ground. He wiggled himself into a position for a back scratch on the cool mat of spruce needles. She wanted to laugh at the expression of doggie delight on his face, but she was too tense. She patted her leg, and the little wiener dog trotted happily to her. She laid down her walking stick and picked him up, taking courage from his warm body and the energetic kiss he gave her. Cradling him under one arm, she picked up her stick and continued on the familiar trail.

She crested the hill, and some burned remains came into view. Fireweed grew through the charred logs. A part of the roof still stood, though most of it had fallen into the center of the cabin. Green moss grew on much of the spongy remains. It was the same and yet different from what she'd expected. The last time she'd seen it, window boxes held bright flowers waving in the summer breeze, and a pile of freshly cut logs lay heaped around the tree stump where her father chopped wood. If she closed her eyes, she might still be able to hear the ring of his axe and smell the sharp tang of wood smoke. Maybe even ghostly laughter would reach her ears as the little girl she used to be played hide-and-seek with Chloe. It was so long ago, and yet just yesterday.

She put down the dog and pulled her camera to her face, then snapped a few pictures. Her wild imagination cooled, and she could see the cabin for what it was again—the sad remains of what once was. She dropped her camera to her chest and advanced to the doorway. It probably wasn't safe to go farther. It wouldn't accomplish much either. These blackened ruins held no trace of what she'd hoped to find here. There were no mementoes, no long-lost chest of old pictures or belongings. No whisper of the spirits of her parents.

She pulled up her camera and snapped a few more shots.

Beyond the cabin, she could see the lake. Its blue shimmer would have been the last thing her mother saw. The thought didn't move her in spite of her deliberate attempt to make herself feel something about the death of her parents. She moved to the tree stump that poked up through the snow. Axe-blade gouges marred the top of it. She stepped on top of the stump and gazed at the view. The hum of insects buzzed around her in spite of the repellent she wore. She felt alone. Abandoned for the final time. But what else had she expected?

Oscar began to bark, as ferocious a sound as she'd ever heard the little guy make. She heard an odd snuffle to her right and turned to look. Her eyes widened. A bear nosed at a rotten tree. Bees buzzed around its ears. The characteristic hump behind its head—a head as big as her back—told her it was a brown bear. The claws digging at the tree looked razor sharp. There was no place to run, no place to hide. Besides, it would do no good. A brown bear could run thirty-five miles per hour. She couldn't move anyway—she could only stare as the bruin took a step toward her. Any minute she expected it to stand on its back legs and roar at her.

She only hoped she was already dead before it began to eat her.

The bear moved toward her again. Oscar launched himself between the bear and her. "Oscar, come," she whispered. One swipe of the bear's paw would be the end of the little dog. The bear moved its head back and forth, then huffed. Oscar cowered and yelped, then tucked his tail between his legs and leaped into Haley's arms.

She held the quivering dog close but didn't take her eyes off the bear as it advanced slowly. She'd seen documentaries on TV that said bears wouldn't attack if you played dead. The information she'd read and heard said to either play dead or to make a lot of noise. She couldn't have pushed a squeak past her closed throat, but she could play dead if she could get her frozen muscles to obey.

Her eyes burned from her unblinking stare at the beast. She stepped down from the tree stump. Her movement caused the bear to stop. She knew she should fall to the ground and lie motionless, but she wanted with everything in her to run. She sank to her knees, then toppled facedown on the ground. She tucked the dog under her neck and covered her head with her arms. Oscar squirmed, and she tried to snatch him back, but he slipped out of her grasp. Barking, he ran around the bear, then stationed himself a safe distance away. She didn't dare call him back.

Breathing in the fresh scent of melting snow and wet mud, she lay motionless. The bear grew closer, and the pleasant aromas that had filled her nose were pushed out by its pungent stink. She heard it snuffle near her head. The dog continued to bark but from a safe distance. She expected to feel the bear's sharp claws on her back, to have its hot breath waft down her neck before it bit into her. She wanted to cry to God for help, but he hadn't been listening for years. Today would be no different. She closed her eyes and waited for death. Her heart pounded in her ears so loudly she could no longer hear the sound of the bear's inquisitive movements or Oscar's frantic barks. Something yanked hard enough on her sleeve that she yelped.

Then she heard a shout. "Get back, Miki! Go, shoo!" A shrill whistle pierced the air, then another longer one that hurt her ears.

The bear snuffled loudly, an agitated sound. He released her sleeve. She wanted to turn her head to see what was happening, but she was still too terrified to move. Moments later she felt a warm hand on her back.

"Are you okay?" The man's voice was rough with concern. He rolled her over gently.

She lay in a snowbank and looked up into the face of the Paul Bunyan she'd seen earlier. Tank Lassiter. A worried scowl hovered on his face. "You need a haircut," she said, then felt idiotic.

His scowl was replaced with a look of surprise that faded to amusement. "I'd guess you're all right if you're criticizing my hair." He grabbed her hand and hauled her to her feet.

"Sorry. I think I'm suffering post-traumatic stress disorder." She tried to smile and found it a bit wobbly. Her face crumpled, and she rubbed her forehead, willing herself not to cry. She couldn't think with Oscar continuing to bark. "Hush, Oscar. Come here." She patted her leg. Oscar snapped his jaws closed and scurried over to her as fast as his stubby little legs would allow. He plopped down at her side and looked up at her like an adoring lawn ornament.

"He was a lot of help," Tank said.

She gulped past the rock that had formed in her throat and looked around for the bear. "What happened to Big Ben?"

"That was Miki. I don't think he would have hurt you, but you never can tell with a bear. He's still a wild animal."

"Miki? You know this bear?" For a wild moment she imagined

him as Ranger Smith chasing Yogi and Boo Boo through the forest. She began to smile and had to cover her mouth with her hand.

He stared at her with his hands on his hips, a puzzled expression on his face. Oscar jumped up and began to yip and race around their feet. "Lucky for the mutt that Miki wasn't particularly hungry for wieners today."

She giggled harder and tried to stop. He would think she had a loose screw. There was nothing funny about almost being eaten by a bear.

"Are you sure you're okay?"

He was beginning to sound annoyed, and she knew he thought she was laughing at him. She snagged Oscar as he passed and finally managed to get her laughter under control. "I'm fine," she said. "Sorry about that. Laughter is my usual response to stress. Stupid, I know, but there it is."

"Hey, laughing is better than crying." His lips quirked up on the ends. He had a nice mouth. Not too full and not too thin. Firm, like he knew what he wanted out of life. She realized she was staring and looked away. "How do you know the bear?"

"I found him after his mother had been shot by poachers. Once he was old enough, I turned him loose. He's about three now. He still thinks he's half human, but wild animals are never truly tamed and can revert to their wild nature without warning."

The dog was wiggling in her arms, so she put him down again. Tank was going to think the dog was a yo-yo. She didn't like the way she felt stupid around him. "I've always heard bears that get too used to humans can be dangerous. Miki was yanking on my arm hard enough to hurt."

Tank frowned. "It's never safe to trust a wild animal. What are you doing out here?" he asked. "These ruins are dangerous."

"I was just looking around." She folded her arms across her chest. Turning to stare at the cabin again, she realized he might know something. "I heard a couple died in the fire here."

He propped a boot on the tree stump. "Yes, it was bad. A couple of archeologists who had worked this site for years died in the fire. Luckily, their daughter escaped injury. She'd gone fishing."

"Their—their daughter?" Haley stammered out the words. She was the only living daughter, and this was the first time she'd set eyes on this cabin in twenty years. "I thought their only child lived in the Lower Forty-eight."

Tank shrugged. "The father's daughter, I guess I should have said. Joy. She showed up about two years ago. She was about ten, I think. A lawyer brought her to the Walshes and told Grady she was his daughter. To Maggie Walsh's credit, she took the girl in and loved her like her own. I heard she looked a lot like the Walsh girl who died in a cave-in when she was little." He nodded toward the burned cabin. "Joy always maintained the fire wasn't an accident, but some folks say she's been a little touched in the head ever since."

Someone had taken Chloe's place. Haley knew she should feel something at the revelation that she had a half sister, but nothing stirred beyond mild curiosity. "How old is this girl?"

"About twelve now, I think."

And she looked like Chloe, according to Tank. Haley didn't see how that was possible. No one could be as beautiful as her little sister. Chloe was the perfect child, obedient and kind to everyone. Quite unlike Haley. "I'd better go," she said. She called Oscar, then turned and hurried away.

ß

Tank watched the woman snatch up her walking stick and rush off. Her auburn curls blazed as they caught the sun. He frowned as he realized he'd been thinking about the vulnerability in her amber eyes. She aroused his sympathy, but he wanted nothing to do with this group of glory seekers. He didn't trust her any more than he would trust Kipp.

He retraced his steps to his cabin. Several times he caught sight of Miki following him from the safety of the brush. He wished he knew what to do about that bear. The animal's persistent desire to be around humans was going to get him shot. Tank winced at the thought. He had to figure out a better way to orient Miki to being on his own. The bear was still too young to mate, so that angle wouldn't work. Right now Miki was solitary.

Kind of the way Tank felt. He reminded himself he had his daughter and sister. They were a definite blessing from God, and nothing was going to disrupt their lives—not even Marley's machinations. Someday Brooke and Libby would be gone too. The thought surprised him. If someone had asked him if he was happy, he would have said yes. He pushed the thought away. There was plenty of time to worry about that. Brooke would be around for another thirteen years at least.

He reached his cabin and realized Chet's truck was gone. He must have gotten a call to head back to town, twenty miles to the north. Though Stalwart was a tiny blip on the north side of Cook Inlet, the town always seemed to be hopping with transients, fishermen, and trappers passing through. Occasionally, cruise ships even stopped and sampled the town's wares.

He started toward the door and heard someone call his name. Turning, he saw Kipp and the older woman coming toward him. "Great," he muttered. He was in no mood to make small talk and pretend he wasn't irritated by the way the animal activist had finagled his way into the area.

Kipp's pale gray eyes were as cool as a winter sky, and his smile was no more warm. He introduced the woman as Augusta Walsh, Haley's grandmother. "Glad I caught you, Tank. I want to get started right away on the documentary. The bears should be coming out to feed later in the day. Where would you suggest we set up camp?"

"Don't you want to rest the first day?"

"Don't try to put us off. I'm ready to get started."

Tank wished he could walk away without another word. "I wasn't expecting you. I have some things to take care of today. I'll be over in the morning."

Kipp's eyes grew colder. "How far is this place you have in mind?"

"About a two-hour walk, though it may take longer than two hours with *cheechakos* along." Augusta looked blank at the word. "Greenhorns," he said. "We have some pretty challenging terrain to travel." But not nearly as challenging as working with this group. Tank realized he was taking a perverse pleasure in waiting for their reaction. It was hardly Christian, and he should be ashamed. The guy riled him, big-time. "We'll camp out a day or two at a time, then come back to our cabins for a day or two and go back."

Augusta grimaced and looked down at her mud-covered boots. "My feet already hurt."

"We saw a couple of bears earlier," Kipp said.

Tank saw the suspicion in Kipp's narrowed gaze. "You can find bears just about anywhere in Alaska. But if you want large numbers, we need to go deeper into the bush. I'll be over at six."

Four

 $\mathcal{J}$ anine Walker's office was a no-frills cubicle lined with books that made it smell like a library. The window behind the desk looked out on the Chugach Mountains. *Tenacious* had been used to describe the thirty-five-year-old female attorney, but Marley would have called Janine Walker *tough*. She was tough in high school, but college and experience had honed that quality to a barbed edge. Just what she needed. Her brother-in-law would be a formidable foe.

Marley Gillespie eyed her lawyer. "So the papers have been served?"

Janine nodded. "Your father took them out himself. Tank wasn't happy. He wants to talk to you. Can you handle him?"

"Of course." Marley wished she could get her hands on Janine to do something with that freckled, blotchy skin. And that black suit did nothing for her. She should be wearing khaki or army green. Marley folded her hands in her lap and studied her nails. It was time for a manicure. She would have one before she went back to the wilds of Stalwart. And a facial too. She'd need all her strength to withstand Tank Lassiter. "What's our next step?"

"The judge has ordered a home study. We can hope it will show Tank is gone too much to be a good father."

"How long before I can get Brooke and get out of there?"

Janine frowned. "I've told you this is a long shot, Marley. Most judges are reluctant to strip custody from a biological father."

Marley's temperature spiked, and she jerked her head up to stare at her attorney. "He killed my sister," she said fiercely. "I won't let him destroy Brooke's life too. Leigh wants me to do this."

Janine's long face softened. "Leigh is dead, Marley. You have to accept it."

This woman understands nothing about love and commitment, Marley thought. Janine was an only child. What did she know of sharing soft giggles in the night with a twin sister, of pacts to support one another forever? Leigh still came in the night, her soft voice begging Marley to save Brooke from Tank. And Marley intended to do just that—even if she had to break the law.

She rose and drew out her car keys. "Just take care of it, Janine. There'll be a bonus if you can get it done quickly."

"I may not be able to get it done at all," Janine said quietly.

Marley didn't answer. She stalked to the door and let herself out into a day overcast with dark clouds that matched her mood. If the law failed her, she'd take it into her own hands.

13

Haley followed the path beyond the charred cabin to the present dig. Out in the open field, she felt safer. In fact, some of her most pleasant memories were of digging in the dirt with her parents. She stopped and snapped a few pictures of the meadow where she and Chloe used to build snow forts. She found the fishing spot she and Chloe loved and took photos of that as well. The memorial scrapbook she planned was shaping up nicely. And so far, there had been no nightmares. Maybe her shrink was right.

A small cabin stood at the edge of the site. It hadn't been here when she was here last. A man shoveled dirt into a handmade sieve of wired screen in a wood frame, her father's favorite tool for finding small artifacts. She stood and watched him a few minutes. About forty, he had black hair that gleamed in the sun as much as the tanned and perspiring skin of his bare back.

He turned and saw her. His eyes widened, and he raised a hand in greeting. "Howdy. It's not often I get such lovely company out here." He grabbed a denim shirt that lay across the wheelbarrow and pulled it on. Still buttoning it up, he approached her. He wiped his hand on his jeans then thrust it out. "Ned Bundle," he said.

She shook it. "Haley Walsh."

His brown eyes studied her. "Walsh. You must be Grady and Maggie's daughter. You look too much like Maggie not to be related."

"That's right." Haley felt tongue-tied at the appreciation in his glance. She suppressed a nervous giggle.

"So sorry about your parents. It was a tragedy. They were brilliant. Thanks to their vision and insight, we know so much more about the first entries of humans into the Americas." He waved his hand over the site. "They are associated with one of the greatest migratory events of human history—the peopling of the New World. The first Alaskans who created these sites went on to spread across North and South America. As far as Native Americans are concerned, all roads seem to lead back to Alaska. It was the original homeland in the New World."

Haley blinked, and he laughed. "Sorry, I'm getting carried away," he said. "You can tell it's my passion. What are you doing here? Come to take your parents' place on the dig?" He gave a crooked smile full of hope.

"Not hardly. I'm a city girl myself. I'm here for the summer to photograph a bear activist. I just wandered over to see where I lived when I was a child." He didn't need to know more than that. She was quickly discovering her parents hadn't talked about her much. It wasn't likely she'd encounter anyone who knew much about her past.

"Too bad. It gets quite lonely out here. Can I show you around?"

She glanced at her watch. "Maybe later. The team is likely looking for me. I'd better get back. Nice to meet you." She could almost hear her father's voice behind Ned's passion for his work. She barely touched her fingers to his, then beat a hasty retreat.

She wandered down to the lake and walked out onto the rickety pier. She sat down to watch a family of loons paddle nearby. She and Chloe used to feed the loons here. She snapped some pictures. The memory sharpened as the smell of spruce mixed with the fresh scent of the lake. Oscar crouched nearby like a cat ready to pounce if the loons got close enough.

She curled her legs under her so they wouldn't touch the

water. She wasn't sure how to feel about the discovery that she had a half sister. Mostly, she felt numb. At least she'd found out something about her family. Maybe this Joy would be able to tell her more. The next time she saw Tank, she would ask him how to find the girl. She heard a child's voice and turned her head. Oscar left the loons and ran to meet the woman and small girl who approached along the path that skirted the lake. Haley stood as well and dusted off her jeans.

The young woman was near Haley's age and had a friendly, open face. Her dark-brown eyes widened when she saw Haley. "Hello," she said. "I hope I'm not disturbing you. Are you fishing?"

The little girl bent over and tried to pick up Oscar. "What a cute little dog," she said. Oscar's tail was wagging hard enough to fall off. He licked the child's face, and she giggled.

"Careful if you pick him up," Haley warned. "A dachshund has a weak back. You don't want to drop him."

"I know," the girl said. "I like wiener dogs."

She talked older than the five- or six-year-old she appeared to be. "Yes, he is," Haley said. "His name is Oscar."

"Just pet him," the woman told the child. She turned a friendly smile on Haley. "I'm Libby Lassiter."

Lassiter. She must be Tank's wife. Haley thought he'd have some Amazon woman to match his size, someone who could chop wood. This woman had curly brown hair that stuck out in all directions. Dressed in jeans, she was tall and slim, and her matching dark eyes looked Haley over with eager friendliness.

Though she wanted to be alone, she mustered a smile. "I'm Haley Walsh. I'm the photographer for the bear project."

"Oh, you're the ones who are putting that scowl on my brother's face." Libby smiled and held out her hand. "I'm glad to see another woman though."

Haley shook her hand and mentally catalogued her. *Sister, not wife.* "Your little girl is darling."

"She's my niece, not my daughter. Tank is her daddy."

So he *was* married. The little girl's shiny curls hung down her back almost like a raven Shirley Temple. She crouched beside the child. "What's your name, sweetheart?"

"Brooke." The little girl touched Haley's hair. "Your hair is like a penny. Coppery. You're very pretty."

"So are you." Haley smiled at her. "You look a lot like your dad."

The little girl's brow furrowed. "I want blond hair like my mom."

Oops, she'd transgressed. "Maybe it will change."

Brooke's smile came out again. "I made cookies. You can come back to our cabin and have some. They're a little burned though. Me and Aunt Libby were making music."

"That's a great idea, Brooke."

"I couldn't." Haley stood. "I couldn't impose."

"Not at all. I've been craving having another woman to talk to. It's not like you have anything else to do, right? The bear project can't go on until you have some bears to take pictures of."

"I already saw one, thank you very much." Haley laughed. "You probably know this one. Miki wanted to eat me."

Brooke's eyes brightened. "Miki is good, but he's not safe."

Libby smiled. "She's been obsessed with *The Lion, the Witch and the Wardrobe* since Tank took her to see the movie in Anchorage in January."

Haley dimly remembered reading the book. "I haven't seen the movie, but I read the book a long time ago. I wish I had it here, and I'd read it again."

"You can read my dad's. Daddy is going to read it to me when I'm six." She ran ahead along the path. Oscar barked and chased after her. Libby followed.

Plunging her walking stick into the ground, Haley glanced at Libby from the corner of her eyes. What could it hurt? Maybe she could learn something about her newly discovered half sister. "Have you lived out here long?"

"About a year. Ever since Tank's wife drowned. I came out to take care of Brooke."

"Oh, I'm so sorry." Hearing the big man had suffered a tragedy raised Haley's level of compassion for him. "It seems lonely."

"It is. Sometimes I talk just to hear a voice. Tank is out in the bush quite a lot, and it's just me and Brooke. I worry about her growing up with no friends or siblings. Tank needs to remarry and give her some playmates that way, but he's too consumed by his work. Besides, he rarely goes to town."

"How far is Stalwart?" Haley had been wondering how long it would take to get to town if she really needed to go.

"Twenty miles or so. But the roads aren't good. When it's muddy, he tends to get stuck. During the winter he uses the snowmobile if the temperature isn't too low."

So a trip to town wouldn't be an easy jaunt. Haley felt even more isolated. She'd hoped Kipp might eventually establish a base in town. At least they were close to the beautiful Cook Inlet.

If Phoenix were on the ocean, it would be perfect in all ways. "Are you ever scared out here?"

Libby smiled. "No, just hungry for girl talk."

They reached a clearing. Haley was getting pretty good at identifying vegetation. She examined the wildflowers. Banks of lupine, black lily, and deer cabbage created a pretty backdrop for the log home, though they weren't in bloom yet. Gingham curtains hung in the windows but did little to soften the harsh reality of the stark dwelling. There was no porch, just a bare door in front. Haley couldn't imagine living here.

"Come on in, I'll start the teakettle." Libby held the door open for her.

Haley shut it behind her as Libby went to the stove in the kitchen. "I'm not the best cook, but I can at least make tea." Haley's gaze wandered the room. The walls were painted a soft yellow, a color she loved. The blue and white gingham curtains added a cheery touch to the kitchen. Haley knew Libby would need all the cheer she could get through the long, dark winter months.

The kitchen and living room were one, an area about twenty feet square. A blue sofa and two yellow chairs sat on a rag rug on one end of the room. A set of weights occupied the far corner. A rough wooden table and chairs sat under one window with four open cabinets on one side. The bare necessities and not much else, though it felt homey and welcoming. A box of toys had been pushed against a wall by the couch. Three doors led to bedrooms. Maybe by cabin standards it was spacious, but it wasn't much by Haley's standards. She was used to carefully chosen pieces that reflected style.

Her gaze caught a cello in one corner. A miniature cello sat beside it. "You're a musician?"

Libby's face brightened. "I played with the Philly Orchestra. I'm teaching Brooke to play as well, and she has a natural aptitude. I'm afraid my poor brother has come home more than once to burned meals because of our passion for music and has had to make do with peanut-butter sandwiches."

Brooke went to a small bookshelf and brought a dog-eared copy of a book. "Here's my book."

"Thanks." Haley took the small volume. "I'll read it and get it right back to you."

Brooke smiled, then went to the toy box and began to root through her toys. She came up with a Frisbee. "Can I throw it to Oscar?"

"As long as you stay where we can see you."

"I will." She called to the dog, and they ran outside to the yard.

Once the tea was ready, Libby joined Haley at the table and sat where she could watch her niece through the window. She pushed a plate of cookies toward Haley. "I'm sorry these are a little burned. Brooke and I were playing Beethoven's *Ode to Joy*."

Haley smiled and selected a cookie. "Thanks. So how long do you expect to stay out here?"

Libby shrugged. "As long as Tank needs me."

She nibbled on the cookie. It tasted a bit charred. "Don't you resent giving up your career for him?"

Libby was silent for a moment. "I couldn't do anything less. He and Brooke needed me. There was no one elsc to care for Brooke. Marley, Leigh's sister, would never live here."

"Tank could move to the city."

"It would kill him. He couldn't study his bears in the city. At least I can still play my music here. And seeing Brooke's natural talent has been amazing."

"Is Tank his real name?" Haley shocked herself by asking the question she'd been wondering.

Libby giggled. "If I tell you the truth, I'll have to kill you."

Haley began to smile. "He's sworn you to that much secrecy?"

"I can't say I blame him."

The big man intrigued Haley. "You say his wife drowned? I don't imagine that's difficult in the lake. It's huge and looks bottomless. And cold." She shivered.

Libby stirred honey into her tea. "No one knows how it happened. Tank found Leigh floating face down in the lake just after dawn. She'd been dead several hours. She always wore a wetsuit, but she didn't that night. It might have been hypothermia."

"She was swimming in the middle of the night?"

"She loved to swim. Everyone said she could have made the Olympics if she hadn't married Tank. She'd been acting weird for a couple of days before, though. Ever since the Walsh cabin burned. Knowing she could do nothing to help them really upset her."

"I'm sorry, it's none of my business."

Libby smiled and patted Haley's hand. "Forgive me. It's been so long since I had someone to talk to, I'm running off at the mouth."

Haley pulled her hand away. "I'm glad to give you an afternoon of diversion." She studied Libby's face. Maybe Libby would know something about Joy. "I saw the burned cabin. Did you know the family that lived there?"

"I sure did. The Walshes." Her eyes widened. "Your family?"

Haley nodded. "My parents." She had to force the words out.

Libby looked stricken. "I'm so sorry. Here I am babbling on. Is that the real reason you've come? No wonder you were upset when I found you at the pier."

She nodded. "My shrink thought it was time I faced the past. When this job came along, my grandmother convinced me to take it. Augusta can be opinionated and pigheaded at times. She was like a pit bull, and I got tired of fighting her."

Libby snapped her fingers. "I just remembered. Your grandmother is Augusta Walsh, isn't she?

"You've read her books?"

"Read them! I own every travel book she's ever written. Her memoirs of her adventures in Africa are masterful. Had you ever visited your parents here?"

Haley shook her head. "I hadn't seen them for ten years, and it was almost twenty years ago when I was last here." A painful, awkward meeting that she'd vowed not to repeat if she could help it.

"Ten years! You never wanted to visit? Why didn't they go back to the Lower Forty-eight?"

"That's where I last saw them. Tank mentioned another daughter."

Libby studied her face. "You say that like you don't know her."

Haley looked away. "I don't. I had no idea I had a half sister until Tank told me a little while ago. What can you tell me about Joy?"

Libby sat back in her chair and exhaled. "I hope I don't offend you, but you have one strange family."

"I know. About Joy?"

Libby shrugged. "She was the light of their lives. I'd met your mom a few times before Joy came. She was always polite, but rather distant and dour. When Joy came, she bloomed. Kind of weird if you ask me. I wouldn't be blooming if my husband presented me with a love child. But Maggie seemed to dote on Joy. And she is a darling girl."

Haley winced. She couldn't help it. That was a position she'd longed for. And it was the place that had belonged to Chloe. "How old is she?"

"Twelve, almost thirteen now. They never told you?"

Not only had they never told her, but not even Augusta had mentioned it. "Where does she live?"

"In Stalwart with a relation of her mother's. She wants to finish school and go into archeology like her—er, your parents."

"Why wasn't she sent to my grandmother?" Augusta must have known. She couldn't imagine her father would keep it a secret from his own mother.

"You're going to have to ask your grandmother about that."

"I'd like to talk to Joy."

"I'm sure she'd love to see you. Your mom had an old album with pictures of the family in it. I never saw it, but Maggie said Joy loved to look at it."

"I wonder why she never wrote me?"

"You'll have to ask her."

"I'll do that." She had to learn all she could. Maybe her

mother or father talked about her or mentioned Chloe. Maybe she could finally find closure.

⁂

Haley's grandmother sat at the table with a pile of leaves in front of her. She was pressing them in a book she'd brought for that purpose. She looked up when Haley entered the cabin. "There you are. I was worried when I got back and you were gone."

Haley shut the door behind her. "I went to the cabin."

"Haley, I told you to wait for me." Irritation flashed over Augusta's face. She didn't like to be disobeyed.

Haley watched Augusta carefully flatten the leaves in the pages. How should she bring up the subject of Joy? Augusta had to know about this. She wet her lips. "Augusta, I heard about Joy today."

Augusta's fingers stilled, and she looked up. "Joy?"

"Don't lie to me, Augusta." She approached the table and knelt beside Augusta. "Why didn't you tell me I had a half sister?"

Augusta put the book down and stared into Haley's eyes. "I did what I thought was best. I tried several times, but in the end, I couldn't."

"Didn't you think I'd find out about her when we came?"

"I thought she was gone from the area, and I didn't think we'd get to town much. I'd hoped to find the right time to tell you. If I'd dreamed you would discover it within hours of our arrival, I would have prepared you. I'm sorry."

"Why didn't you seek custody when my parents died? Aren't you curious to meet her?"

Augusta closed the book. "The attorney told me her mother's parents were caring for her. I thought there was no need for me to intervene. I intended to check on her, of course, when I was sure you wouldn't be hurt." Her grandmother rubbed Haley's cheek with gentle fingers. "I love you, Haley. I couldn't let you worry that you would lose my love too. You're the most important thing in my life."

Haley's knee was cramping, so she stood, then dropped into the chair beside her grandmother. "I'm not sure what to feel, Augusta. I'm more upset for Chloe than for me. I got used to the rejection long ago. I hear this girl looks like Chloe, and even Mother accepted her in Chloe's place. I don't like it." Augusta was silent for so long, Haley began to think she wouldn't answer. After all, how could she argue against the truth?

"If Grady were still alive, I'd take a switch to him," Augusta said finally. "You can't let this eat at you, darling. Chloe's death changed them so."

"It changed us all."

Augusta nodded. "You most of all. I remember how adventurous you used to be. How curious. You bottled it all up after that. Only your pictures betray you. You hide behind the camera. Someday, you need to step out and be yourself again."

Haley heard the rest of the group talking and laughing as they approached the cabin. "Don't say anything to the rest of them," she said. She couldn't handle speculation and pity right now. Maybe never.

Five

What a motley-looking crew. Tank wanted to walk away as he surveyed the ragtag assortment of men and women assembled outside the cabin. Kipp had bags under his eyes, and he still reeked of beer, though he was clearly dressed for the camera. The producer's eyes drooped as he leaned against his backpack. Tank's gaze found Haley. Dressed sensibly in jeans and boots with layers of shirts, her auburn curls sprang from her head as though they were alive. Her pale complexion glowed with health, but her amber eyes looked shadowed. Augusta's slim figure was outfitted with as much common sense as Haley's was, though her clothes were obviously not as new as her granddaughter's.

His gaze traveled to the dog that peeked out of the pack on Haley's back. He frowned. "You're not taking that dog with you, are you?" He scowled at Oscar.

"Of course. We'll be gone too long to leave him behind."

"I doubt you'll see many bears with all the noise he makes," he said dryly. "We'd better get going if we want to be ready for the afternoon feeding frenzy." He adjusted the strap on his backpack and took off down the trail. He heard faint grumbling behind him.

"Hey, aren't you going to help haul the stuff?" Kipp called.

"You shouldn't be bringing more than one backpack per person. Everyone out here needs to pull their own weight. I suggest you stick your clothes in the middle of your sleeping bag." He saw Haley cover her mouth with her hand, but it didn't hide the amusement he saw in her face. Maybe she wasn't quite as bad as the rest of them, though if bringing that dog was any indication, she didn't have much more sense. He raked her with his glance. "And you've got two bags as well. You'd better be prepared to carry them yourself."

Her hand came down, and her gaze was as sharp as Miki's claws. "I'm used to handling my own equipment." She lifted her chin.

He supposed he'd been a little rough on her. Neither of her bags was large. The backpack probably held her photography equipment. "I'll wait fifteen minutes while you all repack and get it down to what you can handle on your own. We've got a two-hour hike, and it isn't a walk in Central Park. We'll be climbing rugged terrain and fording streams." His gaze caught Haley's again. She was sober this time, looking back at him steadily as if she could read his mind. The back of his neck prickled. He was at it again, judging others. He had no right. God was the judge, not him.

"Everyone have on a fresh coat of DEET?" he asked, his voice gruff. "The mosquitoes aren't bad yet, but they're starting to come out, and they'll be worse the farther into the bush we go." They all nodded. "Let's go then."

The group shouldered their packs and fell in line behind him. He noticed Haley's walking stick with approval. Clouds of insects flew up as they walked through the wet leaves and moist vegetation. Their feet kicked up an aroma Tank never tired of— spruce, ferns, moss, and wildflowers.

Sorry for his earlier bad humor, he lifted his head and began to sing "North to Alaska" in a deep baritone. He loved the old John Wayne movie, and the song never failed to lift his spirits. Maybe it would do the same for his traveling companions.

Haley plodded along, already too weary to do more than focus her gaze on the uneven ground. At least her fatigue kept the fear at bay every time a strange sound came to her ears. She hated it here. Hated it. She wanted to be back in her home with the familiar sound of traffic on I-10. She fingered the can of bear spray attached to her waist. Would she even have the courage to use it if needed?

Her head came up when Tank's rich voice began to sing. She studied the back of Tank's head. He almost sounded like Johnny Horton himself as his voice bellowed the song to the treetops. At the sound of the singing, Oscar came romping through the vegetation. He sat on his haunches, lifted his muzzle in the air, and howled along with Tank.

Haley laughed, then looked back to see Kipp roll his eyes. Her grandmother talked her into watching the film one night, and maybe the old movie was a little hokey, but she was enough of a romantic that she'd sighed over the happy ending. Tank intrigued her even more after his unashamed singing. He looked back and grinned. She looked away. There was something about him that raised the hair on the back of her neck. He epitomized the wilderness, untamed and unknown. It was part and parcel of him. She was just going to do her job and get out of here.

An hour later he stopped, and she didn't. She barreled into him, and her stick went flying. His broad back was hard. She rubbed her nose and stepped back. "Sorry," she muttered, her earlier mood returning. She wanted this shoot over with.

"Time for a break." He retrieved her stick, then shrugged off his pack and sat on it. They all collapsed behind him with soft groans. He pulled out a canteen of water and offered it to Haley, but she shook her head.

"I have my own." She pulled two plastic bottles of Perrier out of her backpack and offered one to Augusta. Augusta took the water with a tired smile of thanks. "You okay, Augusta?"

"I'm fine, darling. I'll be ready for bed tonight though."

Haley swigged some water and glanced at Oscar. "Better get a drink," she told him.

The small dog wandered over to Tank and sat at his feet with his tongue hanging out to one side. "I've seen you drinking from the mud puddles," Tank told him. "You can wipe that pleading look off your face."

Haley grinned. "I think you like him already."

He glanced at her briefly then looked back at the dog. "I

never said I didn't like him. I just didn't want him to get eaten by a bear."

"He won't." She chewed on her lower lip. "I have bear spray."

"Yeah, I noticed you using it yesterday."

She bit her lip harder. "Miki took me by surprise."

"That's generally what bears do. This is a hard, unforgiving land. There is no room for mistakes."

"I'll be on my guard next time." The back of her neck itched, and she swatted it. Her fingers came away bloody. "If these bloodsuckers are just getting started, what is the summer going to be like? These things are huge."

He grinned. "You've heard the stories of people needing a blood transfusion when coming from the bush without DEET? Believe them. We're stuck with these bloodsuckers until winter comes. They'll lessen some in July, but you pretty much have to wear insect repellent all the time out here. I buy it by the gallon."

"Lovely," she said with a sigh. She glanced away, then met his gaze again. "I met your sister and daughter yesterday."

"I know. Libby told me. Nice of you to spend some time with her. She gets lonely."

His tone was polite, and Haley thought he would like nothing better than to tell her to stay away from his family. "Have I offended you?" she asked softly.

The silence opened a gulf between them as wide as Alaska. Just when she thought he wouldn't answer, he glanced back at her.

"You're not going to be here long," he said. "Brooke is vulnerable. She chattered about you all evening. I don't want her to be hurt when you leave."

"I see." The last thing she wanted to do was to hurt that precious little girl, especially when she'd already suffered the loss of her mother. "I'll keep my distance." She dug in her pack. "She loaned me a book. You want it back now?"

"Finish it first. Brooke will want to know if you like it."

The chasm between them seemed to grow. Haley studied him with a sideways glance. What made a man come out here so far from creature comforts? His wife had died out here too. Did he feel he was to blame? Haley knew all about blame. They had that in common, if nothing else.

She stood and walked toward a small lake a few feet away. She was careful to keep the others in sight. The thought of being out here alone was enough to make her break out into a cold sweat. Oscar followed her. She found a flat rock and aimed it at a placid pool between two boulders. She flung it and counted as it skipped over the surface. Three times.

She dug in her backpack and got out a powdered-sugar donut. The sweet taste took her away from this place where the sky was too big and the land too terrifying. It reminded her that there was another land out there, home, a place she would soon see. She just had to get this job done, catalog Chloe's life, and get back to Phoenix. It wasn't like she had to live here the rest of her life. She could hack it for a little while longer.

Tank found it difficult to keep his stride slow and deliberate so he didn't lose the group. To their credit, none of them offered much complaint, and they did a fair job of keeping up with him.

To give Haley a break from the little wiener dog's squirming, he'd put Oscar in his own pack for the afternoon. The dog had his paws on Tank's shoulder and seemed content there.

Stepping over bear scat, he began to whistle to let any brown bears in the area know they had visitors. The flattened vegetation showed the imprint of several bears' passage through the lingonberry patch. "We're getting close," Tank said.

Haley shivered and looked around uneasily. "Are we setting up camp here?" She sounded hopeful.

Tank shook his head. "Just a little farther. This is a bear trail to the river. You don't want to be in their direct line of travel. It's too dangerous."

"No, right here." Kipp dropped his pack. "This is perfect. I want the chance to get close to them, show them I'm their friend and brother."

Tank felt his jaw drop, then tried to recover. "You are not their brother. You're a man. They're bears. They'll feel threatened and might attack." The condescension in Kipp's smile made Tank realize he wasn't getting through. He tried again. "They're wild animals, Kipp, not some family pet like Oscar here. You don't just walk up to a bear and introduce yourself." Haley frowned and glanced at Kipp.

"This is perfect," Kipp repeated. He unzipped his pack and began to pull out his tent, a high-dollar unit that looked practically new.

Tank's jaw tightened. "I'm setting up my tent fifty yards off the trail. Any of you who have an ounce of sense will join me there." Too angry to say more, he plunged off the trail in the direction of the river. He heard thrashing behind him and turned to see Haley and Augusta hurrying after him. At least the women weren't as stupid as Kipp.

"We watched two bears feeding yesterday. We were within just a few feet of them," Augusta said. "Now you're saying it's not safe to be so close. We don't know what to believe."

"Bears are wild animals, Augusta. They are unpredictable. There are certain things you can do to minimize the danger. One of those things is to not surprise them. You don't set up camp on a well-traveled path where they generally don't find men. I'll be surprised if their camp lasts the night. I doubt Kipp knows how to cache his food so he doesn't attract the bears. From what I've seen of him, he's liable to leave it out to feed them. He's just asking to be attacked."

"He may order us back," Haley said. "Denny stayed to try to talk him out of camping there."

"He may be a celebrity, but he doesn't have the right to get you all killed. This is no Sunday picnic," he said. "It's serious business. Bears don't usually attack if you give them space, let them know you're here, and don't challenge them. Kipp is doing everything wrong."

"I just want to go home." Haley tossed her backpack to the ground and sat on it. Augusta put her hand on her shoulder.

He'd picked up on her uneasiness in the bush. There wasn't much to say to someone who didn't see the beauty of the wilderness. "This clearing isn't quite as far away as I'd like, but we need to keep the others in sight. Toss me your tent, and I'll set it up."

"Can we assemble it in the tree?" She smiled, but her tone was half-serious.

"You'll be fine. I brought wind chimes to make a racket, and you've got Oscar to protect you. They may be curious and check you out, and that's okay. Kipp wants that to happen so he can video them for the documentary." He dumped the little dog out of his backpack. Oscar went to Haley and jumped into her lap.

"I'll gather some wood," Augusta said.

"I brought some protein bars." Haley rummaged in her pack. "Anyone else want one?"

"I'll take one." Tank knelt to begin assembling the tent.

Haley stroked the dog's head while her grandmother began to pick up wood. Haley's steady gaze never left Tank as he put their tents together. He piled rocks into a firepit.

"Why do we need a fire? It feels pretty warm today," she said.

"The smell will tell the bears we're here and keep the mosquitoes bearable, no pun intended." He grinned.

Her nervous laugh was too loud. Her gaze darted toward the thick forest of spruce. Was that a shudder? She didn't say anything, but she got up and began to pick up small logs at the edge of the clearing, though he noticed she didn't step into the forest itself. The pile she started by the firepit grew steadily. Dusting her hands on her jeans, she sat on a log. "Anything else?"

Before he could answer, a shriek rang out. It sounded like Augusta. The sheer horror in her voice made him fumble for the can of bear spray fastened to his waist. "Stay here!" he told Haley.

"Augusta!" She already had her can of bear spray in her hand. Though her eyes were dark and wide with terror, she snatched up her walking stick and ran after him. She matched him step for step as he ran toward the river. Brambles barred their path, and he thrashed through them and held them back for Haley. They broke free from the thorny shrubs and stumbled onto the mud that surrounded the river.

Augusta stood with her hands over her eyes. Kipp and Denny stood with their arms over their chests. They were staring at something on the ground. Haley ran to her grandmother, and Augusta turned into Haley's embrace.

"What's wrong?" Tank demanded. The men's ashen faces turned toward him. He paused to look around but saw no immediate danger. No bear or anything else threatening, just the gurgling river.

Denny wet his lips and pointed to the ground. "I think a bear got him."

"Stay here," Tank told Haley. He stepped past the men and looked at the figure on the ground. There wasn't much left of the man. Tank forced himself to stoop and examine the pitiful remains. From the prints around it and the evidence in front of him, Tank knew Denny's assessment was correct—a bear had attacked the man.

The bear had also partially buried the remains. Tank carefully dug around the body to reveal the face. He inhaled sharply. Joe Wooten. No wonder no one had seen the doctor for a few days.

"Who is it?" Kipp knelt beside him. He seemed to have recovered his composure.

"A doctor from town. I need to call Chet Gillespie, the trooper. I'll have to hike back to the cabin and use the radio."

"We brought a satellite phone," Denny put in.

That would save him a two-hour hike. Tank stood. "Show me. Stay away from the site."

"You don't have to tell me twice," Denny muttered.

They all went back to camp, and Tank placed the call to Chet's office. His father-in-law wasn't in, so he left a message on the machine. When he hung up, he found Denny and Kipp taking down the tents they'd put up.

"You heading back to the cabin?" Tank asked.

Kipp shook his head. "We'll join you off the path." His voice was deadpan, and he didn't look at Tank.

Tank decided not to comment or say, "I told you so." Maybe Kipp had learned a valuable lesson about bears today. "There's a clearing over here." He led the way to the meadow, where he found the women trying to get a fire started. Haley had a book in her hand that she was referring to. She laid the book down and picked up the axe and a piece of wood.

She pressed the blade on the wood. "It says to shave off small slivers, but this isn't working very well."

"You need some kindling and paper at the bottom." He took the axe and shaved slivers of wood from the driest log he could find and layered the kindling on top of the paper, then finally stacked logs on top. He was conscious of Haley's interested gaze.

"Making a fire looks like an art form," Haley said. "I would have figured it out though. The book had step-by-step instructions."

"Better to learn from someone directly than to read it in a book," he said.

"Don't you like to read?"

"Not really. I'd rather be out doing than have my nose stuck in a book."

"Everything I need to know can be found in a book."

"You must like to play it safe."

"There's nothing wrong with safety." She clasped her arms around herself.

"There is if it keeps you from really living." The newspaper flared and began to crackle. Moments later, the kindling took fire.

"I enjoy my life. I'm perfectly safe and happy in Phoenix."

Her words were a sharp reminder that she didn't belong here. He studied her face a moment, noting her paleness, as her gaze darted to the woods beginning to deepen with shadows.

"The wilderness has a compelling beauty if you take time to see it."

"It's savage and horrifying," she said. "I don't know how you stand to live here. And what about Brooke? What kind of life is it for her to grow up with no friends? Don't you worry about some kind of animal hurting her?"

"Now you sound like my sister-in-law," he said grimly. Tank clamped down on the anger that began to rise. "Brooke is happy and loves the woods."

"What about her musical ability? Libby says she has an amazing talent."

"And she has the best possible teacher in Libby. When she's ready, she can go to Juilliard or somewhere good." That day was eons away. Light years. He wouldn't lose his daughter for a long, long time.

"But what about your sister-in-law? She disagrees?"

"You might say that. She's suing for custody."

Haley put her hand to her mouth. "I'm sorry. That must be difficult for you. But surely she won't succeed."

"She has the judge in her pocket. There's no telling what will happen. But she's not taking my daughter."

"I believe you. You look ferocious." She clasped her arms around herself. "I could never live out here."

He wondered why she was so afraid. It was none of his business though. He turned to Kipp. "If you all want to rest for a while, I'm going to go try to catch some fish for supper. Chet should be here in a little while."

"I'll come with you," Denny said. "I love to fish."

The producer still looked pale and strained. Tank wondered if he was afraid of being left with Kipp and the women. "Bring your bear spray with you," he said.

Denny paled further, but he nodded and ducked into his tent, then emerged with a can of bear spray in his hand. "You have an extra fishing pole?"

"I've got some line. We can string up one for you with a branch. That's what I do." Denny followed him to the river.

Tank was careful to avoid the site where Dr. Wooten's body lay. He wondered how long it would be before Chet showed up. Probably another hour at least. He usually wasn't out of the office long. Tank was anxious to get Wooten's body examined. He held out a slim hope that a bear hadn't killed him. Maybe Joe had died of a heart attack and a bear had found him.

Miki was never far from Tank's mind. He didn't know what he'd do if they found his bear was to blame.

Six

*T*he sound of the plane's propellers cut off, and the craft slewed sideways, then touched down on the sandbar. The stink of plane fuel mixed with the fresh scent of the river as it rolled in white-capped waves toward the shore where Haley stood with the rest of the group. The line of spruce forest crowded behind her, its growth so thick it was hard to see a patch of sunlight strong enough to break through the overhead canopy.

A man in rubber waders hopped down from the plane and waded through the cold waves. Haley's eye took in his bulk, then lingered on the badge pinned to his chest. Another trooper and the pilot, all in waders, followed the big trooper to shore. They paused long enough to discard their waterproof garments.

"Nasty business." The first trooper mopped his florid, perspiring face with a large red handkerchief after the introductions were made. "Was it Miki?"

Tank's lips tightened. "Don't you think you'd better look at the body before you assume a bear got him—or that the bear was Miki?" He turned and stomped toward the body.

The trooper raised his eyebrows but followed without another word. The two other men trailed behind them. Shuddering, Haley turned her back on the men as they bent to examine the doctor's body.

She focused on listening to the gurgle of water over the rocks, the squawks of birds above her head, anything to block out the examination. Footsteps approached from behind her, and she turned to see Tank striding toward her.

"Haley, could we borrow your camera? Chet's isn't working." He held out his hand.

Haley's fingers tightened on the camera. "I never loan my camera. Sorry. Let me see if I can fix his."

His gaze grew steely. "We don't have a lot of time."

She knew he thought she was being unreasonable, but she lifted her chin and stared him down until he dropped his gaze. "Fine," he muttered. "See what you can do."

She motioned for the trooper to bring her the camera. He lumbered toward her, hitching up his pants as he came. "What's it doing?"

"The film isn't advancing."

She inspected it, and then grimaced and popped open the film cavity and showed it to him. "You have more film?"

He blinked, and his jaw tightened. He turned to the closest trooper. "Randolph, would you get me a roll of film from the camera bag?"

The pilot nodded and unzipped the bag, then rummaged through it. "There isn't any more film."

Gillespie looked back at Haley. "Would you have any extra?"

She shook her head. "Wrong kind of film. I use 35 millimeter, and this is an APS camera." Looking at their expectant faces, she tightened her hold on her camera. "I suppose I can take the pictures for you." She generally chose to photograph life in all its wondrous stages. This would be a departure for her. She just hoped she didn't throw up.

She kept her gaze on the trooper's broad shoulders and followed to where the doctor lay on the beach. A gag reflex built in her throat, and she fought it. *Be a professional.* Bringing the camera to her face, she was able to get some distance from the horror of what had happened to the man. *Click, whir.* She snapped several areas of the body that the trooper asked for.

Trooper Gillespie pulled on plastic gloves and knelt, then rolled the body over, and she photographed the other side. She kept herself from dwelling on the parts of the man that were missing.

Chet picked up hair and a loose bear tooth that had been under the doctor, then dropped them into a plastic bag. "We've got bear hair and claw marks in the dirt. I should take a cast. Randolph, go get the plaster. Take some shots of the bear prints, Haley."

Haley shot pictures until the camera began to whir in her hands as the film rewound. She popped open the back of the camera and extracted the film, then handed it to the trooper. "Is that enough?"

His big fist closed around the film. "Thanks. Nice camera you've got. Have you taken many pictures yet?"

"Not many. Just three rolls. I brought two hundred." She glanced at him. "Um, have you been a trooper here a long time?"

"Ten years. Long enough, I reckon." He took off his hat and mopped his forehead.

She glanced around and noticed no one else was listening. The other trooper bent over the bear tracks, and Tank and the pilot were engaged in putting the doctor in a body bag. "My parents were Maggie and Grady Walsh." He gave no indication of his surprise other than a flicker in his brown eyes. "What can you tell me about the fire that killed them?"

"Not much. That kind of thing happens out here. We suspect a spark from the woodstove started it, but there's no proof." Chet swatted at a mosquito. "I wondered what a city slicker like you was doing out here. You come out just to find out what happened to your folks?"

"Among other things. Just reconnecting." Her throat ached with the words she wanted to spill after looking into his kind brown eyes. There was much he could tell her about her parents. "You've lived here all your life?"

"I'm a sourdough. Been here about twelve years. Don't remember ever meeting you before."

"I lived here until I was a little over eight and haven't been back since." She clamped off the tap of memories that pushed toward the surface like a spring flower.

He raised his eyebrows at her revelation but didn't comment. "I wish I could help with more information, but all we know is that Joy came in from fishing to find the cabin engulfed in flames. It was seven in the morning. She ran to Tank's for help, but it was too late."

The stump of Haley's leg throbbed with a sudden pain. She glanced over at Tank and frowned. He was standing toe to toe with the other trooper. Both men had their fists balled and were in each other's personal space.

Chet swore. "I knew Bixby wouldn't wait like I told him." He sprang toward the two men.

Haley knew it was none of her business, but she followed him anyway.

"I loved my wife, Bixby, and I resent your insinuations otherwise."

"Even men who love their wives sometimes see other women." Trooper Bixby was only three inches shorter than Tank but not nearly as wide. He made no move to stand back from Tank's displeasure. In fact, the smile on his face seemed to suggest he relished it.

"I didn't." Tank ground out the words, then stepped back. "My wife's drowning was an accident."

"We'll see. The autopsy results should be back any day."

"You never got over her choosing me over you, did you, Ed? You had to go and make this a personal issue."

"She'd still be alive if she'd picked me. I intend to get to the bottom of her death." Bixby glanced toward Chet when the older man gasped. "Try to let me do my job, Chet."

Chet turned and crashed away. His face was a blinding mixture of grief and rage. Tank went after him. Haley wished she could comfort them both. Tank caught up with his father-in-law, and they stood talking in low tones. They both came back after a few minutes.

"Do what you have to do," Tank said to Bixby. "I have nothing to hide."

"I'd like you to come to town for a full statement in the next day or two," Bixby said.

"I have to come in for supplies. I'll drop by."

"Fine."

The troopers began to load the doctor's body on the plane. Tank went to help them. Haley stopped Chet when he started to follow the men with their burden. "I have one more question about the fire. Was there an autopsy performed?"

His smile faltered. "Nope. I didn't see a need for that. It was pretty clear how they died."

"Which doctor examined the bodies?"

Gillespie nodded toward the body his deputies were carrying toward the plane. "Dr. Wooten."

She winced. "Sorry. I didn't mean to question your judgment either. I would just like to know the details."

He mopped his head and put his hat back on. "Joe Wooten was highly respected in the community. I don't know how I'm going to tell his wife." He turned away, but not before Haley saw the sheen of moisture in his eyes. She hadn't stopped to consider what those who knew the doctor were going through. She watched the trooper plod back through the water toward the plane. His stooped shoulders spoke of the burden he carried.

Tank rejoined the group, and the plane took off. Haley limped a little as they walked back to camp. Tank gave her a quick look. "Got a blister?"

"No, I'm fine," she said shortly. The last thing she wanted was for them to think they had to give her special treatment because of her missing leg. She glanced up at his tight mouth and strained eyes. "This Bixby is going to be a lot of trouble for you, isn't he?"

"Nothing I can't handle," he said.

"Nothing God can't handle," Augusta corrected.

The strain around his mouth eased. "You're right, Augusta. I forget that sometimes. I want to do it all myself. Thanks for the reminder. He's got this all under control. Let's have fun tonight and forget this. I'll leave it in his hands."

Haley made a conscious effort to throw off her pensive mood. "So tell me something about bears. Something I don't already know."

"Oh, you're a bear expert? I had no idea I was in the presence of such a great mind." He grinned.

She grinned back. "I've read ten books on them. So I guess I know a lot about them."

"Somehow I'm beginning to see you think you can learn anything from a book."

"Name one thing you can't learn from a book."

He took her arm and led her toward the water. "Tell me what that is." He pointed to a disgusting mass on the ground.

"Excrement of some kind. Bear, I presume?"

"Bear scat," he corrected. "What's it tell you?"

"Um, I guess that a bear passed through here." She glanced at the water. "Maybe he was fishing here."

"Good guess. And that part's right. Look closely at the scat." He pressed on her back, and she resisted.

"I'm close enough, thanks." She wanted to giggle. Her stupid nervous habit.

He pointed at the scat. "First we take a sniff." He leaned over and inhaled. "No odor, so it's been here awhile, at least three weeks. And this bear had been eating mostly vegetation. I don't see any fur or flesh. He was probably searching for fish though."

"You can tell all that from looking? And, er, smelling?" Her smile widened. Tank was even more likable when he was in his element. A dimple flashed in his square-jawed face. She'd never noticed it before, but then he'd been focused on the seriousness of their trek.

"Can you tell if this is from Miki?"

His eager expression grew stoic. "No. Are you thinking about the doctor's death? I don't think Miki had anything to do with his death. There's no telling what happened, but I bet he died of something else. A heart attack or something."

"I hear worry in your voice. What will happen if they determine a bear killed him?"

"We'll have to find it and destroy it." A muscle in his jaw twitched.

"Even if it's Miki?"

"Especially if it's Miki. Several people in town—Chet included—warned me not to try to rehabilitate him. They've been predicting dire consequences ever since. I was determined to prove them wrong. I hope my pigheadedness didn't cost Dr. Wooten his life."

Seven

The first two days went well, or as well as could be expected with a man committed to pushing the bears beyond what was safe. Tank managed to keep Kipp a safe distance from the bears they saw, but he talked to the bears like they were his children, and more than once Tank had stopped him from trying to feed the browns. By six o'clock the second day, he was bone-tired.

Tank kicked out the fire. "Better get the foodstuffs stowed. The bears will be hungry and looking for dinner. We don't want them wandering through our camp."

"Sure we do," Kipp said. "I want to see all the bears we can."

"You'll see plenty of bears without making them mad they can't get at your food." Was there any way to get out of this assignment? Tank didn't have time to waste on fools. He needed to get back to his cabin so he could see if the lawyer had called him back. And he had to get to town to talk with Bixby.

Kipp's tone held a trace of superiority. "I know how to handle myself around bears. I've even touched them. They know when a man means them no harm."

Oh brother. If this guy wasn't dead before the summer was out, Tank would eat his hat. He decided not to respond. "The bears will be coming down to the river to feed anytime. I have a new spot to show you." He stowed the food in the cache and raised it into place in the fork of the tree. When he stepped back into the clearing where they'd set up camp, he found Kipp, Haley, Denny, and Augusta waiting for him.

Haley's camera nestled against her chest as though it was part of her. He wondered if she ever took it off. He noticed her snapping pictures whenever she got tense or scared too. It was like her shield.

Tank slung his backpack to his shoulder. "I've got a good spot to watch. Let's get going. Make noise, sing or whistle, let the bears know we're here. The last thing we need is to go around a curve and run smack into a bear who doesn't know we're coming."

As he led the way, he watched for signs of bear. Haley walked beside him. She had a strange gait, like she favored one leg. He wondered what she'd done to it.

"Are you worried about Miki?" Haley asked.

He glanced at her. "How did you know?"

"You keep looking into the trees with a worried look on your face. You've been like that ever since we found the doctor's body two days ago."

"I don't believe Miki would hurt him."

"So you said, but he was tugging on my arm pretty hard at the cabin. If I hadn't had on my jacket, I'd likely at least have bruises."

"I don't want to think he'd hurt anyone," he admitted. "The prints around the doctor's body looked like Miki's. He lost a toe somehow before I found him, and the print's pretty distinctive. Of course, that doesn't mean Miki killed him. He may have just found the body."

"And eaten it." She made an expression of disgust.

"Hey, he's a bear. Bears scavenge. That's how they survive."

"What happens if he just found it and ate it? Will he be in trouble?"

He shook his head. "People know about bears here. We've learned to live in relative harmony. We don't leave food out because we know they'll eat it. They're inherently lazy and will eat whatever's handy."

"I still hope Miki didn't eat him. He seemed like a fairly nice bear. As bears go."

He grinned. "You didn't think so the other day."

"I've learned to like him a little more since then." She stumbled and went to her knees.

"You okay?" He stooped to help her to her feet.

She struggled awkwardly with her left leg. "I'm fine." Her face was red, and she didn't meet his gaze.

He didn't pry. It was clear she didn't want to talk about it. They set off again. He paused on a small rise. Alders grew thick between here and the river. The hedge afforded a small measure of protection between them and the hungry bears, yet it was low enough for Haley to see over even while seated. "See the blackberry patch over there? It's a favorite of the bears." He slung his pack to the ground and sat down. Taking out his binoculars, he prepared to wait.

Haley sat beside him. Augusta dropped her pack and dug out her pad of paper. Haley got out a small journal and a book on Alaska vegetation. She began to examine the plants in front of her.

"It's fireweed," he told her. "The Natives use it for boils. They put a piece of cut stem on the boil, and the plant draws out the pus. It's a good source of vitamin C too." She nodded and jotted it down in her journal. Her expression was distant, and she hardly looked at him. He thought back to their conversation by the river. He could recall nothing offensive in their lighthearted discussion. He gave a mental shrug and decided not to worry about it.

Denny set up his equipment, then clipped a wireless mic on Kipp. Kipp settled on the ground and pulled out binoculars, a tiny set of Swarovski roof-prism binoculars that Tank knew cost the earth.

Tank heard a grunt and held up his hand. "Listen!" The sound came again, and then a sow with two small cubs emerged from the forest and wandered toward the water. The sow bounded into the water and ducked her head under the rippling current. She came up with a fish in her mouth. She tossed it to her cubs and continued to fish.

"Amazing," Haley whispered. She stared in rapt attention at the bruins. The color drained from her face, and her knuckles whitened where she gripped her camera.

"Aren't you going to take pictures?" Kipp growled. He stood and started toward the bears.

Haley jumped. "Sorry." She began to snap pictures.

"Get back here!" Tank made a grab at Kipp and missed. The

man broke through the alders and continued to walk slowly toward the bears.

Tank rose to go after him. "He's going to get killed. The sow will take him down if he gets close to her babies."

Denny frowned. "He generally doesn't mess with cubs. At least I've never seen him approach a sow." Vertical lines of worry settled across his forehead as he followed Kipp, camera running.

"What a *cheechako*," Tank muttered. He tugged his Ruger Blackhawk out of the holster and cocked it. If the bear charged, there would be little time to respond. If Kipp's stupidity caused two cubs to grow up without their mother, he'd throttle the man. He stepped over the alder and followed Kipp.

Kipp whistled a tuneless melody. The sow turned to look. She snorted and bounded from the water, her massive paws igniting the water with her fury.

Kipp raised his hands to indicate he was harmless, then turned to face Denny. "This is Kipp Nowak, and I'm in Alaskan brown-bear country. This is a mama bear I've named Sos. Isn't she beautiful with her two cubs?"

The cubs lifted their heads from their meal of fish and looked at the approaching man. One bawled, and the sow charged the men. The cubs squalled, tucked their tails, and ran for all they were worth to the safety of their mother.

"Look down and back away," Tank called. He stopped in place, praying the bear would realize they were no danger. The ferocious expression on the sow's face must have frightened Kipp. He dropped his gaze to the ground and took a step back. He wet his lips and tried to whistle again.

The tuneless sound seemed to enrage the sow. She charged them again, stopping about ten feet away and huffing. She turned sideways to demonstrate her size, then popped her jaw and turned back to make direct eye contact. Her eyes sparked with a murderous rage. "Keep backing away. Don't look at her," Tank said softly. He backed up to allow Kipp room to get past him. If he needed to shoot, he didn't want Kipp in the line of fire. Denny had already hightailed it back past the alders.

The other man was alongside Tank, then moved past him. "Don't turn and run," Tank said as he passed. Kipp didn't listen. As soon as he was three feet away from Tank, he bolted.

The sow snarled and charged again. Tank was going to have to shoot. He held his breath and prayed. The bear swerved off just as Tank's finger tightened on the trigger. She ran past her cubs, then circled back to face him again. She charged once more. Tank tensed and waited. He didn't want to shoot her unless he had no choice. The look in her eyes as she bore down on him told him this was it. She wasn't going to stop.

Maybe he could frighten her. That often wasn't the wisest thing to do, especially with a sow with cubs, but he didn't want to hit her. He took aim and shot over her head. The boom of the gun stopped her forward charge. Her claws dug into the soft ground as she tried to stop. She loped to the side and ran back to her cubs. She nudged them away from the river, and with a last departing glare at Tank, the three disappeared into the woods.

Tank's skin was damp with perspiration. He swiped his sleeve over his forehead. That was the closest he'd ever come to actually having to shoot a bear. Rage began to build in his belly. He stalked back to the rest of the group. "Don't you ever do that again," he said tightly. "Those cubs need their mother, but they came a hair's breadth from losing her today. And all because you had to play hotshot. They are wild animals, Nowak, not cuddly toys or pets. One more infraction like that, and I'm done. You can find someone else to guide you."

Kipp met his gaze, but he was pale. "She was the maddest bear I've ever seen."

"Can you blame her? She was protecting her babies. This was not a circus bear. This was a sow protecting her cubs. What did you think she would do—just let you waltz up and handle her cubs? Think again. If you'd reached out to touch one of them, you would have pulled back a bloody stump."

Haley made a small sound of protest. He glanced over to see her rubbing her leg. He swept his gaze around the rest of the group. "Is that clear to all of you? No approaching the bears." Aware he was overly severe, he softened his tone. "I'm thinking not only of your safety, but of the bears' as well. When they get accustomed to the presence of humans, they tend to wander into camps where they can become nuisances. In the worst cases, someone is attacked and injured or killed and the bear is shot. We're not contributing to that scenario. Clear?"

No one spoke for several long moments. "You'll have to let me use my own judgment on when to approach a bear," Kipp said. "I admit I miscalculated the sow with her cubs. That won't happen again."

"It had better not happen with any bear."

"How am I to get useful footage if I'm not with the bears?"

Kipp had recovered his aplomb. "I'll be able to tell when it's safe. I've gotten close to bears many times in the past. It's part of what I'm famous for. I won't be hobbled by your anxiety."

Tank caught Haley's gaze and shrugged. He'd done all he could. If Kipp ended up in bear scat, there wasn't much he could do about it.

⁂

Rivulets of spring runoff flowed through the streets of Stalwart, turning the unpaved dirt roads into muddy quagmires. Heavy clay clung to Tank's boots in clumps. He paused outside Chet's office long enough to knock most of the mud off on the walk, then stepped inside, where he found Chet and Ed Bixby hunched over a sheaf of papers at Chet's desk.

The men looked up. "Have a seat," Bixby said. "We just got back the autopsy report."

His voice was filled with a satisfaction that sent Tank's gaze skittering to meet Chet's. But his father-in-law kept his head down like a wounded animal. Tank sat and folded his arms across his chest. "What's the autopsy say?"

"There was Seconal in her bloodstream. Enough to knock her out."

"Seconal? What's that?" His gaze went again to Chet.

Chet's head finally came up. "A barbiturate sometimes used as a sleeping aid or as a sedative for nervousness."

"Was that what was in the packet Libby found?"

Ed nodded. "Who did you get it from?" He slipped the question in softly.

Tank leaned over the desk. "Can I see the report?"

"Suit yourself." Ed shoved it at him.

"Makes you wonder what could have been so bad at home, doesn't it?" Ed asked. "Did you ever hurt her, Tank?"

Tank's boots hit the floor, and he stood so fast, the chair he was sitting on toppled to the floor with a clatter that made Chet jump. "I loved Leigh," he said. "I would never have hurt her." The doubt on Chet's face pierced him as he turned and rushed away.

Eight

*T*he bright May sun in a brilliant blue sky caused new life to grow almost visibly minute by minute. Haley watched, mesmerized, throughout the long days. The rest of the crew arrived from their break in Anchorage, and taping began in earnest. There were no more close calls with the bears, who seemed to grow used to the cameras and the man who talked to them.

The day had warmed up, and she snapped pictures, then headed back to camp. She couldn't remember ever having been so tired and knew it was from both mental and physical strain. Tonight she was particularly exhausted as she settled on a log and watched her companions. They were nearly as entertaining as *Survivor.*

Haley glanced at the sky, bright though it was nine o'clock. She didn't know if she'd ever get used to the nearly constant daylight. Lucky for her, she didn't have to get used to it, she reminded herself. This exile was only temporary. Before she knew it, she would be back in the bright lights and excitement of the Valley of the Sun. Just thinking about Camelback Mountain looming over the Phoenix metro horizon made her loneliness increase.

Augusta stood. "I'm restless. I think I'll go for a walk."

Haley looked up. "Want to play euchre?"

"No, I need to think about the book and stretch my legs."

"Not a good idea," Tank said. "At least take the dog. His barking will keep any bears away."

Haley dragged herself to her feet. "I'll go with you."

Augusta laughed. "You said that with all the enthusiasm of a person going to the gallows. I'm fine, darling. I won't go far."

"No, no, I'll go with you." Haley grabbed her walking stick. "Which way?"

Augusta frowned. "I'm not a child. You know I value time alone. I need creative time. I won't be coddled. You all are smothering me."

"I'll be quiet, and you can think. Which way shall we go?"

Augusta sighed, then shrugged. "Toward the hills. Maybe we can climb a bit and get some good landscape pictures." Her grandmother skirted Cary and Erika Waters, the couple in charge of sound and film editing, and took off away from the lake. "I don't mean to be unkind, but those two don't look like they go together," Augusta whispered when they were past. "Erika is a head taller and orders him around like he's her younger brother."

"I think he is."

Augusta stopped, then burst into laughter. "I thought they were married."

Haley giggled. "You're such a romantic. They even look alike if you consider their noses."

"I never noticed."

They hiked for fifteen minutes before they reached the base of the rocky hillside. "You sure you want to go up there?" Haley asked. Climbing would be difficult for her.

"You wait here. I'll just go up a little ways." Augusta stepped to the top of a large black-and-white rock.

Haley sighed. She couldn't let Augusta go alone. Oscar barked and ran past her. He disappeared behind a bush. His barking changed to a frightened yip. She frowned and walked to where he'd disappeared. She prodded the large bush with her walking stick, then flattened it slightly. The opening of a cave yawned in front of her. She stumbled back and dropped her stick.

"What is it?" Augusta came back down the few steps she'd taken. She stooped and peered into the cave. "Oscar, come back here." The dog was practically crying. "I think he's trapped."

"No, he's not," Haley said. "Oscar, come here, boy." She tried to sound excited and coaxing. The dog responded with more pitiful howling.

"He's trapped. We have to get him out." Augusta got on all fours and started to crawl into the cave.

"No!" Haley sprang forward to prevent her grandmother from entering the cave. "Don't go in there." Her knees wobbled along with her voice.

Augusta looked up at her. "We can't leave him, Haley. I'll be fine."

"I'll go." She got on her knees and pushed the bush farther

out of the way. She poked her head into the cave, but it was too dark to see anything. The rush of musty cave scent, hatefully familiar, closed her throat.

She jerked her head out. "I can't." She covered her face with her hands and sat down with her boots splayed in front of her. She was such a failure, such a coward. Hugging herself, she rocked back and forth.

"Oh, Haley, darling, don't." Her grandmother embraced her.

"Don't go in there, Nana, please don't." She buried her wet face in Augusta's neck.

Her grandmother ran her hand over Haley's hair. "You haven't called me Nana in years."

"You told Aunt Caroline it made you feel old."

"It did. Is that why you stopped?"

She nodded, her face still against her grandmother's neck. "I know it wasn't easy to have your life disrupted by an eight-year-old. I thought if I was your friend and not just your grand-daughter, you wouldn't send me away."

Augusta didn't answer right away, but her arms tightened around her. "I won't lie to you, Haley. I was furious with your parents for doing that to me and expecting me to give up my freedom. It was hard to write at times with a child around, not to mention the doctor visits your leg demanded. I know I haven't always been the easiest person to live with. Both of us have an artistic temperament, and that's made life interesting, but I wouldn't give up the years we've spent together. I would never have sent you away. Right from the start, there was a special bond between us."

"I knew that, deep down." Haley pulled away at another whimper from the dog.

Her grandmother stood. "You stay here and keep Oscar calm. I'll go get Tank. We need a flashlight anyway."

With the comfort of her grandmother's embrace removed, Haley felt cold. She watched Augusta hurry away in the direction of the camp. Her facade of competency and self-sufficiency lay in crumbled pieces around her. Oscar's wails sounded tired. "It's okay, Oscar," she called. He knew better, just like she did.

⁂

Oscar's trembling finally stopped, and he lay on Haley's lap. Tank had quickly extracted Oscar from the hole after inserting only the front half of his body into the cave. Haley should have been able to save her own dog. Denny stared pensively into the fire. He brushed at the hair the wind blew over his eyes. Augusta's Alphasmart keyboard made a comfortable clacking sound that filled the eerie quiet.

"Do you ever get used to the silence out here?" Haley asked Tank, who sat on a rock tending the fire.

"I love it," he said without looking up. "No blaring horns, no engines, no people. Just me and the beauty God created. Out here you can get away from the noise and learn what's important."

Haley stroked Oscar's ears as he nestled comfortably against her. "That's a pretty sweeping statement. What's important is different for every person."

He looked up then and closed his notebook. He folded his big hands in his lap. "Not really, not at the heart level. We can easily get sidetracked into thinking ambition or money is important, but you can't take them with you. Love for God and family, finding your purpose in the eternal scheme of things—that's what's really important. The other stuff is just icing. Thinking they're key is like stuffing ourselves on candy so we're not hungry for the food that actually nourishes us."

"Very profound, Tank," Augusta said, setting aside her keyboard.

Haley struggled to hide her irritation. "I don't think anyone can know where they fit in the eternal scheme of things." She'd attended church with Augusta every week for years, but she got tired of hearing Christians spout off about purpose and destiny. One kindhearted friend of Augusta's had even gone so far as to say Chloe's death had a purpose. If Chloe had died for some nefarious purpose of God's, Haley didn't want anything to do with him.

She stood. "I think I'll turn in." Tank's passion for the subject warned her that he was just getting wound up, and she didn't want to be preached at any more tonight.

"I'll be right behind you," Augusta said.

Haley saw the understanding flash between Augusta and Tank, and her irritation rose. Let them think she was a heathen. She didn't care. Others had accused her of the same thing, but they hadn't walked in her shoes. Let one of them watch his or her sister die and see how quick they were to talk about God's love.

She grabbed her backpack with one arm and tucked Oscar under the other, then went to the tent. Lifting the flap and stepping inside, she flipped on the lantern and dropped her pack in the corner. She put Oscar down, and he went to nose at her satchel. The unzipped contents lay open to view. She could have sworn she'd left it zipped and at the head of her sleeping bag instead of in the middle like it was now. Could Augusta have been looking for something? She pulled the bag to her and rummaged through the contents. Someone had riffled through it. The sweats she slept in were no longer on top but had been shoved down the front of the bag.

She glanced around the tent, trying to see where she'd left everything. Her memory pulled up images of how the tent had looked when she last stepped out. Augusta's bag had been moved about a foot from the corner where Haley's backpack now lay. The entire camp had come out to watch Tank save Oscar, and there was no one around the camp for about an hour.

She stepped outside the tent and walked back to the fire. Augusta and Tank seemed deep in some kind of intense discussion. Probably religion. It was a good thing Haley had decided to vacate. "Augusta, were you looking for something in our tent?"

Augusta stopped midsentence. "Why no, Haley. I haven't been in the tent since we left this morning. Is something wrong?"

"I don't know. It looks like someone has been looking through our things."

Tank frowned. "I haven't seen anyone near your tent since we got back. Are you sure?"

"It looks like it to me."

"Maybe a hiker happened through camp while we were out bear watching," Denny suggested. "Someone could have looked through the tents."

"Maybe." Haley shrugged. "I guess it doesn't matter, since nothing is missing. I just thought it was strange. Good night." She went back to her tent. Pouring some water into the tin cup she brought, she brushed her teeth, then sat on her sleeping bag and pulled off her prosthesis. She changed into sweats and crawled into the sleeping bag. Oscar snuggled against her.

She could feel every lump, every transition in the ground under her. Though she was tired, her mind wouldn't shut off. When she heard Augusta coming, she rolled so her back was to the opening and shut her eyes. The last thing she needed to hear was Augusta scolding her for being rude to Tank. Maybe she had been. But that didn't mean she wanted to listen to a lecture.

Augusta moved through the tent preparing for bed. Haley heard her grunt as she climbed into the sleeping bag.

"These old bones don't like sleeping on the floor," Augusta said. "I know you're awake, Haley. You can't fool me."

Haley sighed and rolled over. "I was in no mood for a sermon. I know I was rude. He deserved it."

Augusta sat up and struggled into a cross-legged position. "I can't abide rudeness, Haley Walsh. You owe that young man an apology. Just because you're finally here and facing what you did doesn't mean you can take it out on someone else."

Oscar yelped, and she realized she was squeezing him too hard. "Sorry, boy," she muttered, loosening her grip. "I'm not taking it out on him. The shrink said to face it, and that's what I'm doing. But I hate the sanctimonious type."

"You know what I think about your shrink. God is the one you need to turn to. He can wipe all that away. Your guilt has affected every part of your life. It's crushing the life right out of you. Tank is right. Out here, you can get a handle on what's important. Your sister has been at rest for twenty years. She would want you to find some peace."

"You make it sound so easy!" Haley sat up and faced her grandmother. "You don't know what it's like to be responsible for the death of someone you love." She picked up her prosthesis and shook it. "It's not like I can just forget about it."

"God can heal you if you let him," Augusta said quietly.

"He let my sister die. I prayed and prayed all night long, but Chloe died anyway. What good is prayer when he doesn't listen? He hates me just like my parents did. Maybe Chloe would have lived if I *hadn't* prayed!" Her throat constricted, and she couldn't talk anymore. She flung herself back into the sleeping bag, then curled into a ball with her back to Augusta. Talking never solved anything. It never had.

"Haley, you're acting like a child," Augusta said. "Turn around and talk to me."

"Good night, Augusta," she said with as much finality in her voice as she could muster. "I don't want to talk anymore."

Augusta sighed. "Good night, Haley. I'll pray that you will be able to accept God's love and mercy."

After a few more shuffles, her grandmother settled down. A few minutes later, Haley heard a gentle snore. She punched her pillow and flipped onto her back. Oscar growled in protest of her movements, and she patted his head. Sleep felt as far away as the Lower Forty-eight.

13

Haley rolled over and looked at her watch. 3:00 a.m. Twilight had given way to darkness, but she was wide awake. Oscar snored by her ear, and Augusta kept tune with him. She wished she could close her eyes and forget where she was. Something rustled at the tent opening. She strained to see in the darkness. It was probably the wind.

It didn't feel like the wind. She felt a presence, a deliberate movement. *Chloe?* A shadow moved across the shaft of moonlight that peeked in through the tent opening. She tried to sit, but her muscles refused to obey. The darkness flowed as thick and seamless as midnight around her, and she squinted to make out the dark shadow. It seemed large and hulking—menacing.

Haley froze. She opened her mouth, but her throat was too tight to force out a scream. She wet her lips as the shadow moved into the tent. She reached out her hand for a weapon of some kind. Her hand closed on her prosthesis, lying beside her sleeping bag. *Move.* She heard the sound of a zipper. He was opening her backpack. The figure started to turn toward her. Oscar awakened. He snuffled, then jumped to his feet and began to bark. The intruder turned toward her. A ski mask covered his face. Drawing back her arm, Haley threw the prosthesis at the intruder. It flew through the air end over end and thumped him in the side of the head, driving him to his knees.

He took hold of the artificial limb and swiped at her backpack, catching it up. Haley threw herself across the ground and snagged one handle of the pack. "That's mine," she panted. She tugged the pack out of his hand as he stumbled out of the tent. "Augusta, help me!"

"What is it? Who's there?" Augusta's sleepy voice pulsed with alarm. She raised herself on one elbow

Flashlights flicked on outside the tent. A beam of light moved toward their tent. "Here, in here!" Haley shouted. Her hands shook as she felt for her prosthesis but touched only the slick fabric of the tent floor. She squinted and looked around the dim light of the tent. Surely the intruder had dropped it. She couldn't lose her leg.

The tent flap opened, and Tank rushed inside. He held the lantern aloft, and though the light was weak, it pushed back the shadows. Haley didn't know whether to shrink back into the corner and hide her missing leg or to kiss him for chasing the darkness away. She lifted her chin and decided not to hide.

"What's happened? Are you all right?" His gaze flickered to her face, then to the flat area of her sweats where her bottom right leg should be. His eyes widened, and then he blinked and seemed to hide his surprise.

"I'm fine," she said shortly. "There was an intruder trying to take my backpack. Could someone get me a long stick I can use as a crutch? My prosthesis is gone, and the walking stick is too short to support me properly." Gone. Her earlier dismay began to fade. She'd have to leave, go back to Phoenix. She'd get out of this hateful place. Her gaze fell on her grandmother's face, and her elation ebbed. Augusta needed her here. She'd have to figure out how to get along without her prosthesis. Or get a new one.

Tank cleared his throat. "Did you get a look at the intruder?"

"It was too dark. I heard him open the zipper, so I threw my leg at him. He still tried to take my backpack, but I tackled it and managed to jerk it from his hand. It had my camera in it."

"You think he was after your camera?"

"It's an expensive one," she admitted. "I guess that could have been the target. There wasn't much else of value in it."

Denny brought her a thick stick. "I think it's a little long," he said. He took off the bear amulet around his neck. "Here, a little Native magic will protect you."

Augusta put her hand out and closed Denny's fingers over the figure. "You keep your amulet, Denny. My prayers are protecting my granddaughter."

Haley tried to hide her smile at her grandmother's tact. "Thanks." She struggled upright and leaned on the stick. "Some makeshift crutches would be useful. Something from a tree fork maybe."

"I'll find you something," Tank said.

"You should have told me you were handicapped," Kipp said. "How are you going to hike out of here with only a stick?"

"I'll call for a plane," Tank said. "She can't hike out of here on crutches. Do you have access to another prosthesis?"

"I might have to go back to Phoenix for another one. Or I could call my friend, Savannah. I accidentally left my old one at her apartment when I flew into Savannah to pick up this new one."

"Savannah from Savannah?" Erika Waters lifted an eyebrow. "I bet she gets jokes." About thirty-five, Erika was nearly six feet tall with flaming red hair that had to come from a bottle. Haley wasn't totally positive Erika had been born a woman. There was something about the way she walked and used her hands.

"And hates them," Haley said. She brightened at the thought of talking to her friend. Savannah would help her put this place in perspective. "I'll have her send it out right away."

Kipp turned to leave the tent. "I certainly hope so. I wouldn't be able to find another photographer of your skill and reputation easily. You signed on to do this project, and you'd better do whatever is necessary to finish it." The tent flap closed. "We need to get some sleep before that blasted sun comes up again."

Nine

*T*he loud cacophony of birds in the spruce outside her tent wakened Haley to the full sunshine filtering through the thin tent fabric. The aroma of coffee drifted in the tent opening. Haley sat up and reached for her prosthesis, then dropped her hand. She closed her eyes. "Great, just great," she muttered. She sat up and reached out to grab the stick Denny had brought her last night.

Instead in its place she found two cut from a tree fork. On each one, the crook seemed to fall under her arm just about right and had a knob for her hand to grab about halfway down. Tank's thoughtfulness—she was sure it was Tank who carefully chose them—touched her, though her reluctance to show her vulnerability to the group remained strong.

The other sleeping bag was empty, and even Oscar had deserted her. Haley couldn't believe Augusta had managed to get dressed and out of the tent without waking her. She quickly pulled on some Ezra Fitch jeans and several layers of tops, then tied up the right leg of her pants to keep it from dragging on the ground. Tying off the leg highlighted her stump even more. The mercury had to hover close to forty this morning, and her breath frosted the air. She pulled on her wool jacket, tested the makeshift crutches, then took a deep breath and exited the tent.

The others huddled around the fire in the middle of the clearing. "I never imagined it would be so cold here in May," Cary Waters grumbled.

"It's usually warmer. This weather won't last long," Tank said.

They saw Haley, and conversation stopped. An awkward silence stretched out. "Good morning," she said, forcing a smile. "I hope you saved me some coffee. It smells great." Watching carefully where she put each crutch, she swung toward the fire.

Tank sprang to his feet and pointed toward the tree stump he vacated. "Have a seat, and I'll get you some breakfast."

She hated to be waited on, hated to feel helpless. "Thanks." She sank onto the stump. Oscar came to see her. He had his wiener-in-a-bun rubber toy. "How'd you get that?" she scolded. She tried to take it from him, but he squeaked it and ran off with it in his mouth.

"He was being a nuisance this morning, so I gave it to him. I can't say it helped much," Augusta said. "He's been squeaking it for an hour."

"I can usually only stand it an hour a day," Haley said. "I thought about leaving it at home, but I knew he'd mope without it."

"You act like that dog is a kid." Tank handed her a steaming cup of coffee, black and aromatic.

"Thanks. Got any creamer?" She decided to ignore his comment about her dog. It was none of his business if she chose to spoil her pet. She studied him while he dug through the cache of food for the creamer. Out here he reminded her even more of Paul Bunyan. He wore a green-and-black-plaid wool shirt and jeans with muddy boots.

She looked away to see Erika watching her with a knowing smirk. Haley's cheeks burned, and she shrugged and looked away.

Tank handed her a packet of creamer. "I've called for a plane. It should be here any minute. I guess we're all going to town for some R and R."

"There's no sense in staying out here without a photographer," Kipp said. "We might as well sleep in a decent bed for a few nights."

"I need a manicure," Erika announced.

"I could use a pedicure," Haley said, giggles erupting. "You all don't have to tiptoe around what's happened. I'm fine. I lost my leg when I was eight. As long as I have my prosthesis, I can do anything the rest of you can do. And really, who else has a weapon like mine? I hit that intruder right on the head with it." She raised one crutch in the air. "He'll know better than to mess with Haley Walsh again."

Erika put her hand over her mouth and giggled. Relief ricocheted through the camp. "Really—you've had your leg cut off since you were eight? What happened?"

Haley's smile died. She should have known that question was coming, should have prepared for it. Her gaze found her grandmother's, and she sent her a silent plea.

Augusta stood. "My goodness, if we're going to leave for town, we need to get our tents down and our things ready. The plane will be here in a few minutes."

Erika groaned. "I'm tired. I don't want to move." She got slowly to her feet and went toward the tent. Kipp followed. Everyone else did the same except for Tank. His tent and belongings were already stowed and awaiting the plane.

"I'll take your tent down when Augusta is finished packing." His gaze, strong and intense, never left her face. "Every time someone mentions the past, you close up. It might help to talk about it."

Oscar came running from the woods without his toy. He jumped into her lap. "I've tried that," Haley said. "It just brings back memories I'd rather forget." She looked toward the woods. "What did you do with your toy, Oscar?"

"Losing your leg must have been painful," Tank said.

"I don't remember much about it." She was a liar. She remembered every sleepless, sweat-soaked night in the hospital. She would wake up terrified and reach under the covers, all the while hoping and praying the leg was still there—that it had all been a terrible nightmare. The real pain, though, had been the remembrance of what happened to Chloe.

"You're a real trouper." He squeezed her shoulder and went toward the tent to help Augusta.

If he only knew it was all a facade. The real Haley was a quivering mass of jelly behind the cheerful pretense.

B

Where would that stupid dog have dropped his toy? Tank kicked through spruce needles and soft dirt in pursuit of the elusive hot-dog squeaky toy. Maybe it would be a blessing not to find it. The pooch had annoyed them all with the squeaks. Only the thought of Haley's disappointed face drove him on. She'd been through enough. No wonder she was so attached to the dog.

He caught a glimpse of red and stooped to grab the toy. As he turned to head back to camp, he stumbled over something in the dirt. He kicked the spruce needles out of the way to see what it was. A black pouch with a drawstring. He picked it up and opened it. A camera lens nestled inside the soft leather. It had to be Haley's, but she thought nothing had been taken. This ought to cheer her up.

Whistling, he headed back to the river. The sound of the water rushing over rocks and tree stumps nearly drowned out the voices of the crew, but he followed the faint sound and found Kipp and his group awaiting the plane.

"You found it!" Haley's smile broke out in full force. Oscar began to bark and ran to jump on Tank's leg.

"Sure did." He dropped the toy to the dog. "This yours?" He held out the lens and pouch.

Her eyes widened, and she reached out to take it. "It looks like one of my zoom lenses. Where did you find it?"

"Near Oscar's toy. I didn't remember you going out where I found it, though. I think our intruder must have taken it, then dropped it."

"Why would he drop it? It cost over a thousand dollars." Haley unzipped her backpack and rummaged through it. "Yes, it's mine. I thought I'd accounted for everything. I bet I missed checking the small outside pouch. This isn't one I use often."

"Maybe he didn't know he dropped it," Denny said.

"And it was dark, so he might have had trouble finding it even if he did know," Kipp said. "But all's well that ends well. At least Haley has it back." He shaded his eyes with his hand. "Looks like our plane is coming."

"I have you to thank that we don't have to hike out," Erika told Haley. "I was *so* not looking forward to a two-hour hike."

Tank suppressed a grin. Did the woman think Haley would want to damage her prosthesis just to get out of a hike? His gaze caught Haley's, and he saw the same amusement in her eyes. He winked, and she looked away. *Darn, she was a hard woman to get close to.* The thought took him aback. He didn't want to get close to her.

Stalwart, Alaska, looked like a rough-and-tumble town right out of the gold-rush days. Wooden storefronts in need of paint lined a rough, muddy track they called Frontier Street. It looked the same as it had twenty years ago. Haley saw familiar businesses, and even the hotel was still the same faded color.

The pickup truck trying to jolt the stuffing out of her was driven by a congenial Native Tank called Sam. She and Augusta were squashed on the bench seat while the rest of the group rode in the back of the vehicle, which sported more rust than paint.

"Here we be." Sam threw on the brakes. The truck slid to a halt in the mud outside the hotel.

Augusta opened the door and climbed out. She turned to help Haley climb down, but Tank hopped over the side of the truck bed and held out his hand. "Why don't I carry you? It will be hard to walk on crutches in this mud."

"I can manage," Haley said. She planted her crutches and hopped down. Tank frowned but didn't protest. She hobbled past the door, and he shut it behind her. She wanted to dance with joy at the open sky above her. No trees. And houses and stores, even if they were mostly ramshackle shops. She was actually back in civilization of a sort.

"Thanks," Tank told Sam. While the rest of the group tossed the belongings out of the truck, he moved alongside Haley as she laboriously made her way toward the sidewalk.

She thought she was going to make it with no mishap, but five feet from the walk, her right crutch sank unexpectedly deep in the mud, and she lost her balance. Tank reached out to grab her hand, but his right foot skidded, and he began to slide. He barreled into her, and they both went down in a tangle of limbs. She sat down in the mud with her feet straight out in front of her. The cold mud seeped through her jeans and sucked at her hands. It was like being encased in cold plaster.

She looked down at the black goo that covered her. This was all Tank's fault. She wanted to throw something at him. Before she knew what she was doing, she scooped up a handful of mud. Then it was on his face. She couldn't believe she'd done it, but the smear of black down his cheek was proof.

He staggered to his feet. She knew she should apologize, but the words lodged behind her teeth, then her nervous giggles erupted. He wasn't laughing. He wiped his face, but the mud on his hand just deposited more goo on his cheek.

"Haley Walsh, I'm ashamed of you. It was an accident," her grandmother said.

Haley barely noticed Augusta as Tank's grim face changed to a grin. He loomed over her. "You want a fight?" He smeared mud on her face.

She gasped at the touch of the cold, clammy goop. Her hand came up and touched the wet smear on her cheek. Grabbing up another handful of mud, she flung it at him, and it plopped onto his left cheek. It clung for a moment, then dribbled down onto his shirt. She laughed, challenging him with her gaze to continue the battle.

"You're going to pay for that," he threatened, narrowing his eyes. He scooped another handful and raised his hand to throw it.

"Children, children, that's enough." Augusta stepped carefully through the mud and grabbed Tank's arm.

He looked at the mud in his hand, then dropped it like it was moose dung. A wave of red ran up his neck, and his gaze went past her. Haley couldn't look at him either. What were they thinking? They'd almost been *flirting* with one another, right in front of everyone. She wasn't sure what had gotten into her. The faster she could get out of this mudhole of a town, the better.

Ten

*T*ank left a trail of hardened mud on the sidewalk as he jogged down to see Chet, still a little chagrined over the childishness of his mudslinging. At the same time, he had to admit he wasn't wholly embarrassed. Haley had shown a lot of spunk through circumstances that would have angered and humiliated some women. He liked that about her. In spite of her city ways, she had guts.

Tank's attention turned to more pressing matters as he neared the jail. The door to Chet's office stood open, and a line of people stretched out the door all the way to the window near the end of the wooden building. Loud, angry voices made Tank proceed cautiously. Alaska was filled with strong-willed people who had no hesitation in making their wishes known, and even in a small town like Stalwart, politics could get heated—and physical.

He stepped past the men into Chet's office and found the trooper standing by his desk. "What's going on, Chet?"

"Your bear just ransacked a fishing camp out near Glenn

River. Jed Hoose is going to lose a leg. I told you not to turn that bear loose. You should have sold him to a zoo or something!"

"Calm down, Chet. There's no telling which bear it was."

The trooper dropped into his chair. "If Jed dies, his blood will be on your head, Tank."

Tank laid a hand on Chet's shoulder. "Slow down and tell me what happened. Jed is a friend of mine." Jed Hoose was one of the first people to welcome Tank to the area when he moved here, and the two of them used to play cards over the long, dark nights before Tank married Leigh.

"A bear attacked last night. Knocked over the tent while he was cooking supper, mauled Jed, and hauled away his food. One of the other fishermen got back in time to drive the bear off before it came back for Jed." Chet nodded toward the line outside. "They're demanding action. Your bear has to go, Tank. I'm sorry. I should have done this sooner." His voice lowered.

"How do you know it's Miki? Did Jed say so?" If Jed said it, Tank would believe it.

"He's too out of it to say. But the bear tracks indicated a missing toe."

Tank tensed. "How do they know the tracks were of the bear that did the mauling? Miki could have been nosing around and had nothing to do with the attack." He was beginning to think his hope was futile.

"His prints were found at the site, just like where Doc's body was found. You just don't want to face the truth, Tank."

Tank took off his hat and rubbed his forehead. "Maybe I don't. Did the fisherman who drove off the bear give a description?"

"I'm going to go talk to him now. I'll let you know what he said." Chet rose and grabbed his hat from a hook on the wall.

Tank followed him out the door. "Is Jed going to make it?"

Chet nodded. "Not being able to get out in the bush and go fishing is going to kill him."

"He can still go," Tank said, thinking of Haley's spunk.

"Be pretty hard on crutches to hike the rough ground."

"I know someone with a prosthesis who does pretty well hiking."

Chet raised his eyebrows. "You might get him to talk to Jed when he is well enough to talk."

"It's a her. And I'll do that." Maybe Jed would be ready to talk in a few days. Tank winced inwardly. Losing a limb would be hard to take.

Chet nodded. "There's Lock Lehman now. He's the one who drove off the bear."

"Mind if I tag along?"

"Not a problem. Sorry if I was a little hard on you. It's been a rough day."

Tank fell into step beside Chet. "Any word from Marley?"

Chet shook his head and stopped to gawk at the tourists flocking into the Moose Nuggets shop. "Would you look at that! When Anna said people would buy jewelry and stuff made from lacquered moose droppings, I thought she was nuts."

Tank glanced through the window and back toward Chet. Was he trying to change the subject on purpose? He had to feel caught in the middle between his daughter and Tank. "About Marley," he began.

Chet took off again and intercepted Loch Lehman. A bony

man in his fifties, Loch was Ichabod Crane in jeans and suspenders. He rarely smiled, probably inhibited by his teeth, blackened by years of snuff use.

"I heard you were the hero today, Loch," Tank said.

Loch shrugged. "He would have done the same for me."

"Did you get a good look at the bear?" Chet asked.

"Sure. I was as close as I ever want to get. Big sucker. Old, too,
with half his teeth missing. And gaunt. I'd guess he has trouble
hunting so takes to easier prey."

Tank closed his eyes briefly. Thank God it wasn't Miki. He
looked at Loch. "You ever seen this bear before? Did you notice
his toes?"

"I can't say I was paying attention to his toes." Loch spit a
wad of tobacco on the ground.

"There were tracks found of a bear with a toe missing. We
thought it was Miki," Chet said.

Loch shrugged. "I saw Miki earlier in the day. I shooed him
off, and he went without complaint."

"Sounds like Miki is off the hook. This time." Chet eyed
Tank. "We're starting to get more and more complaints about
Miki though, Tank. Nosing through gardens, hitting the trash
cans. I think I'm going to have to do something about him soon.
Maybe take him deeper into the bush."

"I think you're right." Tank would do whatever it took to
protect the bear, even if it meant having him moved far
away. A hollow space developed between his shoulder blades.
Lately, it seemed like he was in danger of losing everything he
loved.

13

"I'm exhausted." Augusta hung up the last of their clothes and shut the closet. "I'll be able to get some writing done tomorrow."

Haley grimaced. The bedspread had been washed so many times, the pattern was no longer visible. The threadbare carpet was the shade of vomit, and just looking at it made her feel queasy. The bathroom had pink tile from the fifties, and the enamel was chipped in the tub. At least it was clean. The only dirt she'd seen was the mud from her body swirling down the drain.

"We need to get you some real crutches," Augusta said, watching her make her way across the room with the makeshift set Tank had made her. "Those don't have rubber tips and don't look very stable."

"I'm hoping to get my leg pretty quickly. I'll call Savannah now." She didn't have to look up her friend's number. She and Savannah Phillips had become friends when Haley flew to Savannah to photograph a beauty pageant. Savannah was investigating pageant fraud at the time, and they'd immediately hit it off. They talked at least once a week.

The phone rang three times; then Savannah's cheery voice answered. "Savannah Phillips."

"Savannah, it's me."

"Oh my stars! I thought you'd dropped off the face of the earth for all eternity." Savannah's southern accent thickened with her excitement.

"I'm in Stalwart, Alaska. Can you stand it? Where are you?

At the park?" Haley could see her in her mind's eye, one leg curled up under her sitting on a park bench, slurping a Coke from McDonald's as if it were the last one this side of heaven, all while twisting a strand of her sun-streaked brown hair.

"How'd you guess?" Savannah slurped into the phone, then giggled. "How's Oscar? Duke says hey."

"Give Duke a bone for me." Oscar and Savannah's golden retriever were best friends.

"Honey, I thought you'd be lost to me for the summer. I've been reduced to reading the old cards you sent me and laughing at them. How are you holding up in the wilds?"

"I was doing okay until someone stole my leg." She grinned at the explosion she knew was coming.

"Stole your leg? Lord have mercy, child! You're legless? How are you getting around?"

"On crutches made from tree limbs. Do you still have my old prosthesis? The one with the Velcro?"

"Of course. It's in my closet."

"Can you send it to me?"

"Shoot, honey child, I'll fly it to you if you need me to."

Though the thought of seeing her friend was tempting, Haley didn't want to subject her to that long flight. "I'll send you a check for postage."

"You will not! Vicky raised me better than that. I'll overnight it."

"That will cost the earth," Haley protested.

"No, it won't. Vicky is paying. Now give me the address."

Haley could hear her rummaging, no doubt for the Big Star

notebook she was never without. "Ready?" When Savannah had her notebook ready, Haley rattled off the address on the hotel notepaper. "You're a doll, Savannah." She hung up after promising to call when the prosthesis arrived. "Savannah is overnighting it," she told Augusta.

"I knew she'd come through." Augusta stood. "I'm hungry," she announced. "Feed me, or I may turn into a grumpy old woman."

"We can't have that." Haley ran a lip gloss over her mouth. For the first time in days, she felt like herself—Haley Walsh, confident, sophisticated. Her gaze fell to the tied-up pant leg of her jeans. Almost herself. Not having her prosthesis was disconcerting.

Augusta was peering out the window. "There's a café beside the hotel your mother used to talk about. Hazel's. Let's eat there."

"I remember that place. Would you carry my backpack? I might want to change lenses." Propping herself on the crutches, Haley got herself balanced, then followed her grandmother out the door. They'd asked for and received a first-floor room near the lobby, a bonus, because they'd been told most of the rooms were taken by the search-and-rescue workers in town for a training session with their dogs. She'd stopped to admire a few dogs on her way to the room. She made her slow and laborious way down the tiled hall, no luxury like carpeted hallways in this motel.

Out of breath by the time they reached the walk in front of the hotel, she paused to rest. Glancing around, she saw someone watching her with interest. When he saw his perusal had attracted her attention, he turned away and began to study the display in a shop window. Her face burned. She should be used to stares and jeers, but she'd had her prosthesis so long, she'd forgotten how awkward it felt to have people study her when they thought she wasn't looking.

Augusta led the way down the street to the café. The Z in the neon sign over the door was out. Augusta pushed the door open and held it for Haley, causing a brass bell to jingle. The threshold was a step up, and the door was a little narrow to negotiate easily with crutches, but Haley managed to get inside. The aroma of liver and onions struck her in the face, and she wrinkled her nose. Maybe this wasn't such a good idea. She had in mind a nice, juicy steak with steamed vegetables and a salad. Somehow, she didn't think this café could fulfill that fantasy. She vaguely remembered having ice cream sundaes here as a child.

Her stomach rumbled, and she decided she'd make do. Her arms ached from maneuvering the crutches, and she didn't think she could walk up and down the streets looking for something more palatable. The sign told them to seat themselves. She nodded toward the only free table, one for two in the back corner. Augusta nodded and murmured an apology as she asked people to step out of the way for Haley. At the stares, Haley wanted to hurry back to her room, but she gritted her teeth and pressed on to the table. Some of the faces looked familiar, but no names came to mind.

Out of breath again, she slid into the seat with her back to the rest of the room. The old Formica table was speckled gray and white with chrome trim. She picked up the menu and had started to open it when their waitress came to greet them.

About fifty, the woman had salt-and-pepper hair tied back with a red ribbon like a teenager. Her black slacks had flour handprints on the thighs, and she wore a white top with red hearts on it. A square white badge with the name MARGE in bold black letters was pinned near her left shoulder. She had a large frame that spoke of hard work.

"Welcome to Hazel's," she said. "What can I get you to drink?" Her gaze went from Augusta to Haley, and her mouth dropped open. "You have to be related to Maggie Walsh," she said. "Haley?"

Did she really look like her mother? Augusta often said so, and Marge was at least the second person to remark on the similarity since Haley had arrived. "She was my mother." Haley searched the recesses of her memory. "I'm trying to remember the name of my mother's best friend. I was thinking she used to work here."

Marge smiled. "That would be Fannie Coghill. She owns the café. She's back in her office doing paperwork. I'll take you back to meet her after your meal."

Haley nodded politely, not sure how much she wanted to learn about the woman who rejected her in spite of their apparent similarities.

🕊

"Vonnie Bird was ordered by the judge to do the home study. She'll go out tomorrow. We just might have a chance, Marley." Janine's voice radiated satisfaction.

The sun suddenly shone brighter through Marley's window. "Wonderful! How soon before we can get to court?"

"Be patient. Let's find out what Vonnie has to say. If her report comes back in our favor, we'll push for a quick court date."

Marley's glee ebbed. "I've leased an apartment in New York and enrolled Brooke in a private school. I need to be there by the middle of August."

Janine sighed. "I wish you'd talked to me before you did that. These things take time. I don't see any way you can have custody by then, Marley."

"We're going! You just make it happen, Janine." Marley punched off the phone with a vicious stab. She had promised Leigh, and she was going to keep her word. She stood and paced to the hotel window. Her view looked out Stalwart's poor excuse for a park. Brooke deserved to play with Marley in Central Park, to be dressed in Lilly Pulitzer, and to have her hair done by a fashionable salon on Fifth Avenue.

She'd paid an astronomical sum to get Brooke into this school. It was the first step in making sure her daughter was accepted by the highest quality people. Her daughter. She caught herself. Leigh's daughter. She knew the difference. Of course she did.

Eleven

ank crossed the street, avoiding the muddy potholes. The odor of sauerkraut hung in the air from the greasy spoon next to Chet's office, and he wrinkled his nose. He liked most food, but he drew the line at sauerkraut. Judging by the crowd, most others didn't share his prejudice against it. Chet hailed him through the open window of the trooper's office.

"I need to see you, Tank."

Tank switched direction and entered the office. His smile smug, Trooper Bixby leaned against a wall with his arms folded over his chest. Tank glanced at him warily, then stopped at his father-in-law's desk. "What's up?"

Chet heaved a sigh and rubbed his temple. "Got a question for you, Tank. Why didn't you tell me you were taking sleeping pills?"

"What?" Tank glanced at Bixby, whose smile had widened into a triumphant grin. "I've never taken sleeping pills in my life. I hate drugs."

Bixby straightened. "I did some investigation at the doctor's office. He wrote you a prescription for Seconal a week before Leigh died. How did you slip them to her? In her favorite tea?" He spat the last word as his eyes narrowed.

Tank took an involuntary step back. "That's impossible." He tried to marshal his thoughts.

"I don't know what to think." Chet's eyes reddened, and he looked away. "You've been like a son to me."

Tank knew he was only seconds away from being arrested for his wife's murder. "Think, both of you. Chet, you talked to Dr. Wooten when we found that packet of sleeping pills. He didn't say anything about having written me a prescription, did he?"

Chet looked up and shook his head. "Maybe he forgot."

"You know Joe better than that. He had a memory like an elephant. Someone is trying to set me up." He narrowed his eyes and glared at Bixby. "You're the one who found this so-called evidence, Bixby. Are you sure you're not out to prove my guilt any way you can?"

"It was right there in black and white." Bixby grabbed the file and shook it in Tank's face. "I'm placing you under arrest."

Chet put his hand on Bixby's arm. "Hold on there, Bixby. He's right about Joe. We'd better investigate this some more before we make any assumptions."

Bixby jerked away from Chet. "You're not getting away with this, Lassiter. I'm going to nail your hide to the wall. Don't be leaving town."

Tank exited the office without answering Bixby. The cloud of suspicion over him seemed as black as an Alaskan winter. He had to figure out a way to prove his innocence. His cell phone rang. He looked at the screen. Finally, the lawyer was calling him back. He punched it on. "Lassiter here."

The man's voice reminded him of a frog with a cold. "Mr. Lassiter, this is Garth Jagger. I'm sorry it took me so long to get back to you. I've been out of town. My secretary says you need some counsel on a custody case?"

Tank stepped onto the sidewalk and found a bench by a bait shop. "My sister-in-law is suing me for custody of my daughter. She can't get Brooke, can she?"

"Depends on if she can prove you're an unfit parent. And the judge's decision, of course. What's going on?"

"My wife died a year ago. Her twin sister doesn't think Brooke should be brought up in the bush. She wants to get custody and take her to the Lower Forty-eight."

The lawyer's voice sharpened. "Is the child in danger where you live? You work with bears, don't you? I've heard your name. Is Brooke around the bears at all?"

Tank flinched at the barrage of questions. "I'm a biologist. It's my work. She's not around them, though. Other than the cub I raised a few summers ago. I let Brooke help me give him his bottle sometimes, but he was just a cub. Once he grew, I never let her around him. He's been released into the wild now and is no longer an issue."

"Does he come around at all now?"

"Once in a while, but I drive him off. I've told her to stay in the house. She knows she's not to be around him."

"Let me see what your sister-in-law is claiming and get the full story." He quoted his retainer. Tank winced but agreed to it. What other choice did he have? Marley couldn't be allowed to take his daughter. He thought about telling the lawyer about the ongoing investigation into Leigh's death but decided to wait until there was something more to report. Keeping Brooke was more pressing right now.

He clicked off his phone and dropped it in his pocket. He glanced down the street, then bolted to his feet. Was that Marley? Chet had said she wouldn't be back from Seattle until next week. He squinted in the bright sunlight, then took off after her. There was no mistaking the bleached-blond cap of hair or the walk that invited every man in sight to look his fill. Dressed in snug jeans and an even tighter blue top, she was attracting more than the usual attention given to women in town.

"Marley!" he called. She stopped in front of the Moose Nuggets shop and looked back. Her smile faded, and she crossed her arms over her chest. She and Leigh were as identical as two salmon in a stream, or they would have been if Marley had her natural honey hair color. He'd avoided her since Leigh died. Seeing her hurt too much. He forced a smile and a hearty tone to his voice. "I need to talk to you."

"I don't want to talk." Her green eyes looked haunted, and faint shadows smudged the skin under her eyes. "I don't want to hurt you, Tank, but I have to think about what Leigh would want. My sister isn't here to fight for her daughter, so I have to do it for her."

"Leigh wouldn't want you to rip Brooke from me. I love her," he countered, barely holding onto his temper. He told himself not to give her any more ammunition for her suit.

"Move from the bush, and there would be no problem. You let the wilderness kill my sister. I can't let the same thing happen to Brooke. Leigh won't allow me to let it go."

He dropped his smile. "What do you mean, she won't let you? Leigh is dead, Marley. I'd bring her back if I could, but I can't. If you want to blame someone, blame your sister. She knew better than to go swimming at night."

She flushed, then grew pale. "How like you to pass the buck. If you'd been a better husband and had been around more, she wouldn't be dead. I've already heard the autopsy report. She took sleeping pills. I knew she hated it out there. This is your fault, Tank. And you're going to pay."

He flinched and drew back. "So this is about revenge, and not about what's best for Brooke?" He wished he had a witness to their conversation. He might need it.

"Of course not. You didn't exercise good judgment about your family, and my sister is dead as a result of it. I can't let you kill Brooke with your neglect too. Someone will be out to do a home study tomorrow. She'll see how unsuitable you are as a father."

A home study. The whole thing was surreal. He'd never imagined he'd end up in court fighting to keep his own daughter. "I never neglected your sister, Marley," he said quietly. "I loved her. And I love Brooke. I'm a good dad."

"You only love your bears." She spat the words. "Leigh and Brooke were always second. She knew it, and I know it. I couldn't save Leigh, but I'll save Brooke." Marley wheeled and marched off toward the jail, her small heels flinging mud as she walked.

Tank started to go after her but knew it would do no good.

Could her mental state be suspect? She'd never liked him, but now she seemed almost psychotic in her hatred. Leigh had killed herself. Pressure built in his head, and he wanted to hide somewhere like a wounded animal. He didn't want to admit it could be true. He headed toward the little weathered-wood church that he and his family attended. Pastor Steve would help him pray through this.

13

Haley sipped her tepid tea and grimaced. She glanced at her watch. Marge had promised to take them back to meet Fannie, but they'd been waiting nearly an hour. She was ready to go. She drummed her fingers on the Formica. The men in this town seemed disposed to stare, and she wanted to bolt back to her room.

"Quit fidgeting," Augusta commanded. "You're making me nervous."

Before Haley could answer, Marge finally made her appearance. She'd discarded the stained apron, but she still wore the red bow in her hair. Haley's gaze went past her to the woman behind her. About five feet two, the woman's short hair lay in a chic cap that curled behind her ears. Strands of gray dulled the sheen, and her green eyes darted in a wary dance from Haley to Augusta.

"It's Haley all grown up. I'm Fannie Coghill." Fannie extended her small hand. "I'm sorry you had to wait. We had an influx of customers, and I had to pitch in to help in the kitchen."

"I remember you," Haley said, standing as gracefully as she could. "You used to come and drink coffee with my mother."

Fannie smiled and pulled out a chair. "That was a lifetime ago."

The café had begun to clear out, but the remaining men still regarded Haley with interest. Haley sat down hastily. "Why do the men have to stare?" she asked softly.

Marge patted Haley's hand as she turned to leave. "Honey, when a starving man sees food, of course he's going to want his fill. To them you're a caribou roast with potatoes and a huge slice of chocolate cake all rolled into one. Get used to it. It's that way all over the state. Men outnumber women five to one in most remote areas. You're going to attract attention wherever you go, but here you're not just a ten, you're a fifteen at least, and we don't get many of them up here."

Haley kept her eyes averted from the handsome man eying her from the next table. "It makes me uncomfortable. It's as if he doesn't even notice I have a leg missing."

"He hasn't looked lower than your hips." Fannie grinned, then lowered her voice. "You sure do look like your mother. I'm still amazed. I didn't know you were in town."

"I'm here with the bear researcher. I'm also trying to document things about my childhood."

Fannie picked up a napkin and began to tear it into strips. "My memory isn't much good anymore."

"Did you see my mother the day of the fire?"

Fannie's fingers stilled, then she began to shred the napkin faster. "We had coffee the day before. After Bundle left."

Augusta put her hands over Fannie's. "You seem upset. Is everything okay?"

"I'm fine, fine." She pulled her hands away.

"I met Ned Bundle the other day," Haley said.

Fannie's head jerked up. "The biggest loser to ever walk the earth." She curled her lip. "He was always following your mother around, complimenting her, annoying her. She was scared of him. After the fire, Ned took over the dig as if it had been his project all the time. He took credit for the work your dad did." Spots of color stained her cheeks, and her voice rose.

"He didn't seem that type at all!" Haley realized she'd raised her voice and lowered it again. "He was polite and gentlemanly. Very passionate about his work."

"Looks like he's pulled the wool over your eyes. Ask Joy about him. She doesn't think the fire was an accident either. Tread carefully around him, honey. He'll pounce when you least expect it. Your father was blackmailing someone. I think it might have been Ned. Maybe he got tired of it."

"Are you saying this man may have set the fire? You and Joy both believe that?" Augusta asked. "But why? Just to get control of the dig? That hardly seems a motive to kill someone. And how do you know he was blackmailing someone?"

"Maggie told me, but she wouldn't say who it was. Fannie went back to tearing the paper napkin. "Maggie didn't trust Ned—that's why I think it might have been him. And she suspected he might be selling artifacts from the dig."

"Did my mother tell my father?"

"Not that I know of. She was afraid of Ned."

The mother Haley remembered feared nothing. "Did you tell all this to Chet Gillespie?" Haley asked slowly.

"Yes, but there was no proof. They didn't find enough of the bodies to do an autopsy, so we had to go with the fire."

Haley winced at the look on her grandmother's face. Did Fannie have to be quite so blunt? "Did they check to see if it was arson? Can't they tell how the fire started?"

"This is Stalwart. We don't have arson investigators and such. Trooper Gillespie is a good man, but he's overworked from all the shenanigans the men pull in this town. He declared it an accident and left it at that. But maybe you can get him to reopen the investigation."

"On what grounds? This Ned Bundle isn't going to admit anything to me."

"He might." Fannie thrust out her jaw in a stubborn pose. "I just hate to see him get away with this. Don't you want to find out what happened to your parents?"

"Did you date him or something?" Haley asked.

A tide of red swept up Fannie's face, and she looked down. "That has nothing to do with anything."

Her instincts had been right. "I realize you don't like Ned Bundle, but a half-forgotten dig of doubtful value is hardly enough to kill over."

"I hoped you had more spunk than to ignore this," Fannie said. "I heard how you loved to explore. Isn't that how your sister died?"

Haley wasn't going to talk about Chloe. Not anymore. "My parents' deaths is something for the law, not for me. I don't have the expertise to delve into something like this."

"I might ask some questions," Augusta said thoughtfully. "This whole thing makes me uneasy."

"Stay out of it, Augusta! I don't want anything to happen to you."

Fannie smiled. "Honey, if you're so sure I'm all wet, why would you think your grandma might get hurt?"

"The truth? I don't care. If that sounds harsh, maybe it is. My parents died for me a long time ago. They exited my life and never looked back." She expected Fannie to try to make excuses for her parents, and she didn't want to hear them.

The older woman nodded. "I talked to your mother about you several times. She was hard, clear to the end. It made no sense to blame an eight-year-old. You were too young to understand."

Haley didn't look at Augusta or Fannie. "Oh, I understood. I knew what I did was wrong, and that I'd killed my sister. My parents never blamed me more than I blamed myself. If I could have taken Chloe's place, I would have."

"Don't say that, Haley." Augusta put her hand over Haley's restless fingers. "It was the Lord's will. We have to accept what happened."

Haley clapped her hands over her ears. "I don't want to hear anymore about the Lord's will. If he's that gruesome, how can you love him?"

Augusta yanked Haley's hands down. "God promises he'll work all things out for our good, Haley. All things, not just the ones we like. This is an evil world, but God is good."

"I see no evidence of that," Haley said stubbornly. She glanced at her watch. "I'm going back to my room." She stood and dropped some money on the table. "Thanks for the information, Fannie. If we hear anything, we'll let you know." She grabbed her crutches and fled the café.

Twelve

W hat are you doing out of your room?" Tank scooped up Oscar, who was racing up and down the hotel hallway. His yipping would soon bring irate hunters out of their rooms in droves. The little dog wriggled in his arms and licked his chin. He strode down the hall to Haley's room and rapped on the door.

When no one answered, he rapped again, harder, and the door eased open. Sunshine flooded the room from the open curtains. "Haley?" He felt a stirring of unease. "Is everything okay?"

A rhythmic thump came from the hallway to his left. He turned to see Haley coming toward him on the crutches he'd made her. Turning toward her so she could see the dog in his arms, he smiled. "We have an escapee."

"How did he get out?" Her skin was flooded with high color, and a sheen of perspiration beaded her forehead.

"Are you okay?"

She nodded and pushed the door to her room open wider. "Just exhausted. I'd forgotten how tiring crutches are. I need to go to the store and get some moisturizer for my hands. They're sore."

"I'll get it for you. Rest awhile. I'll be right back." He followed her inside, where she dropped her backpack and half fell into the chair.

She held out her arms for the dog. "I'd better get it myself. I'm a little picky about the brand."

"Are you always this independent, or only with me?" He plopped Oscar in her arms. Were those tears in her eyes? "Whoa, I didn't mean it. Are you okay?"

"I'm fine." She dashed the tears from her cheeks with an angry jerk. "It's nothing."

"Looks like it," he observed. "Nothing always makes me look like I'm about to explode. It's good to do nothing and get the blood pumping."

Her angry expression eased, and she sniffled, then smiled, though it seemed a little forced. "I don't want to talk about it." She heaved herself to her feet.

"I'll go with you. What do we do with the mutt?"

"Leave him here."

"He was outside in the hallway."

She paused. "For real?"

"How else do you think I got him? I didn't break into your room."

"I was too mad to think." Her smile was shamefaced. Her gaze wandered the room. "I'm sure I left the door locked. Positive. It was unlocked?"

"And not latched." He shrugged. "Maybe the maid didn't lock back up."

"Why would the maid be here? We haven't even slept in the beds yet." She swung on her crutches toward the bathroom and peered into the tiny room. "It doesn't look like anything is disturbed."

Tank went to the door and knelt to look at the latch. The doorframe had numerous scratches and gouges, but the latch and tongue seemed intact. The screws were firmly attached and tight. "Has your grandmother been back?"

Haley shook her head. "She's been with me. We went for lunch. Augusta is still at the café talking to an old friend of my mother's."

She looked away and didn't meet his questioning gaze. Bingo. Whatever had happened at lunch had upset her. Every time someone brought up her parents, she became tight-lipped. He'd liked the Walshes, but he was beginning to wonder if he ever really knew them.

Haley picked up her backpack. "Let's go."

"I'll carry that." He took her backpack and slung it over one shoulder, then held the door open for her.

13

Haley thought her heart was going to pump out of her chest by the time she got to the shop. She was woefully out of shape, and she promised herself to start an exercise program the minute she got back to Phoenix. She'd see about ordering a prosthesis for running.

"I'll be glad when I can throw these away."

He grinned. "You never know. You might take it in your head

to whack an intruder again like a female Rambo. They might come in handy."

She giggled. Nervous jitters again. Why did he affect her that way? She was usually able to handle male attention with dignity. Not that he was interested in her, she hastened to assure herself. They were as dissimilar as Oscar and Miki. She browsed through the toiletries aisle and found a surprising number of familiar items, though the prices made her gasp. She finally selected a medicated lotion. She paid for her purchase, and Tank tucked it into her backpack.

He followed her out the door onto the sidewalk. "Now what?"

"You don't have to follow me around all afternoon."

"I don't have anything better to do," he said cheerfully. "I called to check on Libby and Brooke earlier to see if they wanted to come to town. Libby wants to finish the laundry, so they'll arrive about three. I'm yours until then."

Hers. The thought made her stop, and he barreled into her. His big hands caught her before she could topple into the mud. "Thanks," she muttered. A giggle fought to rise through her throat, but she stuffed it back down.

"No problem." He seemed reluctant to let go of her.

She was in no hurry to move away either. His huge hands covered nearly all of her forearms, and their warmth seeped through her sweater. She could smell his musky scent, and a tremble started in her knees and moved to the pit of her stomach. She quickly turned her head so Tank wouldn't see and ask what she was thinking about. "Do you know where Joy lives?"

"Sure." He eyed her. "You want to go see her?"

The uncertainty in his face irritated her. "Do you think she should be warned first?"

"No, it's not that. It's just you are already upset, and I wasn't sure you were up to a confrontation."

"Is it going to be a confrontation? She doesn't even know me."

"And you don't know her, but I could feel the prickles coming off you in waves when you just mentioned her name. What do you have against her?"

"Nothing." Haley looked away.

"Well good, because she's a great kid. Mature for her age and so sweet."

She was tired of hearing about how perfect Joy was. She punched her finger in his chest. "Okay, you want to know? How would you feel if your parents disowned you for something you did when you were eight and you saw them only once or twice in a twenty-year span? Now I find out they had another daughter they never told me about, and loved her like they should have loved me. They put Joy in my sister Chloe's place as if Chloe never existed. You think that would make you a little hostile?"

He backed up as she shouted and continued to jam her finger into his breastbone. If she hadn't been so angry, she might have laughed at the dismayed expression on his face.

"Whoa," he said. He caught her hand and held on when she tried to jerk it away. "No wonder you have a hide as thick as a buffalo's. Calm down."

"I'm perfectly calm," she said through gritted teeth. "Or I would be if you'd let go of my hand."

He released her and held up his hands. "If you want to hit me again, go ahead. Maybe you'll feel better."

Her anger ran off like melting snow. It wasn't his fault. It wasn't Joy's fault either. She was as bad as her parents. She passed her hand over her forehead and eyes. "Sorry to take it out on you." She leaned on her crutches and pulled her camera to her face, then stared at him through the viewfinder. That was better. She snapped a couple of pictures.

He took the camera from her hands and dropped it to let it hang on its strap. "Don't hide behind your camera. If you will face this, Haley, it will fail to have any power over you. Let's go see your sister. Maybe you're ready now."

"She's my half sister," she said automatically. She swung along beside Tank.

"Half is as good as full. She's a sweet girl. I think you'll like her."

Haley didn't answer. She didn't want to like her. It might make her own faults seem more glaring. They moved in silence past clapboard and log homes that lined the narrow streets of Stalwart. A few had well-kept yards where phlox grew in profusion, lifting their faces to the Alaskan spring sky. The fragrance of the flowers filled her head and siphoned off her feelings of inadequacy. Okay, so she was out of her element here. She'd had years of practice in faking it.

Tank paused in front of a low-slung clapboard house. "This is it."

The front door had claw marks from a dog on the lower half of the wood, the curtains at the windows were a soft faded-out blue, and moss grew on the shingles. The front yard looked like it hadn't been mown in a month. Haley felt a stirring of something that felt like pity. Her half sister lived in his hovel? Why? What kind of family did she belong to?

Tank stepped to the door and rapped hard. From inside, Haley could hear a child squalling and the blare of a television soap opera. "Shut up!" a woman yelled. Moments later, the door swung open. The woman's low-rise jeans were topped by a light-blue sweater. A blue bandana held back her dyed red hair.

Struggling to maintain her smile, Haley stepped in front of Tank. "Hello, I was wondering if I could see Joy."

"Who are you, some new sales drone?" The woman took out her cigarette and tossed it to the concrete step, where she crushed it under what Haley called Barbie-doll shoes, slip-on high-heeled mules with no back. It joined a pile of other cigarette butts.

"I'm Haley Walsh."

The woman blinked. "Walsh. You related?" A crafty expression crossed her face, and she smiled. "We're so glad to have her with us. I know her mother would approve. Our little boy adores her."

The child's wailing from somewhere in the house was beginning to grate on Haley. She strengthened her flagging smile. "Is Joy here?"

"Sure." The woman turned and bellowed. "Joy!"

The wailing grew louder, and a young girl appeared with a one-year-old boy on her hip. Wisps of hair escaped her long blond braids. Cereal stained the front of her white top, and she looked tired. Haley inhaled, unable to tear her eyes from the familiar face. If Chloe had lived to be twelve or thirteen, she would have looked like this girl.

Joy's blue eyes went from Haley to Tank, and she brightened. "Hey, Tank. How're Brooke and Libby?"

"They're just fine, Joy. I brought someone to meet you."

Joy's curious gaze went to Haley. Haley's throat constricted, and her lips parted. This young girl had enjoyed the love Haley had always craved, but Haley couldn't hate her like she wanted to. A curious mixture of pity, curiosity, and affection surprised her. Maybe it was because of her uncanny resemblance to Chloe.

Haley wet her lips. "I'm Haley. Haley Walsh."

Joy stared, and her gaze traveled from the top of Haley's auburn curls to her crutches and missing leg. "You're Haley? I thought—" She broke off.

"What?"

"Nothing." Her lips trembled.

"Would you like to go for some ice cream?" Tank put in. "The two of you can get to know one another."

"She has work to do," the woman objected.

Joy turned pleading eyes to the hard-faced woman. "Please, Alice," she begged.

Alice gnawed on her lip, then glanced at her watch. "Half an hour. You be back before Craig gets home from work."

"Okay." Joy handed her the child and stepped outside.

Conscious of the girl's rapt expression, Haley wished she could dig out what her parents had led Joy to believe. But did she really want to know?

13

The small ice-cream shop, decorated in red and white, reminded Haley of a Steak 'n Shake in the Lower Forty-eight. The spotless black-and-white tile made an attractive contrast to the rest of the place. Rescue workers and their dogs crowded the café. Haley perched on a red stool at a black Formica table and tried to think of how to open the conversation with Joy. Tank seemed to have no trouble. The young girl chattered to him about school, her friends, and her pet cat. A pet. That might be common ground.

"I have a dachshund named Oscar," Haley said. She pulled her camera to her face and snapped some pictures of the room, then took several pictures of Joy.

"Oh, you have to enter him in the wiener-dog race today!" Joy's dark eyes sparked with enthusiasm. "It's so fun to watch."

"I don't know," Haley began. "I don't know anything about training for a race."

"I'll help you," Joy said. "Can we go meet Oscar after we eat our ice cream?"

Haley glanced at Tank. He was watching them with an expression that said *How are you going to get out of this?* She lifted her chin to meet the challenge in his eyes. "Sure, we'll do that if we have time."

The light in Joy's eyes faded. "Oh, that's right, I have to get home."

"How is it at the Worleys'?" Tank's voice was gentle.

"It's okay. It's not like it was with Maggie and Dad, but it's okay." Joy's eyes were moist. She looked at Haley. "Are you here to figure out who killed them?"

Haley sat back in her chair and exhaled. "I heard you don't think it was an accident."

Joy shook her head. "Do we have to talk about it now? I wanted to get to know you first. Otherwise you might think I'm crazy." She tipped her head to one side. "You look like Maggie. She had hair your color."

"Someone else told me that," Haley blurted, then wished she'd kept silent. Her admission would prove to Joy that she didn't know her own mother. "And you look like . . ." She looked down at her hands.

"Like Chloe?" Joy nodded. "Everyone says that. We both look like Dad."

"How did you come to live with my, er, our parents?" Haley asked. She'd work up to asking about the fire later.

Joy examined Haley's face. "Mama was an archeologist who worked with your parents. Your mom was sick, and I guess Dad noticed Mama. I didn't know who my dad was until Mama died in a diabetic coma when I was at school one day. I freaked at first, sure I was going to get stuck living with my aunt and uncle Worley. Our lawyer gave me a letter from Mama that told me everything and said I was to go to my father if anything happened to her. It was pretty wild going to the door that first time. I was scared, but Dad took me right in. And Maggie was great to me right off." Her smile didn't reach her eyes. "I know now it was because I looked so much like Chloe. I didn't know for a long time that they had another daughter. It was kind of weird the way they never talked about you."

Haley's eyes burned, and she couldn't have vocalized a sound past the lump in her throat if her life had depended on it. This wasn't news to her, so why was she upset? She took several shallow breaths and willed herself not to feel the ache in her heart.

"What did you do?" Joy asked. "They always acted like it was too shameful to talk about. There's nothing that bad."

Haley looked into Joy's curious eyes. "Chloe was the perfect child. I don't remember ever hearing her cry. I was into one scrape after another. It was natural they would prefer her."

"Parents aren't supposed to play favorites," Tank said.

"Maybe not, but it was hard not to with Chloe. She brightened all our lives."

"So what did you do?" Joy asked again. "Something you did when you were a kid is nothing to get a wedgie over." She took a bite of her ice cream.

It would have been so easy to accept Joy's way out, to not take the blame for what happened, but Haley had to be honest. She shook her head. "I could be vindictive sometimes."

"All kids can be."

"Not to the extent I was." Haley was suddenly tired of hiding the truth. Once they knew, they'd let her alone to take her pictures. She rubbed her forehead. "I killed my sister when I was eight."

Joy put her spoon down. "I'm sure it was accidental."

Haley shook her head. "Chloe had broken my favorite doll, and I hit her. I got in trouble when she cried, and I decided she needed to get in trouble herself. She was never in trouble, and though I loved her, I got tired of it sometimes."

"I can understand that," Tank said.

His soft voice urged her on. She'd show him there was nothing about her to be admired. "At an archeological dig in the Wrangell Mountains, there was an old mine we were never supposed to go into. It wasn't safe. We were camped there, and I talked Chloe into going with me to explore. I was going to tell my mother that it was Chloe's idea." She smiled. "Stupid, really. My parents knew both our temperaments well enough to know whose idea it was. But I was only eight, and it seemed perfectly logical then."

She took a deep breath. "We went to the mine. I had a flashlight, and we went down a narrow tunnel that looked interesting. We were just about to go back when it fell in." Even now, she could smell the choking dust, hear Chloe's screams. And her own. "We were trapped by the cave-in, and we just had to hope our parents would find us in time. Rocks fell on both of us. That's how I lost my leg."

She patted her pant leg where it ended below the knee. "But Chloe died. Not right away. My flashlight was lost in the cave-in, and I talked to her through the hours. Her voice kept getting weaker and weaker. Finally, she didn't answer no matter how much I begged." She fell silent. A fresh wave of grief overwhelmed her. "I loved her so much," she choked. "I never wanted to hurt her."

"You were just a child." Tank's big hand covered hers. "You can't blame yourself."

Haley didn't look at him or Joy, but pushed on to finish the story. "My parents were devastated. They tried to pick up the pieces at first—to go on loving me. But gradually the full story came out about how I wanted to punish Chloe. They changed after that. A month later they sent me to my grandmother."

"Did they never come to see you?" Joy's voice was a horrified whisper. "I can't believe it. They were always so kind to me."

"I saw them a couple of times," Haley admitted. "They came home one year for Christmas, and another time they visited on my birthday. I ran to hug my mother, but she pushed me away." She noticed the horror and censure on the faces of her companions. "It's okay," she assured them. "I got used to it. And my grandmother filled the void. She loves me in spite of my faults."

Tears were streaming down Joy's face. "I hate them," she muttered. "How could they?"

"They were right," Haley said. "I deserved their hatred. I learned at an early age what I was capable of. I've never forgotten it, and I've tried so hard to become a better person because of it."

Tank shook his head. "You were their daughter. Parents are supposed to have unconditional love for their children."

"I don't blame them. I have to pay for my mistakes. That's justice."

Tank took her hand. "It's time you forgave yourself and put it behind you. You were a kid, Haley. Kids are kids. You didn't maliciously set out to hurt her."

"Now you sound like Augusta." Haley stirred her melting ice cream.

"God loves you," Joy said. "I don't think you know that, but he does."

"If that's love, I don't need it," Haley said. "He let my sister die though I begged him to save her. He doesn't listen."

"God never said we wouldn't have sorrow," Tank said. "I find it odd that you'd excuse your parents but not God. He is the ultimate judge and makes correct decisions on everything, unlike our earthly parents. He was with you in that dark hole, and he's with you now. He can turn even this out for your good if you'd let him."

"I don't want good to come out of it—that would make it worse. Besides, the difference is that God could have done something about Chloe, and he didn't."

"Your parents could have chosen to forgive your childish acting out too, and they didn't."

Haley stood and tossed her warm ice cream in the trash receptacle by the door. "I'd better go check on Augusta. Thanks for listening." She grabbed up her crutches.

"Can I meet our grandmother?" Joy asked.

"It's getting late," Haley pointed out. "How about later? If you can get permission, call me, and I'll come get you."

Joy stood and rushed to hug her. Haley let the girl enfold her in her arms, but it was as though she stood outside the scene watching it through her viewfinder.

⁂

Tank wasn't sure how to breach the awkward silence. Haley swung along on her crutches without looking to the right or the left. Her face was set and strained, and he knew revealing her past had taken a huge toll on her mental state. Poor kid. She was beating herself up over a foolish childhood mistake, and it looked like she intended to continue for the rest of her life.

He cleared his throat. "That took guts to tell us." She glanced up at him, then quickly looked away, but not before he saw the moisture in her eyes. She didn't answer, so he tried again to break past the wall she was busy erecting. "Talking about it helps. Keeping the pain bottled up just makes it hurt worse."

She didn't look up from her scrutiny of the path in front of her. "I don't notice you talking about things much. You never mention your wife's death."

He winced. She knew how to turn the tables on him. "Sorry. You're right. It's not easy to talk about things you feel responsible for."

She stopped and looked at him then. "I thought she drowned. How can you feel responsible for that?"

Her amber gaze pinned him in place. He shuffled his feet and looked away. "I should have realized she needed more of my time. Brooke's birth threw her for a loop, and she wasn't herself after that. When I wasn't catching up on my research, I was doting on Brooke. I think Leigh felt left out. Just before she died, she said she needed some space, that she needed to talk to her dad about it. She was unhappy, and I didn't do what I needed to fix it."

He took off his floppy hat and rubbed his head. "I got home late that night, and she wasn't there. Brooke was sleeping like a baby. I went out to look for Leigh. I never found her, so I called in help on the radio. Early the next morning, I found her in the lake."

"I'm sorry." Haley put her hand on his arm. "I know it's hard to think about. But you still have Brooke."

He covered her hand with his. Being this close to her somehow eased his pain. "The autopsy report just came back. Leigh had a high amount of a sleeping aid called Seconal in her blood. Ed Bixby thinks she killed herself." Or worse, that Tank killed her, but he bit back the words.

Her fingers tightened on his; then she pulled her hand away. "Will that hurt your custody case?"

He hadn't considered the possibility. A sudden pain flared at his temple. "I'd better let my lawyer know. Brooke is my life. I can't lose her." He checked his watch. "Libby should be here with her any minute. I thought they'd be here by now."

They reached Chugach Street. A few beat-up trucks rumbled past, and Tank pulled Haley out of the way of the mud that came slinging up from the tires. Some light, appealing scent rose from her hair. The sunshine made it glow with even more fiery red. It was all he could do to resist bending down and pressing his lips to the top of her head and inhaling.

She looked up at him, and her eyes widened. He wondered if she felt the same pull he did. It was useless with so much separating them. He'd never live in a big city, and she would never live here. There was no way to reconcile their differences. Her spirit and courage drew him, but he had to resist it.

Thirteen

Someone had been cooking in the hotel. The odor of sausage and sauerkraut filled the hallway. Haley wanted to fling open the windows at the end of the hallway, then caught herself. It wasn't the sauerkraut that made her feel she was walking through a nauseating mist. It was her own self-loathing. Telling the story to Joy and Tank had brought it all back.

She was thankful the hallway was deserted. Haley wouldn't have been able to smile and greet another soul. She wanted to get to her room and curl up on her bed. Pull the covers over her head and forget where she was and why she was here. The warm sunshine of Phoenix seemed distant, though the cold she felt had little to do with the gray, cool air. She didn't belong in this hallway with its faded green wallpaper that was peeling and bubbled in the corners. She longed to lift her face to warm Arizona sunshine, to pick up the threads of the life that had helped her to forget what had happened in this land of wide spaces and cold hearts.

But she was stuck now. She'd have to see it through. She fumbled with the key in the door. It slipped from her stiff, cold fingers and dropped onto the worn gold carpet. Balancing herself with the crutches, she stooped to retrieve it. Before she could try the lock again, the door swung open.

Augusta stood looking down at her. "You were gone so long, darling. I was beginning to worry. Where did you go?"

"To meet Joy."

"How did it go?"

"Fine." Haley stepped past Augusta and advanced to the bed.

"What was she like?"

Haley tried to ignore the eagerness in her grandmother's voice. The hollow feeling between her shoulder blades wasn't jealousy, she told herself. She looked at the faded bedspread and wondered how many people had sat on it other than herself. She folded it up and moved it to a chair. At least the sheets were clean and white. Pulling off her boot, she lay down on top of the bed.

"Don't you dare take a nap when I'm dying to know everything that happened!" Augusta sat on the bed beside her.

Pinned by her grandmother's blue-eyed gaze, Haley realized she wasn't going to be able to escape in sleep. Hugging the pillow, she sat up and pushed her hair out of her face. "She's perfect, okay? Wide-eyed, innocent, and totally deserving of my parents' love." She softened her tone at Augusta's stricken face. "She wants to meet you. She looks just like Chloe, Augusta."

Augusta leaned forward, and the familiar scent of Augusta's peppermint breath whispered over her face. Augusta cupped

Haley's face in her hands. "Haley, you will always be my special one. You don't have to worry about anyone taking your place in my heart. But there's room for more in our family. Don't let fear keep you from doing the right thing."

Her cheeks burned. Augusta's face blurred, and Haley blinked rapidly. "I want to go home, Augusta."

Augusta straightened, and Haley recognized the Doris Day determination. "No, Haley. Running away won't solve anything. I want you to face this, to forgive yourself once and for all."

Haley pulled her face free. "I thought I might be able to do that here, Augusta. I would chronicle Chloe's short life, face my fears and all the things I'd done like my shrink said, and be done with it, but she was wrong. The guilt is still there. I am to blame. My sister is dead because I wanted to hurt her! How can I forgive myself?"

"You know why you can't forgive yourself, Haley?" Augusta asked, her voice quiet. "Because if you do, you think that will make it okay that Chloe is dead. You think you'll be letting Chloe down a second time. But listen—forgiving yourself doesn't make it okay. When you recognize you're part of the human race with all our foibles and frailties, you can let it go. When we sin or make a mistake, we try to learn from it. We don't hold onto it and nurse our feelings of unworthiness. God loved you when he formed you in your mother's womb, though he knew even then every choice you would make. If he can love you—and me—in spite of our faults, can't you learn to love yourself a little too?"

"It always goes back to God. If he loves me so much, why do I have this?" She slammed her palm down on her stump. "Why did he let my parents reject me? Why did he let my sister die?"

"We have no easy answers this side of heaven, Haley." Her grandmother's voice was so quiet, Haley had to strain to hear her reply. "Romans 8:28 says we know all things work together for good to those who know Christ and are the called according to his purpose. We can't see the big picture on this earth. We can only trust he's got it all in hand."

"I stopped believing that when he killed my sister," Haley said.

Augusta plowed on. "Deep down, you know I'm right, Haley. You're angry with God and angry with yourself. I know you sometimes feel aimless and wonder why you're here on this earth. You need to get in touch with God's purpose for your life. He has one. You just need to let him reveal it to you."

Haley didn't want to feel jealousy toward her newfound sister, and she hated upsetting her grandmother. Augusta had done so much for her over the years, and she didn't deserve this. "You want to meet Joy now? We could go back to her house." She rubbed her eyes. "I want you to see what she's living in now. We probably ought to do something to help her."

"Not now. You're tired. Take a nap, and we'll take a walk later. I saw a cute park on the way home from the café. Some fresh air might blow out the cobwebs."

Haley nodded, then lay down and pulled her knees to her chest. If only there was some way to be absolved of her guilt.

The radio squawked once, then died. Chet swore and threw the receiver down, making Tank's ears ring. "Radio gone again? I wanted to check in with Libby and see if they're on their way yet."

"Piece of junk," Chet muttered. He sighed and picked it up again, then rattled it. It surged back to life with a high-pitched squeal of an incoming call. He answered it and listened, then hung up slowly. "Got the autopsy back on Joe Wooten."

Tank studied his father-in-law's face, which was set and hard. "And?"

"And he was shot. The bear got him after he was dead."

Tank inhaled quickly. Murder. While violence always loomed just around the corner in Alaska, he hadn't expected this. It was in his neck of the woods too. The hair on the back of his neck stood at attention. Who could have killed Joe—and why? It seemed like death had stalked the area for a year now. First the Walshes, then Leigh, and now Dr. Wooten. It left him looking over his shoulder, even though he knew the incidents weren't related.

"Mind if I use the radio?" Tank asked.

"If you can get it to work."

Chet moved out of the way, and Tank took his place. No one answered. "Libby and Brooke must be on their way to town." He disconnected, then swung around to watch Chet going through paperwork on his desk. "Do we have any idea what happened to Joe? What caliber gun, any information?"

"Yeah, but what we have doesn't tell me much. He was shot through the temple with a shotgun."

"Ugh. It's going to be hard to figure out whose gun did it."

"Probably why the perp used a shotgun. It will be harder to trace." He rubbed his forehead. "I don't want to tell Sue about this. It was hard enough announcing her husband was dead."

"So where do you start with Joe's death?"

"The usual places. Talk to his acquaintances, see who saw him last. I'll probably start with Sue."

"She's not a hunter."

"No, but she can give me details of what he was doing the last time she saw him."

Tank glanced at his watch. He had some time to kill until Libby and Brooke showed up. "Want some company?"

"I'd better handle this. Thanks anyway." He nodded toward the window. "The park is hopping today. Go take a stroll, and let me worry about the murder."

"Don't you think it's a little odd that we've had all these deaths lately?" Tank said.

A shadow darkened Chet's eyes. "You don't have to tell me. When we found Leigh, I didn't think I could go on living. I was drinking myself into oblivion when Joe Wooten dragged me into the bathroom and pushed me into a cold shower. He poured all the booze down the drain and came over every night for a month to play cards and drink coffee until I got my feet under me again. I don't know what I'm going to do without him."

Chet kept his grief for his daughter very private, and Tank never realized the trooper had nearly unraveled. "Sorry, Chet," Tank said quietly.

Chet waved his big hand in the air. "I'll find out who did this." The radio squawked. Chet held up a finger in Tank's direction. "Hang on a minute." He went to the radio.

Tank glanced at the pictures on the wall while Chet was on the radio. A burned-out cabin arrested his gaze. The Walsh cabin. While death was a part of life out here, he couldn't remember another period of time where so many people had died. Could they all be related? He shook his head. Where had that thought come from? They had nothing in common. Only Joe Wooten's was murder. But the thought lodged in his brain like a burr. Maybe he'd ask around a little about the Walsh fire. It couldn't hurt. If he found something, he could ask Chet to test for accelerants.

13

The park's tranquility washed over Haley. A Native, his face brown and wrinkled, carved tiny ivory seals and swans from a cigar box full of seal tusks. His legs crossed and his back straight, he sat on an old army blanket in the middle of a field of wild-flowers. To the man's right, Haley saw a woman with salt-and-pepper hair drawn back into a tight bun. She was mounting some kind of little creature on a wooden plaque. Boughs of spruce lay heaped in a basket beside her.

They'd been moving toward the park when Libby and Brooke pulled up in a pickup truck. Brooke had begged to go with them to the park, and Libby had seemed happy to oblige. As they walked, she told Augusta how much she loved her books.

Haley paused to watch the Natives work. Libby saw Haley staring. "That's a hoofaboo," she said. "It's made from a caribou hoof. You're supposed to hang him on a south-facing wall, and he'll bring luck to your home."

"Charming," Augusta said.

Haley stared at the cute little hoofaboo and wondered how it would look on her pale-lemon walls in the elegant home that looked out on White Tanks. Probably ridiculous, but the little face was cute. Oscar nudged her chin with a wet nose, and she pushed him down then put him on the ground.

A crowd began to gather. A dachshund ran over to rub noses with Oscar, then more wiener dogs yipped and tore across the park. "What's going on?" Haley asked Libby. She loved to watch the dogs. Dachshunds always looked like they were smiling.

Libby's delighted smile spread across her face. "I'd forgotten. It's our annual wiener-dog races."

"I've heard of them but never seen one. Joy mentioned it."

"You should put Oscar in it." Augusta patted the dog's head. "He's fast."

"Oscar wouldn't know what to do. He's never raced before." Haley shielded her eyes with her hand. "Here comes Tank now." He strode across the park and joined them.

His smile broadened as he looked around at the dogs. "The wiener-dog races! Brooke loves them."

"Oscar is eating up the attention. Augusta wants me to enter him."

He rubbed Oscar's head, and the little dog wriggled with delight. "Go ahead. You might as well enjoy the evening. You may never see another wiener-dog race."

A small boy of around ten tugged on her sleeve. "Hey, lady, we need another dog in the race. Can we race your dog?"

"He doesn't know how," Haley told the child.

"The dogs are good at figuring it out. You stand at the end of the run and call to him. He'll come running to you."

"Go ahead," Tank said. "Me and Brooke will cheer you on."

"Okay. Show me where to stand."

The boy took Oscar. "Right there," he said, pointing toward a gnarled spruce tree. "You'll be able to figure out when to call him. I've got to get a numbered shirt on him."

Tank and Libby went to stand with Augusta and Brooke. Haley joined the group of dog owners. They ranged from women about her age to men with long, straggly beards who looked like they'd be more comfortable mushing across the snow with huskies. A few teenagers talked excitedly as they waited to call their dogs. She stood beside a young couple with a big handsome German shepherd.

"Nice dog you've got," she said.

"This is Samson. He's a search dog," the woman said. She had hair a little lighter than Haley's own coppery locks and an open, friendly expression. "I'm Bree Matthews from Rock Harbor, Michigan."

"You're a long way from home," Haley said. She introduced herself. "My dog is in the race, and we have no idea what we're doing." She pointed him out as the young boy brought Oscar to the starting line. He wore a tiny red shirt with the number ten. Smiling, she moved to the left directly across from her dog. Oscar liked to run. Maybe he would do okay.

A man with a bullhorn stepped up. "We're about ready to start. Our prizes this year range from hoofaboos to free dinners. The grand prize is five hundred dollars."

The crowd cheered. The woman to Haley's left poked her in the ribs. "I'll take the money and splurge on a rug for the living room in my cabin. The floor gets mighty cold in the winter."

"Which dog is yours?"

"The red one next to the dapple. Which one is yours?"

"He's the dapple."

"I haven't seen many of them. He's cute." The woman stopped talking as the moderator waved a flag in his hand.

"When I drop the flag, you can call your dogs," he said. He waved the Alaska flag imperiously. "Get ready, set, GO!" He dropped the flag in a grand gesture.

"Oscar! Come here, boy!" Haley leaned on her crutches, clapped her hands, and continued to shout. Oscar hesitated a moment, then flung himself into the sport. Floppy ears flying behind them like silken banners, the tide of wiener dogs moved down the track. Their short legs were almost a blur. Each doggy face wore an expression of joy in the mad run.

With difficulty on only one leg, she knelt and patted on the ground, calling encouragement to Oscar. He was lagging behind, but when he saw her kneel, he put on an additional burst of speed. She heard Tank's hoarse shout from the sidelines and Augusta's high-pitched squeak of approval. Oscar had only two dogs ahead of him now. He seemed to smile even wider as his broad little chest put everything he had into the run for glory.

"Come on, Oscar, you can do it. Come here, boy!" Oscar pulled ahead of the dog in front of him, which inexplicably decided to put on the brakes. The other dog's short legs skidded to a stop, and then she loped off to the right, colliding with another dog. The two tangled and reminded Haley of the long red balloons that clowns twisted into the shape of animals, only in this case, the shape wasn't recognizable.

Now there was only one dog ahead of Oscar. Haley's pet gave a giant leap—or as giant as his short legs would allow—and drew neck-and-neck with the lead dog. He growled as if to say *Back off*, then leaped into Haley's arms. He was wet and panting as he lolled his tongue over her face. The crowd roared its approval at Oscar's win.

"Good boy!" She patted him and praised him. "You won."

"Hey, lady, you want to sell him?" The little boy scratched his head. "I'll give you ten dollars for him."

"Sorry, he's not for sale."

The kid frowned, then shrugged and ran back to his parents. Oscar wiggled to be put down, so Haley put him on the grass and followed him to the rest of the group. The man with the bullhorn announced Oscar's win. Oscar raced off to jump into Brooke's lap. She giggled when he licked her chin. Haley went up to accept the trophy and award money, then rejoined the group.

Haley was trying to look everywhere except at Tank's face. She didn't like this attention that warmed her blood.

Tank put his hand on her arm. "I'd like to talk to you for a minute."

"Is something wrong?" She finally tipped a glance up into his face.

"The autopsy came back on Joe Wooten. He was shot. The bear got to his body after death."

"So at least we know Miki didn't kill him."

"Yeah. But I wanted to ask if you knew any details about the fire that killed your parents."

"Not really." She hesitated. "Fannie Coghill thought it might not have been an accident. She said my mother told her she sus-pected Ned Bundle of selling artifacts. She suggested we talk to Joy about it. I meant to do that, but it seemed a pretty far-fetched notion. And I'm not sure Joy would know anything about it any-way. Why are you asking about the fire?"

His gaze bored into hers. "There have been so many so-called accidents lately, and now a real murder. I just wondered if we were maybe missing something where Leigh and your folks are concerned. I think I'll talk to Joy about it. I'd like us to test for accelerants in the cabin's ashes."

"Hasn't it been too long?"

He shook his head. "I asked a buddy in the fire department. Most lab tests are sensitive enough to detect the accelerant even after considerable weathering. He can put me in touch with a lab that does it."

Something inside her cracked at the thought. She'd never imagined she had any emotion left for her parents besides bit-terness. "You think someone set their cabin on fire? Who would do that?"

"Maybe no one. But I think we need to find out."

She nodded, but she didn't know what to make of the strange sensation she felt inside, something like new life stirring after a long winter hiatus. She wanted to dig a hole and bury those feelings, but she was curious to see what they were. "Augusta wants to meet Joy."

"See if she'll come now. We can stop by the Worley house, then meet up with Libby and Brooke for supper."

"I doubt we'll find out anything. I think Joy was just upset when our parents died and had to blame someone."

"You might be right. People like to have someone to blame."

She realized he was talking about her. "That's hardly the same thing."

"Isn't it? I've been thinking about your experience. You didn't make that mine collapse, Haley. It was an accident. You didn't pick up a gun and shoot her."

She wished she could believe it was just an unlucky accident, but she knew how wicked her own heart was. "Let's not talk about it."

"You're going to have to let it go sooner or later."

"Then later." She giggled and clapped her hand over her mouth.

"Nervous, huh? About talking to Joy or dealing with your past?"

"Maybe both. Wait here, and I'll get Augusta. I'll tell Libby what we're doing."

⁂

Tank, Haley, and Augusta walked the three blocks to the Worley house. Tank tried to look at the town through Haley's eyes. The residents of Stalwart lived up to its name. Most of the houses were no more than eight hundred square feet, if that. There was no beauty, no aesthetic appeal in any of the homes. Plain Jane, boxy wooden structures. A splash of green occasionally broke the brown sameness. It was a world Tank knew and loved, but watching the bleak expression on Haley's face, he realized it held no appeal for her.

Toys lay in the Worleys' yard. This time when they knocked on the door, a male voice answered. "Joy, get the door!"

Augusta's nostrils flared at the peremptory tone in the man's voice. "He's talking to her like she's some kind of servant," she hissed.

Haley nodded. "The woman treated her like that too. That's why I said we need to do something."

Tank peered through the screen door and saw Joy coming toward them. She had a dark mark on her arm. A bruise? He clenched his fists.

Joy stopped before she got to the door. Her hand flew to her mouth. "Oh. I didn't expect . . ." Her gaze went to Augusta. "Are you . . . ?" She pushed open the wooden screen door and stepped outside.

Augusta patted her hand. "Hello, Joy. I'm your grandmother. Call me Augusta like Haley."

The two inspected one another. Joy wasn't usually so tongue-tied, and Tank knew two encounters in one day had thrown her. "There are some questions Haley forgot to ask you. Do you have a few minutes?"

Fear flashed over Joy's face. "I don't think Craig will let me go with you. He was mad when he got home and found out Alice allowed me to leave with you."

Her hand touched the mark on her arm. It was a bruise, Tank saw, his anger ramping up immediately. "Let me handle it," he told her. He stepped past her to the door and pounded on it with all his might. The door shook, and the windowpanes rattled from the force of his fist.

The gruff voice down the hall swore viciously. Feet pounded on the wooden floor inside, and a big man punched open the screen door and stepped outside. His head thrust forward aggressively, and his hazel eyes narrowed—he looked ready to take on all comers. "What do you want?" Tank's size didn't seem to deter his belligerent stance.

"These ladies are Joy's family. We're taking her out for dinner."

"No, you aren't. She has chores to do. She spent all afternoon gallivanting around town."

"You put that bruise on her arm?" Tank jabbed his thumb in Joy's direction. The women gasped, and he saw them dart quick looks at Joy's arm.

"She fell," Craig said quickly. His eyes darted from Tank's face to Joy, then back again.

"I don't believe it. You touch her again, and you'll answer to me. You got that?" Tank was nearly yelling. He wheeled and took Joy's arm gently. "I'll have her back by nine." Haley and Augusta scurried ahead of him.

Joy came without resistance. "He'll make me pay for that," she said. "I know you were trying to help, but next time . . ." She bit her lip.

"There won't be a next time. You're not going back there," Haley said. Her color was high, and she swung along the rough streets on her crutches with a scowl that said she'd like to stomp Craig under her boots.

"Hold up." Tank stopped. "If that's your intention, we need to do this legally." He turned to Joy. "Did Craig put that bruise on your arm?"

She nodded. "Next time he'll make sure he puts them where people can't see."

"Will you tell Trooper Gillespie that?"

Joy hesitated and looked at the other women. "What am I going to do? Where will I live?"

"With me," Augusta said staunchly.

Joy's eyes lit with light. "You're moving here?"

"I live in Phoenix. You'll love it there."

Joy's smile faded. "I love it here. It's my home."

"We'll figure something out," Tank said. "For now, let's get this documented." He took her to see Chet, who listened to the stories of abuse. Haley snapped pictures of Joy's bruises, including some on her legs that her jeans had hidden. Her back had scars from beatings with a belt.

"What about the other children?" Haley asked.

"He never touches them. Only me. I think he resents the money he has to spend on me. They expected a boatload of money from my dad, and it's all been tied up in the estate. Once it comes through, I thought it would get better."

"I'll send a trooper to get your things," Chet said, his mouth in a grim line. "And I'm also going to ask the judge to do a home study to make sure the other children are not in danger."

"I kind of hate to leave them when they need me to watch the kids," Joy said. "The little ones are sweet."

Tank told Chet where to find them, and the group walked back toward the café. Joy was subdued, and he knew she wondered what would happen to her. She would be a polar bear in the desert if they tried to transplant her. Maybe she could live with him and Libby. Libby would like the company, and Brooke adored Joy.

Haley paused by the park. "Let's talk before we meet up with

Libby and Brooke. I don't think Brooke should hear the questions I have." The women sat on the bench together while Tank leaned his back against a fence post.

"We talked with Fannie," Haley said. "She said you don't think the fire was an accident."

Joy's eyes widened; then she ducked her head and shook it. "I think they were killed, but no one believes me."

"Who did you tell?" Tank asked.

"Fannie believes you," Augusta said.

"No one who can do anything about it," Joy amended. "I told Chet, but he said there was no evidence of anything weird." She splayed her fingers on her jeans.

"What makes you think it wasn't an accident?" Tank was beginning to wonder if Joy was just stubbornly refusing to face facts.

"See, you don't believe me either."

"Give me some facts, and maybe I will."

"I don't have any facts!" Joy rubbed her forehead. "I walked in on Ned Bundle one day at the dig. He shoved a crate out of the way when he saw me. Later, I went back and looked at it. It was full of artifacts. I told Maggie, and she started wondering if he was stealing them and selling them. She'd noticed several things missing. She told him she was going to tell Dad about it." She hesitated. "I think she didn't want to tell Dad about Ned. Dad liked Ned. He was always saying he'd never had a friend like him before. I think Mom didn't want to wreck that if she didn't have to."

Tank tried to think it through. "When was this?"

Joy bit her lip. "Two days before the fire." Her chin jutted out. "I think he didn't want to be found out, so he killed them."

"I could talk to him," Tank said. "If I can get some kind of proof, maybe Chet could have the bodies exhumed and autopsied. Or he might not have killed them. He may have just set fire to the cabin and the smoke got them."

"Fannie said there wasn't much to autopsy." Augusta's voice was low.

"There wasn't, but if they're looking at murder, they might find something."

Joy examined her short, stubby nails, decorated with chipped pink nail polish. "There's something else. I wanted to tell you sooner, but I didn't think you'd believe me."

Her voice quavered, and Tank focused on her tense and fearful face. "What is it?"

"Ned saw me looking at the crate." Joy's gaze came up to meet Tank's. "He said for me to keep my nose out of his business or I might end up in the lake."

Tank's arms came up in a defensive posture across his chest. "Like Leigh," he said. "Could he have had something to do with Leigh's death?"

Joy wet her lips. "I caught him watching her through binoculars once. He said she was hot."

Tank exhaled sharply. "I'll talk to him." He didn't know what to make of Joy's story. Could she have an overactive imagination? She seemed so mature and levelheaded for her age. He thought of the pills. Could someone have forced Leigh to take them? His mind didn't want to go there.

Fourteen

$\mathcal{S}$upper was a grim affair. Brooke chattered all through her meal of caribou burger and macaroni and cheese. More macaroni ended up on chipped tiled floor than in her. Libby kept shooting curious glances into their faces but didn't ask questions until they rose to go back to the hotel.

She caught Haley's arm as Tank went to pay at an ancient relic of a cash register that looked like it came into Alaska during the gold rush. Augusta and Joy took Brooke to a bubble-gum machine. "What's going on? It's like someone has died."

Libby didn't know how close she'd come. Haley told her what Joy had said and decided to focus on the story as it pertained to Tank first. "Did you ever notice Ned hanging around the lake, or the Walsh place?"

Libby shrugged helplessly. "I didn't stay out there much while Leigh was alive. She and I didn't get along very well."

"Why not?"

"I think she was jealous. She wanted all of Tank's attention

166

when he was home. He and I have always been close. It was a hard time for me, making myself back away to give him a chance to bond with his new wife. That's one of the reasons I took the cello seat in Philly, much as it killed me to leave here. When Brooke came along, I forced myself to listen to Leigh's snipes and to deal with her irritation every few months. I wasn't going to allow my niece to grow up without knowing me."

"So you never saw her with Ned? Or saw Ned do anything inappropriate?"

Libby shook her head. "I don't know the man well. I went over to watch the dig a few times, but it was kind of boring. Just digging in the dirt and sifting it for artifacts. I'd go bonkers doing that all day when I'd rather be playing my cello."

"What about at the dig? Did you notice him watching my mother or anything like that?"

"Like I said, I only went a few times. He worked in one part, and your parents in another."

Haley glanced over at Joy, who was getting gum out of the machine for Brooke. "Do you think Joy would lie or stretch the truth?"

"No way! Joy has a passion for the truth. Even when she got in trouble for being late, she never tried to wiggle out of it with a lie."

"I'll go see Ned at the dig tomorrow."

"Not you! Tank or Chet. If this guy is dangerous, you need to stay away. You're a beautiful girl, and you don't want to get him fixated on you."

Haley grinned. "I'd say you need to get your eyes checked."

She pulled her camera to her face. "Let me take your picture, and I'll show you beautiful."

Libby laughed and stood still while Haley snapped some pictures. "You never did say where he lives," Haley said, putting the lens cap back on her camera.

"Oh no, you don't. I'm not that easy to trick. Tank knows where to look. You stay out of it."

If only it were that easy. Haley had thought she'd destroyed all love for her parents, but like a seed exposed to sunshine, it had come bursting out when she discovered some maniac might have deliberately killed them. The emotion she hadn't been able to name earlier was *grief*. She was grieving for her parents for the first time.

The next morning, Haley went to the front desk to check for mail. When the pimply-faced young man brought out the long box, she nearly kissed him but resisted the impulse. She thanked him and took the box back to her room. She unwrapped it and lifted out her old prosthesis. It might not be the most advanced version, but she'd never seen a prettier limb.

Joy was watching, her bright blue eyes alive with curiosity. "Is that thing uncomfortable?"

"No, it's great. I'll be able to get along much better. The one that was stolen distributed my weight better, but this baby got me through for a lot of years." Haley patted the artificial limb, then strapped it on and pulled her jeans down over it. She put her sneaker on the fake foot.

"You'd never know if you didn't know," Joy said.

Haley stood and walked around. "Model-perfect now." She seized Joy and waltzed her around the room. "I feel like it's Christmas or something. I'd forgotten how hard it is to get around with crutches." She released her giggling sister, then called Savannah and thanked her for sending the leg. When she got off the phone, she saw Joy studying her.

"It must have been hard losing your leg."

"It was." Haley remembered the terror of seeing that flat sheet where her leg should be. "That reminds me, another man in town lost a leg to a bear. I should go talk to him. Jed Hoose, I think Tank said his name was."

"I heard they took him to the hospital in Anchorage."

"Oh, okay. Maybe another day then. I want to go talk to this Ned Bundle."

Augusta came out of the bathroom in time to hear her last comment. "Tank told you to stay out of it. And just yesterday you told Fannie you didn't want to get involved."

"I didn't believe her, not really. But I believe Joy." Oscar came to her, and she scooped him up.

Her sister's face lit with relief. "Thanks, Haley."

"Don't go without Tank," her grandmother ordered.

Looking at the two of them, Haley was struck by how much they looked alike. That same blond hair and blue eyes. A lump formed in her throat. She grabbed her camera. "Don't move." She snapped a couple of pictures. They belonged together. She wasn't sure she fit with them.

"Are you going to call Tank, or shall I?" Augusta pressed the issue.

"I'll call him. You're making a mountain out of a pile of bear scat." She grinned. "Don't tell Tank I said that."

"Maybe you should ask Chet to go too," Joy said. "Ned scares me."

"I'll have Tank. He could take on a brown bear with one arm tied behind him." Haley's spirits rose at the thought of spending the morning with Tank. She told herself it was just because she was doing something different, taking action.

She called Kipp's room and got no answer. She'd leave a message with the desk to tell him she'd be out today. He wouldn't like it, but right now, Haley didn't care.

Tank saw the woman through the window of his cabin before she saw him. Vonnie Bird had been Dr. Wooten's nurse for as long as he could remember. He opened the door, and she entered with purposeful steps. Nearly six feet tall, from the back she could be mistaken for a man. She was dressed in her usual attire: bib overalls over a checked shirt. Her hair stuck up in front, giving her the appearance of a startled ostrich.

She nodded at Libby and Brooke. "Hey, Tank. As I told you on the phone, I've been appointed to do your home study in the pending custody case." She glanced around the cabin. "Thanks for meeting me on such short notice. I need to see where Brooke lives and make sure the housing is adequate."

Libby gasped and put her hand to her mouth. "I'd better take Brooke out of here."

"No need for that. I'll need to assess Brooke to see how

well-adjusted she is, though she looks healthy and happy to me."

Brooke ran to climb into his arms. "What's going on, Daddy?" she whispered.

"Vonnie has a few questions," he told her. "Your aunt Marley loves you a lot, and she wants to make sure you're taken care of right." He saw Vonnie's smile of approval, but he didn't care whether she was impressed. Brooke was all that mattered. He didn't want her scared.

Vonnie's sharp gaze took in the neat cabin. "Nice," she said. She settled on the sofa and clicked her pen as she got out her pad. "I'll be real honest with you, Tank. I resented being pulled into this matter. You're Brooke's father, and much as I dislike children growing up in the wilds, I hate seeing kids ripped from their parents without good cause even more. But I'm going to be fair about this. Tell me about your life at home."

Tank leaned back and launched into a description of his work and the time he spent with his daughter. Libby offered an account of the family routines. Vonnie asked Brooke questions about her day, and his daughter played her miniature cello for the nurse. When they were finished, he realized nearly an hour had passed.

"I think I have all I need," Vonnie said. "I'll leave you and get back to town."

Her noncommittal remarks left Tank uneasy.

13

The old truck struck a pothole and went airborne. Haley clung to the door handle with both hands. The wind blew in through her open window and snatched away the gasp that escaped her lips. Tightly packed spruce trees crowded against the side of the truck as the forest thickened.

"What are you going to say to him?" she shouted over the sound of the wind.

Tank slowed to miss a moose that meandered onto the side of the road. It lifted its massive head and stared at them, as if asking what right they had to disrupt him. This place was like Jellystone with Ranger Smith and all the animals.

Tank pulled the truck off the road and got out. "The dig is just over the hill. Let's walk from here. I want to watch him when he doesn't know we're here."

"You still haven't told me what you're going to say. We can't just waltz in there and ask him if he's stealing artifacts and selling them." She opened her door and hopped out with her walking stick.

"If he is, I'd like to find out who he's working with. He has to have a partner. He isn't gone from the dig enough to be handling the sale by himself, and Joy never noticed anyone else hanging around the site."

"I didn't think about that. He's not likely to tell us anything."

"That's why I want to watch him." He took her arm and helped her walk along the trail. "You're limping more."

"This prosthesis isn't as good on rough ground." Warmth rushed up her neck. They reached the top of the hill and looked down onto the dig. Nothing moved below. Even the wind was still. "I'm not sure he's here."

"Perfect. We can look around a little." Tank took her hand and helped her down the steep slope.

His big hand completely covered her small one. The warmth radiated up her arm and touched her heart in ways she wasn't sure how to deal with. At the bottom of the hill, he tucked her hand into the crook of his elbow in a curiously courtly gesture that she found pleasant. She didn't think men like Tank Lassiter existed anymore. Maybe Alaska was a throwback in more ways than one.

"I'll check the tent," Tank said in a low voice. He ducked inside, then stepped back out, shaking his head. "Just artifacts inside. Some are boxed like they're being taken out. No address though."

"Let's find a spot to wait and watch," she suggested.

"There's a cave over there," Tank said, pointing.

Haley was shaking her head before he even finished talking. "No, no, I'm not going in there." Her vision wavered, and she thought she might need to sit down and put her head between her knees. Her chest constricted.

"Easy," Tank said. "Are you having a panic attack?"

She nodded, but couldn't squeeze any words out of her tight chest. He grabbed a camp chair and pulled it to her, then forced her down into it. Haley tried to drag another breath through her lungs but felt like she was trying to breathe through a straw. She wanted to run from this place and never look back.

"Is it the cave that's causing this?" Tank's mouth was next to her ear.

She nodded and leaned forward to put her head between her legs. Her vision began to clear, the pinpoints of darkness fading. *Don't look at the cave.* She turned her head, but her panic came rushing back. She stumbled to her feet. "I have to get out of here!"

Tank grabbed her and pulled her against his chest. He smoothed her curls with his big, rough hand. "Shh, it's okay. You're safe. We're not going anywhere near the cave. You're not trapped. There's plenty of air." His voice was a soothing rumble through his chest under her ear.

She clutched him, and her panic ebbed again. In his arms, she felt as though nothing could touch her, no wave of fear or destruction could swamp her. The clean scent of soap and the fresh aroma of fabric softener from his shirt wafted up her nose like the best aromatherapy. If she could bottle it, she would make her fortune in Phoenix, where she could ease the stress of living.

Tank's caress on her hair and back changed in quality. The tightness that spread through her chest then had nothing to do with panic. She lifted her head and looked up. Big mistake. She was lost looking into the dark, fathomless depths of his eyes. His lips parted, and then he bent his head.

Her heart slammed against her ribs. She stepped back. "I think I'm okay now." She felt curiously bereft when his hands fell away. She wanted to defuse the romantic tension between them, didn't she? Her gaze lingered on his lips, and his eyes darkened again. She tore her gaze away and swallowed. A sound distracted her.

"I think someone is coming." Tank glanced around, then took her hand and tugged her toward a thick patch of fireweed. He pushed her down, then flung himself beside her on his stomach. "Keep your head down."

That would be easy to do. She needed to recover from the effects of nearly being kissed by a man she found too attractive for her peace of mind. Peeking up over the fireweed, she saw Ned approaching the dig. He looked around in a furtive manner, then stepped inside the tent. He exited a few minutes later with a box in his arms.

"That's the box I saw. It's full of artifacts," Tank whispered in her ear.

His muscular arm lay over her back. Haley had a crazy impulse to snuggle against him. What had gotten into her? She'd always run the other way whenever an attractive man showed interest in her. Now she was not only hanging around but encouraging him. It had to stop. She shifted slightly, but he didn't take his arm away.

"I'm going to follow him. Wait here." He left her. Crouching, he skulked through the site and trailed after Ned.

The bugs and mosquitoes were beginning to swarm. She'd forgotten her DEET. Getting to her feet, she waved at the insects then hurried after Tank. She caught up with him behind the tent.

"I told you to stay put," he whispered.

"I don't think he's dangerous," she mouthed back. Peering around the corner of the tent, she watched Ned toss the box into the back of his SUV, then get inside and drive off. "He's selling artifacts. We're too far away to follow him in your truck."

"This time. I'll tell Chet about it. Maybe he can do some sleuthing."

Tank seemed to have resumed his impersonal manner. Maybe she'd imagined the passion she saw in his face, but there had been no mistaking her own. She needed to keep her heart as far away from Tank Lassiter as she could.

Fifteen

*T*ank decided he'd been out in the wilderness too long. That was the only explanation for his overwhelming attraction to a city girl like Haley Walsh. She wasn't his type at all. He liked blondes; she was a fiery redhead. Tall, willowy figures caught his eye, but she was the round, squeezable type. Sitting in front of a fire with popcorn was his idea of a good time, but he couldn't imagine Haley content with anything less than a fine dinner and a movie. He must have been off his rocker to have even been tempted to kiss her. From now on, he was going to keep his distance.

He found Chet in The Trappers Store. The place always reeked with the pungent odor of skins, kerosene, and taxidermy chemicals. Steel traps hung from nails that had been pounded high on the wooden walls and ceiling. Guns lined several racks behind the counter, and camping gear lined narrow walkways around and through the conglomeration of pots, tents, and heaters.

Chet pocketed the ammunition he'd just purchased and moved to join Tank at the door. "You look about as happy as a wolf cub dropped in the middle of Cook Inlet. What's eating you?"

"I've been following up on Joy's claim that Ned Bundle might be selling off artifacts. You ever check that out?"

Chet pushed open the screen door, waved away the flies that made a beeline for his head, and strode outside. Tank followed. "Be careful spouting off that nonsense. That's how you get rumors started."

"Are you so sure it's nonsense? Haley and I scoped out the dig today. We saw him haul out a box of artifacts." He hurried to match his stride to Chet's. The trooper stopped, and Tank nearly mowed him down. "Anyway, about the Walshes—Haley and I sent off a test for accelerants on the ashes of the cabin. We'll have that back in a few days."

Chet frowned. "Why didn't you tell me? It looks bad to go behind my back like that."

"It's Haley's right as next of kin to check it out."

"She should work through the local law enforcement. My job is on the line here, especially with Bixby breathing down my neck."

"We'll try not to stir up anything. But she wants to know what happened."

Chet frowned. "I guess that's okay, so long as you keep me in the loop. What about Ned and those artifacts? For all we know he was sending them out to a museum."

"Maybe. But Joy is certain of what she saw. Did you ever check it out?"

"I asked him about the allegation. But he laughed it off, and

I had no proof. I couldn't find any evidence that he spends more money than he makes. No unsavory types have been hanging out around town."

"Other than the usual ones, you mean?" Tank grinned.

"Other than those," Chet agreed, matching Tank's smile. "Let me handle this, Tank. You've got enough on your plate with Marley's custody suit."

"I don't think that's going to be a problem." Tank told his father-in-law about the home study. "I think it went well."

"That's good news, but I'm worried about Marley's state of mind. I'm not sure she might not try something desperate when she hears this."

"Desperate how?"

Chet chewed his lip. "No telling. But she keeps talking about Leigh as though she's still alive. I wish her mother were alive. Marley always listened to her. I've tried to get her to a doctor, but she won't go."

"I picked up a little on her Leigh obsession when I talked to her."

"I'd keep close tabs on Brooke," Chet advised.

"I intend to do just that," Tank said grimly.

⅓

Tank had barely said two words to her since their foray into Ned's domain four days ago. Haley's tension grew as they trekked back into the woods. Kipp wasn't willing to stay in town any longer. He must think the bears would disappear if he actually enjoyed a real bed for a few days. The chilly recesses of the forest on each side of her didn't help her disgruntled mood. She wanted civilization and a soft bed, not a sleeping bag on the hard ground.

The group formed a line that marched along the narrow trail. Tank was in the lead, followed by Kipp and Erika. Denny lagged about five feet back with Cary. Haley had talked Augusta into staying in town with Joy and working out the details of Joy's custody transfer. Haley tried to keep up, though she was almost last. Only Libby and Brooke were behind her.

A small hand crept into hers, and she looked down to see Brooke smiling up at her. Her irritation faded. "Hey, sweetheart, are you doing okay?" Libby had pleaded to be allowed to come along for a few days of camping, and Tank had agreed as long as she and Brooke stayed in camp when the rest went to watch the bears.

Brooke nodded. "Daddy said I could ride piggyback if I wanted. Sometimes I ride on his back and pretend he's Aslan and I'm Lucy. Riding across Narnia on Aslan's back in the spring might be just like this. Have you started the book yet?"

"No, I haven't. I need to do that." Brooke's imagination stirred Haley's faint memories of the story. Aslan was supposed to be Jesus, wasn't he? She couldn't remember. Brooke was the most amazingly precocious child, probably because Libby spent so much time with her.

Libby jogged to catch up with them, though the narrow track was barely wide enough to walk two abreast. "I'm ready for a break," she panted. She wiped her forehead and left streaks of dirt across it. "You're limping a little. Are you doing okay?"

"I'm a little tired," Haley admitted. "Your brother keeps a grueling pace."

"I'll ask him to let us take a breather." Libby grinned. "Don't worry, I'll tell him that me and Brooke need it." She jogged to the front of the line and spoke to Tank. He glanced back down the line of hikers, then nodded.

"We'll stop here for a break," he said. He dropped his pack and uncapped his canteen, then took a swig of water.

"Finally!" Erika dropped her pack and nearly collapsed onto it. "How much farther?"

Tank glanced up the trail. "Only another hour or so. Keep your eyes peeled for wildlife. This is a particularly abundant area."

Haley picked up Brooke, who was still clinging to her, and walked up to join the other women. Tank's face darkened when he saw his daughter in Haley's arms, but she ignored his glowering expression. She wasn't going to deliberately hurt the little girl. He needed to distract her if he didn't want Brooke getting too close.

She dropped her pack beside Erika's, then eased down onto it with Brooke still in her arms. Perspiration dampened the back of her shirt, and her leg ached.

"Look," Tank whispered. He pointed to the brush to their left. A small fox lifted its sharp nose out of the vegetation. Tank reached into his pocket and withdrew a granola bar. He broke off a piece and tossed it to the fox. The animal grabbed it with his sharp little teeth and disappeared.

"Not even a thank you," Haley said, smiling.

"Foxes are shy. It's rare to see one, but there's plenty of game for them. Look, Brooke." Tank pointed ahead in the trail. His daughter's eyes grew wide. A group of marmots—similar to prairie dogs—rolled in playful abandon ahead of them on the trail.

Oscar crouched like a tiger and approached the animals. "Oscar, come here," Haley hissed softly. The dog ignored her. He raised one leg in the air, then put it down with the lightest touch possible.

"He won't hurt them," Tank said. "They're fast." His grin widened as he watched Oscar approach. The little dog pounced, and the marmots scattered. Oscar tried to follow one down a hole, but his belly got stuck. Brooke giggled as he wriggled around and finally backed his way out.

Tank touched Haley's arm and pointed up. She felt as awestruck as Brooke when she saw dozens of bald eagles roosting on the tree branches above their heads. Much as she surprised herself to admit it, the wilderness had an unmatched beauty. Her artist's eye noted the rich hues of green and gold in the vegetation that seemed to sparkle in the sunlight. The trees juxtaposed against the brilliant blue sky made her bring her camera to her eyes and snap some photos. She had to have proof of so many eagles in one place.

"It kind of gets into you, doesn't it?" Tank asked. He lifted Brooke from her arms and settled her on his knee.

"For some people," Haley admitted. "Have you always wanted to live without creature comforts?"

"What comforts am I without? I have my daughter, a warm, snug cabin, all the food we need, clothing, books. What else is there?"

Erika was listening to their conversation. "Don't you miss

electricity and a television? And when was the last time you saw a play or a movie?"

"A book is always superior to a movie. Haley is a big fan of books too." He pointed to the two books sticking out of the top of her pack.

Haley nodded. "But I don't know how you stand the isolation. And aren't you ever afraid that something will happen to the ones you love?"

"Bad things happen anywhere. In the city, you have to worry about—well, you know," he said, glancing at his daughter. "Here, we're generally safe if we obey a few normal rules. And with Brooke and Libby around, I'm not isolated."

Haley glanced at Libby. "Your sister might have a different opinion. Women need the company of other women."

Libby nodded. "She's right. I get pretty lonely for someone to talk to about things only women like to discuss. Like hair and makeup, our feelings. When was the last time you told me how you felt about something, Tank? You men keep that all bottled up inside."

Tank looked away.

"See," Libby persisted. "Even now you don't want to talk about it. Especially after Leigh." She broke off and glanced at Brooke, who had fallen asleep in her father's arms. "You never talked about how you felt."

"What good would it do?" he mumbled. He pressed his lips against Brooke's curls. "It was just something I had to deal with." He looked at Libby. "You've never told me you're lonely, Lib. I'll try to get you to town more often."

"I can go anytime I want. It's not up to you to entertain me." Libby smiled and patted her brother's hand. "Don't stress over it."

Haley decided to take pity on Tank and give him something else to talk about. "How did you get into bear research? Seems a kind of obscure profession."

His shoulders relaxed, and he leaned against a tree trunk. "I had a run-in with a bear early on. I think I was about twelve, and we'd gone to Montana. We were camping, remember, Libby?"

His sister nodded. A thoughtful smile played around her mouth. "You were Indiana Jones that summer, complete with the same floppy type of hat you still wear."

Tank grinned. "It comes in handy to swat flies. Anyway, it was the middle of the night, and I had to go to the bathroom. I sneaked out of the tent and went into the woods. There were grunts and the sounds of something big moving through the brush. I froze, sure I was going to get eaten. I could smell the stink of my own fear and figured the animal would smell me and come eat me. I didn't know if it was a cougar or a bear or what, so I started to climb a tree."

Haley leaned forward as she listened. "I would think that would make you not want to be around bears. It was a grizzly?"

He nodded. "The grizzly came charging out of the trees at me, but I was already higher than it could reach. I screamed for my dad, and he came running out of the tent with his gun." Tank fell silent, then sighed. "He shot the bear. I climbed down out of the tree. That dead bear was the saddest thing I'd ever seen. It had once been strong and powerful, full of life. It was dead because of my fear. If I'd waited, it would have left. I would have been fine, and it would have been fine. We were in its territory."

"It gave up its spirit to you," Denny put in. "That was your sign of what you were to do."

"I got back home that summer and started to study everything I could get my hands on about bears. By the time school started, I was hooked. I decided then I was going to do what I could to find out more about bears, to help keep them from being wiped out. I was determined to face my fear." His gaze slid to Haley. "When fear rules us, we are nothing more than a slave to it. It keeps us from making good decisions. I decided I wasn't going to let fear run my life—or anyone else's."

She knew what he was saying, and she bristled. "I do exactly what I want with my life," she said. "Just because I prefer the city doesn't mean I'm letting fear rule me."

"If you say so."

He said the words so softly only she caught them. She looked away. There was no sense in talking to him about it. He thought there was no place like Alaska. She thought Phoenix ruled the world. They'd never see eye to eye on that.

Tank rose with Brooke in one arm and shouldered his pack on the other. "We'd better get going again. I'd like time to get our camp set up before dinner."

Kipp bounded to his feet and helped Erika up. "Will we see any bears today?" he asked

"Probably. We should get to our site before they come down to feed at the river." Tank began to walk briskly through the brush.

By the time Haley donned her pack and picked up her walking stick, the rest of the group had disappeared. Panicked, she hurried after them. She tripped on a tree limb hidden by a fall of spruce needles and went sprawling. Her camera bag had opened, and all her film and lenses lay among the moss. "Wait," she called out, scrambling to pick up her belongings. Her voice didn't seem to carry farther than the berry bushes in front of her. She staggered to her feet and hurried in the direction she thought they'd gone. How could she be so stupid as to get left behind? Hadn't anyone missed her?

Erika had been chattering to Libby, but surely one of them should have noticed Haley wasn't with them. If they discovered her missing, could they even find her? She picked up her pace and strained her ears to hear the sound of voices, but the only noise the wind carried back to her was that of rushing water. Maybe they were following the river. She turned in that direction.

As she stepped over some low-lying branches, something yanked on her backpack. She went sprawling again, her face buried in a three-foot-high bank of cottongrass. She heard a low grunt as someone struggled to get her backpack off her. She gripped both shoulder straps and hung on.

She had no weapon, no way to defend herself. Her left shoulder socket popped, and a wave of agony spread down her arm as the attacker tried to wrench the pack off her shoulders. She cried out, but spruce needles pricked her lips and muffled her scream. Her vision wavered, but she hung on with grim determination. The scuffle seemed to last for hours, but it could only have been a few seconds before she heard the sound of voices calling her name. The tugging on her back ceased, and she heard thrashing through the underbrush. She rolled over but caught only a glimpse of a dark shape melting into the forest.

Sixteen

*T*ank wished someone else could do this. He didn't want to inflict the pain he knew he had to. "This is going to hurt." Tank's gripped Haley's forearm and popped her shoulder back into place.

She let out a shriek, and beads of perspiration popped out on her forehead. She sagged against his chest, and he eased her back onto the ground. Her closed eyes fluttered, and then she opened them and stared up at him. Her jaw was set, and she swallowed.

"You okay?"

She nodded weakly. "Thanks. The pain is easing now."

"I'd better do something about those scratches too." He pulled out iodine and dabbed it on her face.

"Ouch! Do you enjoy inflicting pain?"

"Blow on it, Daddy," Brooke instructed.

Tank grinned. He doubted Haley would appreciate it, but he blew gently on the injury. "Better?"

Haley glanced at Brooke and bit her lip. Tank could tell that only his daughter's presence spared him from the tongue-lashing she wanted to deliver. His grin widened, and Haley's eyes narrowed. "I think you'll live," he said, putting his first-aid pack away.

Kipp paced around the clearing. "You never saw your attacker? Are you sure there was an attacker? These things keep happening to you, and no one else sees anything. I'm beginning to wonder if you're trying to sabotage the shoot. Were you hired by a rival network?" He put his hands on his hips and glared at Haley.

"Don't be such a jerk," Erika said. "She's hurt, and you're acting like she's some kind of axe murderer. You're being melodramatic."

Tank raised his eyebrows at Erika's staunch defense. Haley inspired loyalty in everyone. He shouldn't be surprised his sister and daughter were on her side too.

The angry glare Kipp shot toward Erika should have sizzled the hair on her head. He turned and stomped off toward the river. "Call me when we're ready to get back to work." He said the last word with pointed emphasis as if to remind Haley she was his employee.

Her lips tightened, and her brows drew together. She blinked rapidly, and Tank knew she wasn't as immune to Kipp's barbed words as she'd like everyone to believe. He held out his hand, and she grasped it.

Once she was on her feet, she brushed at the mud on her jeans. "I'm fine. Let's get going."

"Not so fast. Is there anything you can remember about the man? What he looked like, what he was wearing, anything?"

Haley hesitated. "I saw a bit of his sleeve. It looked like a khaki shirt."

Tank looked at Denny. "You've got on a khaki shirt, Denny."

Denny held up his hands. "Whoa, I wouldn't hurt Haley. What reason would I have?"

Tank shrugged and turned back to Haley. "Could you tell what he wanted?"

"He was trying to get my pack off."

"To steal it? Or . . ." He hesitated and looked at his daughter.

Libby took the hint. "Brooke, I'll read you a story before you nap. Come with me." She led the little girl off toward the tent.

Haley flushed. "It didn't feel like a sexual attack. I think he wanted my pack for some reason. But that makes no sense. The camera equipment isn't valuable enough that someone would keep trying to get it."

"May I?" Tank held out his hand for her pack. She nodded, and he took it and unzipped it. He knelt beside her and began to pull out the contents. Several books on living in the wilderness, clothing, toiletries, camera equipment—nothing that surprised him.

"See? I don't get it." Haley began to repack everything.

"Did you turn over all your film to Chet? Maybe it has to do with the pictures you took of Joe Wooten's body. What else have you shot?"

She shrugged. "Just the bears, some scenery. Nothing that would warrant an attack on my person." She fiddled with her hair, twirling a curl around her finger. "I gave Chet the film of Joe's body."

He opened her camera bag and rooted through it. "Looks like you have about twenty rolls of film here. Maybe we should get it all developed and see what it shows."

"Where?"

"We'll go back to town in a few days. We can drop it off at the general store. They'll send it out to Anchorage, and it will be back in about a week."

"A week!" Erika shook her head as if that was not an option. "She's been attacked several times. We need to find out what is going on before she's seriously hurt." Erika dug in her pack and pulled out a wide-toothed comb. "Let's get the dirt and spruce needles out of your hair."

"Thanks, Erika." Haley looked up at Tank. "I'll be back in Phoenix soon, and this will all be a bad dream."

The pang Tank felt when he heard her eagerness to get back to the city surprised him. He needed to remember she was as much out of her element here as a salmon atop Mount McKinley.

He rose and dusted his jeans. "I could call in a plane to take the film."

"There's no need to jump through hoops," Haley said. "I'll just stay close to the rest of you."

◇

The fire snapped and crackled outside her tent. Haley lay wide-awake. The sun was finally fading, and night was falling with a suddenness that took her by surprise. Libby lay sleeping with Brooke in the sleeping bag next to her. Haley wasn't a bit sleepy. They'd reached their camp and set everything up. They'd even gotten some good bear shots. It was after midnight, and she ought to be exhausted, but her eyes refused to stay closed.

She wished Libby were still up. It would be nice to have someone to talk to, but maybe Tank's sister wouldn't be the best one. Every time she was around the big man, she felt as tongue-tied as a junior-high girl with her first crush. Not that she had a crush on Tank, she hastened to assure herself. He did intrigue her though. Learning how he'd decided to be a bear biologist had moved her more than she expected. That kind of bravery and dedication would affect any woman, especially when the man in question looked like Paul Bunyan and made her feel every inch a woman. He was so large, yet had such intensity and gentleness. A potent combination.

She sat up and pushed her hair out of her face. Maybe a snack would help her sleep. Light still filtered through the tent. The moonless twilight intrigued her. It never got fully dark. Sometimes Haley thought her life since Chloe died was like walking through this blue haze—never really awake but going through the motions. She rummaged in her pack but found no crackers left. The ingredients for s'mores were there though, if she dared go outside by herself to melt the marshmallows. She looked again at the half twilight. It wasn't really dark.

She pulled out a Hershey's bar, marshmallows, and a pack of graham crackers, then eased her stump into her prosthesis and pulled her sweats back down over it. She opened the flap on the tent and stepped outside. Tank was sitting on a rock by the fire. A pulse throbbed in her throat. She knew she should go back to her tent. Tank attracted her way too much to be around him without the restraint provided by the presence of other people. But her right boot betrayed her and moved her closer to the fire.

Tank must have heard her, because his head snapped up, and he turned to stare at her. "Couldn't sleep?" He moved over on the log and patted the space beside him.

She held out the chocolate and marshmallows. "Here I thought I wouldn't have to share them tonight if I waited late enough."

He grinned. "I'll arm wrestle you for them."

"You'd win."

"That's the idea." He got up and picked up his pack. "I've got skewers especially for marshmallows." He pulled out some stainless-steel skewers, then poked them through the fluffy white treats.

She took the stick he handed her and put it into the fire. "I like mine burned."

"Not me. Lightly toasted, just enough to melt it."

They sat in companionable silence surrounded by the aroma of warm sugar. "I think mine is done," Haley said. She broke off some chocolate and handed half to Tank, then assembled her s'more. She bit into the warm, chocolaty treat. Sitting so close to Tank, her insides felt as warm as the fire that melted her s'more. She glanced at him from under her lashes as he took a bite of his own dessert.

He was staring back at her. The gooey treat didn't want to go down past the constriction in her throat. She tore her gaze away. She should have turned around and gone back when she saw him out here. Nibbling at her s'more, she managed to get it down. Her face felt as hot as the red embers radiating at the base of the fire.

He rubbed his hands on his jeans. "Thanks for sharing with me. Not every woman would give up her chocolate."

"Chocolate I can share. But don't ask for my powdered-sugar donuts." She smiled and rubbed her palms against her sweats.

He leaned over to throw another log on the fire. When he sat back, his arm brushed hers. If her face got any hotter, she'd have to go plunge it into the lake. She could only hope he assumed her color was from the heat of the fire.

"I'd better try to get some sleep," he said abruptly. He stood.

"Me too." She scrambled up so quickly, she lost her balance and nearly fell against him. He put out his hands and caught her. The press of his fingers against her forearms felt as hot as the warm s'mores, and just as inviting. She stared up at him. His gaze bore into hers.

He bent his head, and his lips found hers. Haley closed her eyes and kissed him back. Her knees went weak, and she clung to his chest for support. His hands on her back pressed her closer to him, and she was drowning in the emotion she was too cowardly to name.

He tore his mouth away, and his hands slipped to her forearms. "You're so beautiful," he whispered. "Why did you have to come here?"

She pulled away. The power of his kiss was unlike anything she'd ever experienced. Her legs still trembled, and she found it hard to think. Tank dropped his hands, but he continued to stare at her. All she could do was hold his gaze. She didn't want to care about him, didn't want to fall in love with him, but she was afraid it was too late.

Seventeen

ank avoided Haley for the next few days, but he found his gaze wandering to her when he wasn't vigilant enough to keep his attention elsewhere. He liked to watch her, enjoyed seeing the way the sun glinted off her auburn curls. She had a quick smile for Brooke, and his daughter adored her, even though he'd asked Haley to keep her distance. Why should he expect his daughter to resist Haley when he couldn't?

The memory of the kiss they'd shared kept him tossing on the hard ground most of that night, and he was only partially successful in keeping his mind from wandering there. He prayed for God to guard his heart. Haley had issues with God, and he didn't want to get in the way of God's dealing with her.

Monday morning, he led the group to a large berry patch he knew brown bears frequented. He took along his rifle and a tranquilizer gun. He might as well get some of his work done this trip. Tank got the group settled in a thick patch of alder that would offer them some protection, then got out his tranquilizer gun and loaded it.

"What are you doing?" Haley asked. "Do you think we're in danger?" Brooke tossed a ball for Oscar while she and Libby watched indulgently.

He didn't look at her as he worked. "With your idiot boss around, you can never tell." He grimaced. "Sorry. I shouldn't have said that. At least he cares about the bears."

She looked over toward Kipp, who was shouting and waving his arms as he instructed Denny, Cary, and Erika. "He cares about his image." She squatted beside him. "So why the gun?"

"A friend is meeting me out here today. We're going to chase down some bears by helicopter and put radio transmitters on them. Brooke loves to go watch, and there's no danger."

"You're leaving us alone here?"

"No, I'm taking you all along. There will be two choppers and enough room for all of us. I thought it might make an interesting addition to your book and video."

"Have you mentioned it to Kipp? He might have other ideas."

"Not yet. I thought it would be a nice surprise. You think he won't want to go?"

"He likes to look like a hero where he's up close and personal with the bears."

He grinned at the disgust in her voice. "You can get some shots of him right next to the bears when they're knocked out. Oh, hey, here's an idea—we can roll the sleeping bear on top of him so it looks like they're fighting."

"That hardly has the drama of a live bear showing its teeth."
She smiled at him.

Something in her smile put a hitch in his breathing. He looked
away, then stood and shouldered his bag of darts. He heard the
sound of rotors. "Here come the helicopters."

She brightened. "Hey, we could send my film back with the
pilots, couldn't we?"

"Sure, Max will drop it off at the store for me. We'll be heading back to town for more supplies next week. The prints should
be back by then." He frowned and looked down at her. "I've
been thinking about the attack on you. Is there anyone down in
the Lower Forty-eight whom you'd consider an enemy?"

A slight smile tipped her lips. "Enemies? I beat out Rachel
Lambert for a photography prize in high school, but I hardly
think she'd be stalking me here in Alaska."

"You never know. A woman scorned and all that," he said
playfully.

"I just can't imagine why anyone would care about my backpack. It has to be related to that."

He shrugged. "Maybe someone wants a designer backpack.
We don't see fancy city packs like yours often." He rubbed his
chin. "Seriously, does anyone know who your parents are?"

She thought. "Joy. Ned Bundle. And a few people in the café,
but the attacks started before we went to town."

"Still, someone could have recognized you or heard you were
coming."

"Why would anyone care?"

He frowned. "The family that was caring for Joy. I wonder . . ."

"What?"

"Remember what she said about your dad's estate? She stands to inherit their land. It's a sizable chunk and worth some money. What if they want to make sure she gets it so they can get their hands on it?" It sounded ludicrous even as he said it. When he saw the pain crash onto Haley's face, he wished he could take back the words.

"They left everything to her? I guess what Joy said didn't register. You'd have thought they would have at least left something to Augusta, even if they hated me."

"They were very private people. A bit odd. Do you remember much about them?"

She nodded. "I thought my dad hung the moon, and that my mother was the most beautiful woman alive. I was always trying to get them to praise me like they did Chloe, though it never happened. That's probably why I acted up so much."

He could hardly bear to think about what it did to a child to have such hateful parents. His glance went to Brooke. It was impossible for him to imagine ever letting her go. She lit up his days with happiness. He knew the Walshes had a daughter in Arizona, but he wished he'd known the circumstances. Maybe he could have talked to them, made them realize how wrong they were. Scripture could sometimes get through when nothing else could.

He shaded his eyes and looked across the open plain. The helicopters hovered, and the sound of their rotors began to block out other noises. He waved, and the pilot waved back, then lowered the craft to the ground.

Kipp stalked to Tank. "What are they doing here? They'll scare off the bears."

"We're going for a ride to find the bears. I need to put radio collars on a few today, and I thought you'd all like to come along and watch. You'll see bears feeding in places we can't get to on foot."

Kipp's brows raised. "Maybe I can get some good video as they're awakening. They'll look alert then."

"That's pretty dangerous. They might charge you. The drug affects their eyesight, and they don't see well."

"I'll take the chance." Kipp gestured to his crew. "Head to the helicopters. We're going for a ride."

Haley leaned out of the open window. The wind whipped her hair into her eyes, and she pushed it away with an impatient hand. Below her, the tundra undulated in a golden green expanse. The breeze brought the scent of fresh air, moss, and spruce to her nose.

"There's one!" The pilot, Max McCarthy, pointed a stubby, tobacco-stained finger toward a dark blob running flat out for the safety of a mountain crag.

"I see him." Tank aimed the tranquilizer gun, then squeezed off a shot.

The bear kept galloping, and Haley thought he must have missed. Tank laid the rifle back down and watched. The helicopter followed the animal, and the bruin looked up, then ran faster. It had almost reached the safety of the rocks when the bear stumbled. It rolled over, then staggered to its feet and galloped forward again. It paused, then tumbled to the ground and lay still in a heap of reddish-brown fur.

"He's down," Max said. He took the helicopter lower and landed near the bear's still form. The other chopper landed moments later, and Cary and Kipp emerged with huge grins.

"Excellent shooting," Kipp proclaimed. "Haley, get some shots of this. The rest of you get the film rolling."

Haley clambered out of the helicopter and joined her boss beside the bear. Libby and Brooke stayed inside with Oscar while the crew got the film tripod set up.

"Stand back," Tank ordered. "Let me make sure he's out. I've been fooled before." He approached cautiously and prodded the bear, then checked its eyes. "Hand me that bag, would you, Haley?" he asked, his gaze still on the bear.

The rotors whirred above her head, and she kept her chin down as she dragged the black nylon bag from the helicopter seat. The wind whipped her hair into her face with such force it stung her cheeks. Bending over at the waist, she ran back to join Tank beside the bear. The pilot cut the engine, and the resulting quiet was a relief.

"Thanks." He took out a yellow transmitter attached to a collar.

"Hey, I want some pictures before you put that thing on," Kipp yelped. He scrambled to reach the bear and motioned for Denny to join him. "Can I put the collar on? That would play well with the viewers."

Tank glanced at Haley, and she could see the irritation in his eyes. "Sure," was all he said.

Kipp straddled the bear like a conqueror, then flashed a smile at the camera. Haley sighed and fingered her camera. Too bad she couldn't just walk away. *Snap, whir.* She walked around Kipp and the bear to get some different angles as she shot a whole roll of film. Denny filmed the action from about six feet away.

Kipp flashed his famous smile. Without moving his mouth, he managed to throw his voice so it seemed to be coming from the bear. "I wouldn't hurt you, Mr. Nowak. You're my friend."

What a ham. Haley rolled her eyes, and she grinned when she saw Tank shake his head.

"The bear is starting to come around," Tank said, peering into the bear's face. "Better wrap it up, Kipp."

"Did you get enough video?" Kipp asked Denny.

"I think so. Looks good, boss." Denny put the lens cover back on his video camera and took it off the tripod.

Haley became vaguely aware of Oscar barking frantically, though the noise barely carried above the wind. Tank made a sound beside her, and she looked up. A bear as big as a glacier stood on its hind feet and looked at them. Though it was twenty feet away, it looked massive and dangerous. It was gaunt with mangy, matted fur. One ear looked clipped. Those eyes seemed to look right through her and see her as a tasty meal.

"Back slowly away," Tank instructed. "Try to get to the helicopter. This guy is nothing to mess with." Tank waved his hands in the air. "You bear! Get away. Go!" As big as Tank was, surely the bear would think twice about approaching. Instead, it dropped to all fours and began to advance slowly. Tank grabbed Haley's arm as she began to back away.

"Slowly," he hissed. The others were moving away already. Kipp's eyes were wide, and even he seemed to understand this bear wasn't acting normally. "It's a predatory bear," Tank muttered. He placed himself between Haley and the bear.

A crack echoed above the sound of the wind. The bear flinched and bit at its flank, but it continued to approach. Another shot came, and this time Haley saw the dart plow into the bear's chest. She didn't think the drug would take effect in time and expected the bruin to charge them at any moment.

Her hand touched the helicopter, and she felt for the floor, then scrambled inside the chopper. The bear roared, then galloped toward them. Tank threw himself into the helicopter and slammed the door. The bear's snarling face rammed the window. "Get us out of here!" Tank yelled.

The chopper rotors roared to life, and the bear turned tail and ran. Haley never did see it fall down from the effects of the drug. Her heart was still slamming against her ribs as the chopper rose in the air.

Brooke scrambled onto her lap. "I didn't like that bear." She leaned over and patted her father's face. "He wasn't good like Miki and Aslan."

"No, he wasn't." Tank mopped the sweat from his forehead.

His gaze met Haley's, and her mood plunged at the expression of alarm in his eyes. They had been in more danger than she'd thought. "Explain to me what a predatory bear is. I thought all bears were predators."

"They are to some degree. A predatory bear is one actively on the hunt for humans. Most bears are just scavengers and would rather run than hunt a human for food. But when animals are sick or too old to get food in the normal way, they can lose their normal fear of humans. Once they discover humans are easy prey, they can be deadly. This bear is old and sick. And dangerous."

"That bear was like the wicked White Witch in Narnia," Brooke said. "Maybe Miki could show him how to be good."

"I don't think he'd listen, Brooke. He's sick and old. Not really bad."

"God should take him home. He'd be happy in heaven. Mommy would take care of him."

Brooke's perfect faith brought tears to Haley's eyes. What must it feel like to believe God had everything under control? She couldn't fathom it, but a new yearning made her wish she could be that young and trusting. It felt like a tiny tendril of green reaching for the sun. "I haven't read your book yet. I'll get started on it tonight."

"Read it to me!" Brooke said.

"Okay, we'll start it tonight after supper," Haley promised. Maybe it could melt the glacier around her heart. For the first time, she was beginning to wonder what it would be like to be free of her burden.

The phone rang in Marley's Anchorage apartment, and she snatched it up. It had to be her lawyer. She'd promised to call today.

"The home study is back, and the news isn't good."

Marley exhaled and gripped the phone so hard her hand shook. "What do you mean?"

"The report recommends that Brooke stay with her father."

The finality in Janine's voice stole the protest from Marley's voice. "That's not possible," she whispered finally. "I have to get custody of Brooke."

"I'm sorry, Marley. Without a home-study report in your favor, I don't believe we stand a chance in court. I'd recommend you drop the suit now and work on mending your relationship with Mr. Lassiter so you can spend time with Brooke. Pursuing it now will only harden his stance against you."

"I'll never give her up. Never." The tears trembling on Marley's lashes dried as rage began to flare in her chest. "Leigh will be livid. You have to fix this."

Janine's voice softened. "I think you need to talk to someone, Marley. I know it's been difficult for you to come to grips with your sister's death, but you have to accept it."

"Brooke belongs with me," Marley insisted. "I want to take my plea to the judge."

"Then you'll need to find another lawyer. I'm too busy to waste my time on a lost cause. I'm sorry. This is something you need to accept. I told you from the beginning it was a long shot. I've found no one who can testify that Tank is a bad father. It would be your word against his. Even your father won't testify against him."

"My father is a weakling," Marley shot back. "He was taken in by Tank right from the beginning."

"It's over, Marley. That's all I can tell you. Let me know if there's ever anything else I can do for you."

The phone clicked in her ear. Marley pulled it away from her head and stared at it with disbelief. This couldn't be happening. She had to get custody of Brooke. Leigh insisted on it. Marley stared with wide eyes out the window in the direction of Denali. The mountain rose in the distance, and its peak punched through the clouds and disappeared in the mist.

She would just grab Brooke and get to New York where a competent lawyer would make sure Marley kept possession of her. Possession was nine-tenths of the law, right? These back-woods yokels would never know what hit them once she got a *real* lawyer to take her case.

Eighteen

Something was going to have to be done about that bear. Tank had never run into a predatory bear that was this aggressive. He'd heard stories but had never come up against one himself. Bears were generally safe if left to themselves. They'd rather run than fight most of the time. Several things could cause a bear to begin to see humans as prey, however. This one looked old, which was the most common reason. A bear that lost some of its teeth would have a hard time finding enough to eat. Sometimes close contact with humans showed a bear how easy it was to obtain food from them. The bear comes to associate humans with easy food and then one day makes the leap to seeing humans as food themselves.

Whatever the reason, he was going to have to get rid of this bear. He would push for moving it to a remote place, but his superiors might insist on destroying it. If only that could be avoided. At least he wouldn't have to do it. Hunters would be called in to take care of the problem.

He became aware of Haley's gaze on him. Her amber eyes studied him, and he could still see fear in their depths. The encounter had shaken her, as well it should. Shoot, even he had felt the effects of fear and adrenaline pumping through his veins. It was a good thing Libby and Brooke had never gotten out of their chopper.

"Enjoying living dangerously?" he asked with a grin.

"About as much as a polar bear likes the desert."

To give her credit, she was trying to smile, though her poor attempt looked more like a grimace. The color that had leached from her cheeks came surging back, so he took encouragement. "Or as much as a lizard likes the ice."

Her smile seemed more genuine. "I think you just described me. The desert seems even more appealing after today." She glanced outside the chopper window at the gray clouds. "I always thought there would be more sunshine in Alaska in the summer. We've had so many gray days. Is this usual?"

"Some years we get more than others. But we're near the coast. If we were farther inland, there would be more sunshine."

She stretched her leg out and rubbed her knee. "You ever been to Phoenix? Valley of the Sun, we call it. You can always count on the sun to be up there shining down and making everything more cheerful."

"I've never been, but you make it sound very appealing. Do they have bears there?" He grinned and winked at her.

"In the zoo." She laughed and unzipped her backpack, then extracted a small package of powdered-sugar donuts. She offered him one, but he declined. "We have black bear in

Arizona. The last grizzly was killed in the early nineteen hundreds. 1902, I think."

"Tragic." Tank shook his head. "The grizzly used to roam all over the West. Its habitat is reduced to the Yellowstone area, a bit of Washington, and here in Alaska."

"When man and animal clash, animal loses," Haley said. "I have to admit I wouldn't want to worry about a grizzly roaming the desert where I live."

"You've had some bad experiences. Bears are fascinating."

"I've already seen that."

The chopper flew over the cluster of buildings. Kipp turned around in the front seat and glanced back at Tank. "Are we landing at Stalwart? Aren't we going back to our campsite?"

Tank shook his head. "I need to report that predatory bear and figure out what we're going to do about it." He eyed Kipp. The bear activist still looked a little pale.

Kipp nodded. "I don't mind admitting I've never seen a bear act that way. The look in its eyes—I think it thought we were caribou or something."

"It was definitely looking at us for lunch," Erika put in. She shuddered.

The chopper flew lower, over the roofs of buildings to the north side of town, where it hovered over a grassy field, and then finally touched down. The pilot kicked off the motor, and the rotors slowed. The other chopper landed behind them.

"How long do you plan to stay here?" Kipp asked. "So far, this trip has been a bust. I've gotten little video of bears and even fewer pictures. And what about the gear we left at camp?"

"I'll pick it up for us later. Besides, you've got all summer to get your video," Tank pointed out. "I can't let you go back out there until we deal with the predatory bear. Cool your jets. Learn a little about the people of Alaska while you're here. Take some video of some of the characters in town. It will add to the drama of your story."

Kipp's blue eyes brightened. "You might have something there." He motioned to Denny and Erika. "Let's head for the café and see what we might learn. Coming, Haley?"

"I need to drop off some film at the general store," Haley said. "I'll join up with you when I'm done."

"Can't it wait?" Kipp sounded petulant. "I want to talk about the project with you."

"She's been attacked twice," Tank said. "I'm hopeful there's something on her film that will give us a clue to what's going on. So no, it can't wait." He handed Brooke to his sister. "Why don't you get us rooms booked, sis? I'll go with Haley to the general store and have them put a rush on the film."

"Got it. Can we all meet for supper later? I'm starved."

"Me too," Brooke put in. "I want chicken fingers."

Tank glanced at his watch. "It's almost five already. Give us half an hour, and we'll meet at the café for supper." He took Haley's arm and hustled her across the muddy street. "Got all your film?"

"I think so." She stopped just outside the rickety screen door to the store. "I think you've got more important things to worry about than my film. I'll be fine. You go report your bear, and I'll see you at the café."

"This won't take long. I want to make sure Gus realizes how important this is." He opened the door for her, and they stepped inside. The scent of cinnamon, cloves, and bear grease greeted them. Barrels of flour, sugar, and other necessities stood at the end of the counter. "Hey, Gus. We've got film to send to Anchorage. You got a good lab to send it to? These are professional pictures, so we need a quality place."

Gus General was a man of indeterminate age. He had enough wrinkles on his face to pass for a sea lion, but Tank was never sure if they were from age or exposure. He'd been a trapper in his early years, and the harshness of the Alaska weather could have made the tracks on his face. He was never without his suspenders and a flannel shirt, no matter how hot the day. Nearly as tall as Tank, he was as grizzled and humped as a musk ox.

Gus wagged his huge head. "Got just the place." He accepted the rolls Haley shoved across the counter. "Should be back in about a week."

"That long? Can you hurry them up? It's important."

"No sooner than three days," Gus said.

"We'll take it." Tank leaned over the counter. "You still do much trapping, Gus?"

"Yep."

"Ever see a big brown bear with a missing toe on its front right paw? It has missing teeth too."

Gus chewed the stick of cinnamon in his mouth. "Old one?"

"Yeah."

Gus nodded. "'Bout took me out two weeks ago. Had to climb a tree to get away from it."

"Have you seen it more than once?" Tank asked.

"Once was enough."

He thanked Gus and got directions to where he'd seen the bear, though Tank doubted it would do much good. Tracking the bear down was going to be difficult. He needed to put out a warning to Stalwart residents about the danger. And get it reported to his boss.

13

Haley was tired of tossing and turning in the too-hard bed. Her wristwatch said it was four in the morning. Oscar was restless as well and kept running to the door and whining. He was going to wake Augusta and Joy if Haley didn't let him out. She strapped on her prosthesis and tiptoed to the door. She slipped a room key into her pocket and opened the door as quietly as she could. Oscar dashed into the dark hall.

The hallway smelled musty with faint traces of cooking mixed with old carpet. She snapped a leash on the dog, then pushed open the outside door and exited the building. Oscar tugged at his leash, and she let him take the lead. He stepped off the sidewalk, then nosed a patch of grass at the end of the street.

She used to love walking the city at night. This small village had a different feel to it. Safer, more quaint. It had its appeal. The thought took her by surprise. Haley glanced up and caught her breath at the stars in the not-quite-dark sky. This time of year, though it never went totally dark, the stars still glimmered in amazing abundance. She'd never seen so many stars in the sky. God's handiwork lay before her as priceless as the Alaskan oil fields. If she were on speaking terms with God, she'd thank him.

She tugged on Oscar's leash and guided him toward the park. There was no use thinking about it. God had cut her off long ago. She passed the general store, and Oscar paused to lap at a mud puddle. She heard a sound behind her—a strange *fwump*. A whoosh of air rushed past her cheek. It left a stinging sensation. She passed her hand over her face and stared at her bloody fingers. The sound of shattering glass seemed to come from all around.

Oscar whined and tugged at his leash, his head pointing back toward the store. Haley heard a crackling noise and turned to look. Tongues of red flame licked voraciously at the windowsills. Small shards of glass, glittering in the glow, lay around the building. Her hand to her mouth, Haley backed away. She saw a shadow move from behind the building, and she shrank back into the concealing darkness of a spruce tree's shadow. The needles brushed her cheek, and the scent of spruce tar covered the odor of smoke.

The figure was carrying something, a gas can maybe? The shadow flitted past the well house in the back, then was gone. Haley swiped at her stinging cheek again. She felt something hard still stuck there, maybe glass. Her knees felt weak and shaky. She turned and took off toward Chet Gillespie's office.

Behind her, the fire gained in intensity, and she heard a shout. Two men ran across the street from the Caribou Bar by the café. She heard distant shouts of *fire* and knew they would handle it. But Chet needed to know what she'd seen. Though she couldn't identify the man, she was certain the fire had been deliberately set.

She threw open the door to Chet's office and ran inside. A young man, his boots propped on the desk, was snoring in the chair. She slammed the door behind her, and he made a snort like a bull, then opened his eyes. Blinking in confusion, he staggered to his feet.

"Fire!" She pointed out the window where the conflagration was threatening to spread to the next building. "I saw a man sneaking behind the store with what looked like a gas can. You'd better call Chet."

Nineteen

*T*he ruins of the general store still smoldered, though the fire had been extinguished nearly twenty-four hours earlier by the volunteer fire department. Tank stood looking at the remains. Haley stood next to him.

"My film is all lost," Haley mourned. A butterfly bandage on her face marked the place where flying glass had cut her cheek. It could have been worse. A few inches higher and she would have lost an eye.

Tank nodded. "I have to wonder . . ." He glanced at her and shut his mouth.

"What? You think someone didn't want my film developed?"

"You'd thought of it too?"

"Pretty hard not to. All these things seem to be related to my camera or my film. It makes no sense."

Tank saw Gus wandering the ruins with a dazed look on his craggy face. "Let's see if Gus has any idea what happened. It may not have anything to do with you at all." She followed him as he moved to intercept Gus.

Gus had soot on his face and arms. A pile of goods lay at his feet, but Tank didn't think the stuff was salvageable. Still, he supposed if he were Gus, he'd have to try to save what he could too. He doubted the old man had insurance. Most didn't out here.

Tank clapped Gus on the shoulder. "I'm sure sorry, Gus. Anything I can do to help?"

Gus grunted. "Clean up. Could use able bodies."

Haley began to snap pictures of the scene. Tank moved out of her way. "I'll be glad to pitch in. Any idea what happened?"

Gus glanced at Haley from under bushy gray brows. "Your girlfriend saw more than me."

Tank ignored the girlfriend remark, but he saw Haley blush. There was something between them, and others could see it, but it had about as much chance of surviving as a lupine in saltwater.

Haley shook her head. "I didn't see much. I wish I could have identified the man."

"You have any enemies, Gus?" Tank asked.

Gus spat a brown stream of tobacco onto the charred ground. "No more than the next man." He glanced at Haley. "Leastways you didn't lose your film. Sent it off on the last plane out."

"Oh, you darling man!" Haley planted a kiss on Gus's grizzled cheek. "I wasn't even going to ask. I figured you had enough to worry about without me whining about my film." She stepped back and snapped a picture of Gus with his mouth hanging open.

Tank tried not to grin, but Gus must have seen the amusement in his eyes. He flushed a dull red and backed away, mumbling something about having to get to work. Tank didn't try to contain his laughter any longer. "I bet the last time someone kissed him was at the turn of the century."

Haley took a picture of Tank. "This is proof that you know how to smile."

"You've seen me smile before."

"Yeah, like this." She barely lifted the corners of her mouth. "I can actually see your teeth in this one."

He burst out laughing. "Have I been that dour?"

She nodded. "You take your responsibilities very seriously."

"I'll try to do better. I actually like telling jokes. Your boss rubs me the wrong way, and I've been taking it out on everyone else. Sorry."

"You're forgiven." She snapped another photo. "I'd kill for a latte. Does anyone in this town have an espresso machine?"

"We don't drink froufrou coffee. The coffee at the café is strong enough to grow hair on your chest. You could ask them to heat some milk and try to cobble together something that tastes like a latte. It's not espresso, but it might do."

She stopped and stared up at him. "You know what a latte is?"

"I'm not a complete backwoods Joe. I've been to Anchorage."

She rolled her eyes. "A true metropolis, Mr. Paul Bunyan."

"Paul Bunyan lived in Minnesota. This is Alaska, in case you were lost. Though it might be a pretty apt description of me if you'd ever seen me wield an axe." When her smile came again, he realized he'd been watching for it. They were engaged in a flirtation, and it felt good. Wonderful, in fact. He hadn't felt this alive since Leigh died. He took a step back. "I guess I'd better help Gus clean up. See you later."

He told himself he wasn't running away.

13

Haley hummed as she walked Oscar. He tugged her in the direction of the park, and she let herself be pulled that way. She glanced over at the burned remains of the store. Tank had his shirt off and was shoveling charred debris from the floor. She averted her eyes at the sight of his muscular back and arms. He was too beautiful to be real. She giggled nervously at the thought of how he'd react if she told him that.

Augusta sat on the park bench watching the cleanup. Oscar leaped into her lap, and she petted him. Dark circles rimmed her eyes. She hadn't slept well last night, and it showed today.

Haley sat beside her. "You doing okay?"

"I think you're right. We should never have come here. I'm not sure what I've gotten us into."

"We have Joy as a result. It can't be all bad."

"I'm not sure how we're going to work out living arrangements though. She's adamant about staying in Alaska."

"You could always move to Anchorage." Haley smiled, knowing Augusta would be horrified at the idea.

"I've been thinking about it."

Haley gaped. "You're kidding."

"You're grown and are off trotting the globe most of the time. I should think about slowing down, and I can write anywhere. I don't have to stay in Phoenix."

"But what a change! Cold, dark days through the winter when you're used to warm sunshine? I couldn't do it." She shivered. Augusta said Joy would never take Haley's place, but it looked like the young girl was going to succeed in that as well. A hollow feeling lodged under her left rib, and she told herself it wasn't jealousy. She was already beginning to love Joy too. Or at least she thought she was.

"I've seen the way you look at Tank, Haley. Don't shut love out just because you're afraid."

"I could never live here." Haley stood. "Where is Joy, anyway?"

"She helps out at the health clinic." Augusta pointed to a corner building.

"That girl is as energetic as Oscar." Her dog's ears perked at the mention of his name. "We'll be back in a little while." She went down the street.

A clapboard building housed the clinic. The peeling clapboards sorely needed a new coat of white paint. A red sign proclaimed it the Stalwart Health Clinic with morning hours only. Dr. Joe Wooten's name hung below the sign. Had he been the only doctor in town? Haley wondered how the clinic stayed open with the doctor dead.

She pushed open the door and heard a bell above her head tinkle. Oscar crouched at her feet, then barked ferociously at the sound. "Shh, Oscar. That's enough." She pulled on his leash, and he subsided. He'd get them both thrown out of here. The waiting room was empty and had the sharp sting of antiseptic in the air.

"Be right with you," a female voice called from beyond the closed door to Haley's left. It didn't sound like Joy.

Haley looked at the picture and certificates on the walls. Dr. Wooten's awards covered the smaller wall by the door, and pictures of Alaska wildlife decorated the larger one. The photographer was good. One shot of a wolverine was particularly artistic and showed the ferocious glare in the animal's eyes.

The door to the exam room opened, and a large, rawboned woman dressed in denim overalls stepped out. Her gray hair was pulled back in a neat bun at the nape of her neck, and she wore what looked like bear claws around her neck. Haley gave a tentative smile, assuming it was a patient until the woman pinned her in place with a pointed black-eyed glance.

"You're not from Stalwart," she stated. "I'm Vonnie Bird. Can I help you?"

"I was looking for Joy," Haley stammered. The woman's supreme self-confidence made her feel like a kid.

"Joy!" Vonnie yelled through the open door.

Joy came through the door holding a cat. The feline saw Oscar and arched its back. It hissed and swiped its claws over Joy's arm. "Ow!" She loosened her hold on the cat, and it shot out of her arms and landed on Oscar's back. Oscar's howl sounded like a scream. He tore off under the chair with the cat still clinging to his back. The ensuing scuffle overturned the chair, then the cat emerged with a victorious swagger, its tail held high.

Haley dropped to her knees to check on her dog. Oscar was a quivering mass of gray and white fur. "Come here, boy. It's okay. The mean cat is gone."

"I don't know what got into Sesi." Joy scooped up the cat and deposited it in the other room, then shut the door.

"No harm done." Oscar was still quivering in her arms, and Haley rubbed his ears.

"Vonnie, this is my—my sister, Haley Walsh," Joy said.

"Oh, you're the new sister." Vonnie gave Haley's hand a decisive shake. "You found my boss's body, isn't that right?"

"I was with the group, yes. I'm sorry about his death."

Vonnie nodded. "It was a shock. He was a good boss. I've wanted to meet you. Now that you're here, and so is Joy, I think we need to have a talk. Have a seat, and I'll get us some coffee. How do you take yours?"

"A talk? What do you mean?" Haley perched on the edge of a chair, and Joy did the same.

Vonnie went to a cart that held a Bunn coffeemaker and cups. She poured out two cups of coffee. "Cream and sugar?"

"Please."

Vonnie handed her a cup. "You want some tea, Joy?"

"No thanks." Joy's voice was subdued, and Haley spared a quick glance at her. She sat twisting her hands together in her lap, and she wouldn't look at Haley.

Haley took a quick sip of her coffee and forced it down. The bitter, burned flavor clung to her tongue. She set the cup on the table and looked at Vonnie expectantly.

Vonnie pulled a chair up to face the other two. "I've held my tongue for years. With Dr. Wooten dead, I think I need to tell the truth now. Joy doesn't want me to tell it, but I've got to." She shot a glance toward the girl.

Haley's curiosity roused further. If it affected her and Joy, then it must have something to do with her parents. "Okay. I'm listening."

Vonnie sipped her coffee, then grimaced. "Sorry, this stuff is undrinkable." She leaned forward and set her cup down beside Haley's. She pursed her lips and blew out a breath. "Dr. Wooten was a good doctor, but he had his faults too." She fiddled with the buckle on her overall strap.

Haley remained silent. Vonnie needed to tell this in her own way. It was obviously hard for her to betray her boss, even though he was dead.

"I already know," Joy said in a low voice. "He was having an affair with Maggie. I saw them together once, kissing."

Haley felt nothing. Her mother was such a distant figure, and she'd long ago toppled off the pedestal Haley had once put her on. "Did my father know?"

"I don't know," Joy said.

"He did," Vonnie stated. "He and Dr. Wooten had a ferocious argument here in the office two days before the fire. Your father said he was filing a complaint with the medical board ethics committee."

"Over the affair?"

"I'm not sure. I thought at first it might just be sexual misconduct. She was his patient. But somehow I thought it might be more than that. Dr. Wooten seemed enraged over it. I heard him tell Grady he'd better keep his mouth shut or he wouldn't like the consequences. Two days later, Grady and Maggie were both dead."

"Are you saying you think Dr. Wooten had something to do with my parents' deaths?" Haley couldn't hide her skepticism.

"Maybe. I considered going to Chet Gillespie, but I needed

my job. It's not pretty admitting I was such a coward. But it's time the truth was known."

Haley wasn't sure she could take any more truth. A headache began to build behind her temples. What kind of woman had her mother been?

Twenty

*T*ank's steps were slow and heavy as he approached the shop where he was meeting Libby. Brooke skipped along ahead of him. He was in no mood to buy new sneakers for Brooke. Not after his boss informed him that he was to arrange for hunters to track and destroy the bear. He'd hoped to be able to transplant it.

The bear would die anyway if they moved it, he told himself. It was too old to get food in the natural way. This was more humane, but it still felt wrong. He put his problems away and pasted a smile on his face as he stepped inside the shop and looked around.

Brooke ran to meet Libby. "Aunt Libby, we're here!"

Libby's pensive expression brightened, and she turned to show Brooke a pair of pink sneakers with flowers on them.

Libby's loneliness bothered him, and he wished he could do something about it. A brother's company was a poor substitute for the camaraderie she needed. Too bad Haley wasn't staying around. The two had really hit it off. He joined the two women in his life and agreed the shoes were perfect. Ten minutes later and fifteen dollars poorer, the three of them were back outside on the sidewalk.

Libby guided them toward the hotel. "I hope you don't mind, but I invited Haley along. She came back upset about something. I thought, between the two of us, we could worm it out of her."

"Where is she?"

"She should be right down. She went up to drop Oscar in the room." Libby tipped her head up to look at him. "I see that look in your eye. You can tell me how you feel about her, Tank."

"I like her," he said, avoiding her gaze. "That's all."

Libby sighed. "She avoids the subject, just like you. I think she's the one."

"Oh yeah? You ever seen a marriage that worked when the couple didn't live together? She'd never live here, and I'd never live anywhere else. Solve that one, Sherlock."

Libby sobered. "Okay, that's a problem. But if you love each other, it can be fixed."

"Who said anything about love? I like her, okay? That's as far as it goes."

"You could love her if you let yourself."

"Maybe I could, but I'm not going to let myself. There's no future in it, and plenty of other puzzles to solve right now. Besides, she has issues with God she needs to clear up, and I don't want to get in the way."

"Do you have to analyze everything? You're always talking about trusting God. Don't you ever want to step out on a limb without scientifically examining it first? There might be a pleasant surprise out there."

"Yeah, a broken neck." He grinned. "Drop it, sis. This isn't going anywhere."

"I'd like her for a sister-in-law." Libby thrust out a stubborn chin. "It could be worked out."

"Six months here and six months in Phoenix, right?" Tank couldn't believe he was even discussing this with his sister. He couldn't deny he cared about Haley, but he had no interest in pursuing her. It would be like picking up a bear cub with the sow in the same den.

Kipp and Erika came out the hotel door. Denny, Cary, and Augusta trailed behind them. "We're going out for a stroll to look for bears," Kipp said. "I'm looking for Haley. Have you seen her?"

"You shouldn't be going out until Tank tracks down the predatory bear," Libby said.

"I'm tired of waiting, and we're not going far. A trapper said he saw a couple of bears out by Crystal Lake an hour ago. I just want a few shots."

"I wouldn't go out there," Tank said.

"I know you wouldn't. But I'm not afraid of the bears."

"You were plenty afraid when the bear came at us," Tank pointed out. The man's cocky manner made him want to take a swing at him. Red ran up Kipp's neck, and Tank realized he'd merely succeeded in egging him on.

"Let's go," Kipp snapped. "If you see Haley, tell her we'll be back in a couple of hours, and that she missed the adventure. I hope her pictures are worth the trouble she's been." He and his entourage marched off.

Tank watched them go. He was more than ready for this summer to be over. "I saw how you skirted his question. Why didn't you tell him Haley was upstairs? I'm surprised Augusta didn't know."

"Haley doesn't need to deal with Kipp's grandstanding all afternoon. Augusta was in the shop next door when Haley came by, so they didn't see one another."

"I should have stopped them somehow," Tank said. "It's not safe until we find that bear."

The postmaster beckoned him from the post office. "Hey, you got a fax, Tank."

"It's probably the accelerant report. I'll be right back," he told his sister. He stepped to the doorway of the post office and took the paper the man handed him, then gave him five dollars. "Thanks." He scanned it and sighed, then folded it up and rejoined his sister. It seemed all he got to do was be the bearer of bad news.

Libby nodded toward the door. "Here comes Haley."

Tank's pulse quickened when he turned toward Haley. It was one thing to deny his attraction, and another to lie to himself. He'd tried not to think of how soft her lips were or how she had felt as though she fit in his arms. Even though his head knew there was no future, his heart wasn't listening.

"Ready for ice cream?" Libby tucked her arm into Haley's and took Brooke's hand, and the three went ahead of Tank toward the soda shop, where they were meeting Joy.

13

Haley spooned the last bit of her ice cream into her mouth. "Thanks, I needed a break." Glancing at her watch, she realized they'd been there nearly two hours. Libby and Tank were easy to talk to. She enjoyed watching their obvious affection for one another as they interacted. She missed having a sibling like that. Her gaze fell on Brooke and Joy chattering. Maybe Joy could fill that void.

Libby wiped her hands with her napkin. "You seemed upset. You want to talk about it?"

"I'm glad you asked. I don't know how much to believe," Haley began. She told them what Vonnie had said.

"I find that hard to believe," Tank said. "I've known Joe Wooten a long time. But I got the accelerant report back," Tank said. "Someone set fire to their cabin. They found traces of kerosene."

His grim voice was enough to curdle the ice cream in her stomach. "You're kidding." She ran her hand over her forehead. *Murdered.* Her parents were murdered. It was all true. "But why?"

"That's something we have to find out."

Haley's gaze wandered to the window, and she saw men and women pouring by. Many had their fists raised. The sound of shouts and screams radiated through the plate glass window. "What on earth?" She half rose. Tank turned and saw the commotion. He sprang toward the door and threw it open. The women followed him outside.

Libby nodded toward Joy, who stood outside the hotel. "Tell Tank I'm going to take Joy and Brooke with me to get some more things from the cabin. I'll be back in an hour or two. Whatever is going on, the girls don't need to see this. He can call me on the radio." Haley nodded, and Libby went toward Tank's truck.

Haley flinched at the angry roar of the crowd as they converged on the health clinic. She scurried to catch up with Tank. Trooper Gillespie stood outside. His attempts to calm the crowd had no effect. Haley followed Tank as he pushed through the crowd to where Chet stood. There was too much noise to figure out what had happened.

"Chet, what's going on?" Tank shouted above the din.

Chet glanced at Haley. "Sorry, guys, your bear activist has gone and gotten himself killed."

Haley inhaled sharply. "Where's my grandmother? Is she okay?"

"She's fine. No one was hurt except Kipp. He approached a bear out by the river. It was our four-toed predator."

Augusta had watched it. Bile burned the back of Haley's throat. For all her practicality, Augusta was a sensitive soul. She would have nightmares for months. "You're sure he's dead?" she whispered.

"The body is inside. So's your grandmother and the rest."

"I need to see her." Haley darted past the trooper and flung open the door to the clinic. Augusta sat beside Erika in the chairs by the door to the treatment room. Both women were as pale and green as sea foam. Erika cried steadily as she twisted a paper napkin to shreds in her hands. "Augusta?" Haley said in a quavering voice.

Augusta lifted her head. Her face crumpled. "Oh, Haley, it was terrible," she sobbed.

Haley dropped to her knees and embraced her grandmother. It felt strange to be the comforter after so many years of being the recipient of her grandmother's reassuring hugs. Augusta felt frail somehow, her bones poking through her blouse. Haley was suddenly struck with the realization that her grandmother might not always be with her. She hugged Augusta fiercely. She would never be willing to let her go. Never.

Tank came inside with Chet. "Can someone tell me what happened?" Chet demanded over Erika's wailing.

Erika shook her head violently. "I don't want to remember," she sobbed. A scratch marred her right cheek.

Haley looked at a white and shaken Denny, who leaned against the wall by the door. His lips trembled, and he seemed smaller and shrunken. "Can you talk about it, Denny?" She didn't want to put her grandmother through any more.

He nodded jerkily, and his throat worked. "I was videoing Kipp as he approached a bear. He was singing and talking in a soothing tone of voice. The bear looked at him but didn't run away. I got some good footage." He stopped and swallowed. "The forest was just to his left. He sat on a rock and started throwing bread to the bear. It got a little closer, then closer still until it ate right out of his hand. He even petted it. When the food was gone, it wandered back to the water. I got it all on camera."

"He knew better than to feed a bear," Tank muttered.

Denny nodded. "I tried to talk him out of it before we got there. He was determined to get it on film. Anyway, he got up from the rock and started back to me when another bear came out of the forest. A big bear. Huge. It kept coming toward him like that bear the other day when we were tagging. Kipp shouted at it and waved his hands, but it just kept coming. Then it got right up to him and lunged at his head." He closed his eyes, and his voice quavered. "It was over fast."

"I can't get his screaming out of my head," Erika moaned. She rocked back and forth.

Tank slammed his hand against the wall. "I told him not to go." His anguished voice quaked.

"It's not your fault," Haley said. "He wouldn't listen." She rose and went to Tank. He shrugged off the comforting hand she put on his back.

Chet turned back toward the door. "Tank, you know what we have to do. We can't wait any longer. Do you want to go out with us?"

"I'd better. I don't want them going after Miki by mistake."

Twenty-One

$\mathcal{M}$arley Gillespie drove down the narrow, unpaved road. Spruce trees crowded her mother's old Jeep. It hadn't been driven in months, but she'd found the keys in the drawer, and it had started right up. Her knuckles were white from gripping the steering wheel, both from fear and determination. Marley felt an overwhelming need to see Brooke and make sure she was okay. It was going to be up to her to save her niece. Tank obviously had no idea of the danger. Just as he'd ignored the dark forces swirling around Leigh.

Her breath left her at the thought of her sister. She'd failed Leigh, but she wasn't going to fail Brooke. No matter what it took.

Her vehicle bottomed out in a particularly vicious hole, and Marley bounced so hard her head hit the top of the SUV. She swore and jerked the vehicle to the right to avoid another pothole. How she hated this place. Hated it and feared it. It was capable of stripping away everything she loved.

The muddy track turned, and a clearing opened in front of

her. *The Lassiter cabin looked even more ramshackle than usual,* she thought, curling her lip. What had possessed Tank to bring Leigh here? Leigh deserved a fine home with plush carpets and fine paintings. Seeing her here had been like seeing a fine diamond set in pot metal.

Lost in thought, Marley almost didn't see her niece standing at the edge of the clearing. Brooke moved, and the bright splash of her red top caught Marley's eye. A bear loomed over the little girl, dwarfing her. Marley froze, then scrambled out of the SUV. She tried to call out, scream for Brooke to run, but her throat closed, and only a squeak emerged.

Brooke reached up and patted the bear. "Good Miki." She dropped a piece of a sandwich in the bear's cavernous mouth as it leaned down toward her. For a heart-stopping moment, Marley thought the bear would swallow the little girl's hand along with the food. It was that bear Tank had raised. Marley had warned him about that.

Cautiously, Marley approached. She kept her voice soft so the bear wouldn't become startled and more aggressive. "Brooke," she called softly, "come see Aunt Marley."

The little girl turned. The delighted expression on her face told Marley she was doing the right thing. Brooke loved her. She needed a mother. Raising Leigh's daughter would be her final act of service for her sister.

Brooke shot across the few feet that separated them and hurtled into Marley's arms. Marley hugged her, breathing in the aroma of little girl, a mixture of baby shampoo, perspiration, and dog. It shouldn't have smelled good but it did.

"Aunt Marley, you're squeezing me," Brooke complained.

"Sorry, sweetie." Marley loosened her hold and bolted for the Jeep. The bear disappeared into the woods. "Let's go for a ride." She cast her gaze toward the cabin. "Where's Aunt Libby?"

"In the backyard watering her flowers. But don't say anything." Brooke held her fingers to her lips. "I'm supposed to be taking a nap. Then we're going to town to meet Daddy."

"I won't tell." Marley opened the back door and buckled in Brooke. "We're going for a ride."

"With Aunt Libby and Joy?"

"No, just the two of us." Brooke needed rescue from this. Tank said she was never around the bear, and here she was outside by herself and feeding the monster.

"I'd better tell Aunt Libby."

Marley ignored the comment. "We'll get some ice cream later, okay?"

"Can I have a brownie sundae?" Brooke settled back in the seat.

Marley started to get into the car, but a figure came dashing from the house. Marley's gaze darted toward the teenage girl. Still no sign of Libby. She could always ditch this girl at the water's edge. She turned her best smile on full wattage. "Hi, I'm Brooke's aunt, Marley. Tank sent me after the two of you."

The girl stopped, and uncertainty replaced the panic on her face. "Tank sent you?" She glanced at Brooke. "Is this your aunt, Brooke?"

Brooke nodded. "She looks just like Mommy." She patted the seat beside her. "We're going to get ice cream, Joy. You can come."

Marley went around the other side of the car and opened the

door. "Tank is in a hurry. He already radioed Libby. Get in."
With a last doubtful look toward the house, Joy went around the
back of the SUV and climbed inside. Marley slammed the door
shut behind her and hurried around to the driver's side. She got
in and jammed the key home. The engine sputtered but finally
fired, and she drove off.

Her thoughts skittered feverishly to her escape plan. She
hadn't planned to do this yet, but the opportunity was too good
to miss. Tank would assume Brooke had wandered into the forest
and search for her there. By the time he figured out Marley had
taken Brooke, they would be far away in New York. She would
get a real lawyer who would protect Brooke from a lifetime of
being a hick. Lost in her rosy dream, it took a few moments for it
to sink in to Marley that the vehicle sounded funny. It surged and
began to thump. *Had hitting that pothole done something to it?* No
sooner had the thought formed than the SUV gave a final lurch
and a loud rattle, then died in the middle of the muddy lane.

"No!" Marley pounded the steering wheel. "This can't be
happening, not now." She turned the key frantically. The engine
ground. She tried again, and it coughed to life. A cloud of smoke
billowed from the back and from under the hood. It wouldn't
make it. Marley's mind raced for an alternative plan. If she
could just hide the vehicle somewhere, Tank wouldn't be on to
her very quickly. She and the girls could walk to Cook Inlet,
where she could get a boat to take her across the bay to Kenai,
where she could catch a plane to Canada and on to New York.

"Come on, come on," she muttered as the vehicle crept forward. There. She spied a parting in the spruce just big enough for

the old Jeep. She coaxed it into the spot and pulled forward until she could go no farther. The engine gave a final cough and died.

"Get out," she snapped at Joy. Grabbing her purse, Marley scrambled out, then opened the back door and unbuckled Brooke. Marley pulled the little girl out and took her hand.

Brooke tried to pull away. "I want to go home, Aunt Marley."

Marley didn't answer her. She thought the bay was to her left. Surely it wasn't far. She glanced at her shoes. The heels would not be conducive to walking. She dropped Brooke's hand, then took off her shoes and knocked the heels off. Another thought struck her. They'd need insect repellent. The mosquitoes would be vicious. She opened the back. Her father had always insisted her mother carry a backpack of gear for the bush. It was still in the back of the Jeep. She grabbed it and slung it on, then went back and motioned for Joy to follow her. By four o'clock, they should be to the Inlet. Another few hours and they'd be safely aboard a plane headed out of this wretched country.

Tank rode shotgun with Chet driving his SUV. Six other vehicles followed them. Some had bear-hunting dogs. Tank felt sick over what would have to happen today. It would be like seeing his dad shoot the bear when he was a kid. He never got used to it. But this bear was a killer. It had attacked Jed Hoose and had now killed Kipp.

"Don't look so grim. I know you hate it when a bear has to die, but you know as well as I do that this is necessary."

"I know it, but I don't like it."

"I don't imagine Kipp Nowak was too fond of what happened to him either," Chet said dryly.

"I'm sorry about that. He was misguided, but I wouldn't wish his end on anyone."

"Where do we start?"

"At the scene of the attack." Tank rolled his window down and let the fresh air help blow away his disgruntled mood. "The bear will likely hang around for a while. We may get him right off the bat." He glanced at his watch. "It's already going on four. I don't particularly want to be out all night hunting."

"Me neither. Especially with a bear like that lurking out there." Chet turned toward the lake.

They rode in silence. Tank didn't know what Chet was thinking, but he wouldn't want anyone privy to his own thoughts. They strayed way too often to a certain young woman with hair the color of burnished leaves and eyes like smoked honey. He nearly laughed. Who would have thought he could have such a poetic thought? He'd surprised himself a lot lately.

Chet parked beside the lake, and the men got out. The other vehicles parked behind the SUV. Carrying guns and shushing their barking dogs, they walked purposefully to join Chet and Tank. The dogs sniffed the bloodstains on the ground and began to strain at their leashes. They could smell the bear and knew what they'd been brought here to do.

Tank knelt and looked at the bear prints. Two bears had been here, both with a toe missing. Miki's was likely the smaller set of prints. He motioned to Chet. "Make sure the men know not to follow this set. It was the bigger bear that attacked Kipp."

Chet nodded. "These Miki's?"

"Probably."

Chet waved the men over and gave them their instructions. "Make sure your dogs know which bear we're tracking. We want the big one." Hunters usually weren't allowed to hunt bears with dogs, but it was allowed in special circumstances like this.

Mort Winters, the leader of the group, nodded grimly. "We'll get this guy before he hurts anyone else."

Tank shouldered his gun and his backpack and followed the baying dogs. He prayed Miki stayed out of the dangerous fray.

13

"Your pictures are here." Gus thrust a bag full of photos into Haley's hand.

"That was quick. It's only been two days."

"There was an extra plane flying this way, and he brought them in for me."

She peeked into the plastic bag to see it full of picture envelopes. Maybe they would help figure out who had attacked her. She'd have Libby look with her and Augusta.

Libby. Libby had gone to the cabin with Brooke and Joy. Haley had forgotten all about it. Libby knew nothing about the bear's attack on Kipp. She needed to call and tell Libby to stay inside. She thanked Gus and left his temporary store set up in a tent, then took off at a run for the troopers' office as fast as her prosthesis would allow. Bursting in, she asked the volunteer if she could use the radio. The woman made the call, then handed Haley the handset.

No one answered. She was about to give up when Libby's breathless voice came on the line.

"Tank, is that you? You have to come quick!"

"Libby, it's Haley. What's wrong?"

Libby was sobbing in short bursts of pants. "I can't find Brooke. She's gone!" Harsh sobs rattled through the line.

Haley stopped breathing. "What do you mean, gone?" Adrenaline kicked her in the gut. *Not again. Please God, not again.* The prayer bubbled to her heart before she could stop it.

"I stepped out back for a minute to water my garden. Brooke didn't sleep well last night, so I thought she could use a nap, though she seldom takes one at her age. When I came in, she was gone. I thought maybe she'd gone to the bathroom, but she wasn't there either. I need Tank! We have to find her!" She burst into a fresh round of sobs.

Haley realized she'd been holding her breath. "What about Joy?" She tried to quell the panic that dulled her thoughts.

Libby put her hand to her mouth. "I forgot about Joy! She's not here either. Could she have taken Brooke for a walk? She was getting some of our things together for me when I went out back."

"I can't believe she'd take her for a walk without telling you. Tank is out looking for the predatory bear. It killed Kipp today. That's what the commotion was about."

"Oh, dear God, no," Libby moaned. "Be with my Brooke, Jesus."

The blood in her veins was like ice, but Haley knew she didn't have the luxury of falling apart. "Do you have a gun?" Libby was sobbing so hard, Haley couldn't understand the answer. "Libby, calm down, I can't understand you. Do you have a gun?"

"Yes, yes, there are guns here."

"Get a gun, the biggest one you can handle. Keep looking for Brooke. I'll be there as quick as I can." She practically threw the receiver back onto the table. "We've got two missing children," she told the volunteer. "Tank's little girl is missing, and so is my sister Joy."

The woman's eyes widened. "Brooke?" She put her hand to her mouth.

"I need some help."

"Everyone is out looking for the bear. I'll try to raise Chet on the radio. I'll see if I can get some search dogs too."

"Tell them I'm heading out to the Lassiter place now." Haley ran for the door.

13

A cold drizzle fell over the cabin in the clearing. The day darkened in spite of the sun that had to be up there. Haley had begged a truck from the boy behind the reception desk at the hotel. Her gaze swept the dark recesses beneath the wind-whipped spruce branches, but she saw no small forms. The truck slewed sideways in the mud, then came to a stop by the cabin. Haley had the door open and her left leg out before the truck came to a stop.

A blurred form came running from the forest. Tears and mud streaked Libby's face, and her right cheek bore the marks of a recent encounter with a branch. A tiny bead of blood dribbled from the wound. "Haley, thank God you're here." Libby's chest heaved, and she dropped the rifle in her hand and threw herself against Haley.

They embraced. "Tell me what happened." Rain struck Haley's face and matted her hair.

"I was checking on my garden behind the house. Brooke was napping. At least I thought she was. When I came inside, I peeked into her room to see how she was doing, and she wasn't there. I thought maybe she'd gone to the bathroom, so I checked there. No sign of her. I freaked and ran around the house calling for her. She didn't answer. I found these over by the tree." She held out a doll dressed in a pink sleeper and an empty plastic bag with cookie crumbs inside. "So she has to have been outside."

"And Joy?"

"She was in my bedroom getting me some clean clothes. I was only outside maybe ten minutes."

Haley took the doll. She cupped her mouth to her hand. "Brooke! Joy!" She looked at Libby, who was still sobbing. They had to reach within themselves and find a way to be strong. "Let's fan out and find her." The drizzling rain made the trees seem even darker and more sinister. Haley dug through her pack, then pulled out a compass. "I've got a compass. Where have you looked, Libby? Let's do this in a smart way."

Libby seemed to recover her composure. She picked up the gun. "I'll show you where I found the bag."

Haley nodded and followed Libby. The rain wouldn't make things any easier. "A volunteer in Chet's office was going to get some of the search-and-rescue workers to bring their dogs out. There are a few left in town."

Libby pointed. "I found the plastic bag here."

Haley's gaze swept the rain-soaked ground and grass. An indention in the mud caught her attention, and she knelt to examine it more closely. Bear tracks. "Are these Miki's?" Haley could only hope they didn't belong to the other four-toed bear.

Libby knelt beside her. "I think so."

Haley's gaze went to another mark. It looked like small holes in the ground. "What would cause marks like this?" She brushed away twigs and debris, but still couldn't figure them out, not that she was an expert tracker. "Snake holes?"

"I don't know. There are no snakes in Alaska."

Libby stood and cupped her hands around her mouth, then shouted again for Brooke. Haley turned and stared at the muddy lane that led into the clearing. The tire tracks of the truck she drove overlaid those of another vehicle. Could someone have taken the girls?

Libby looked at the tracks. A frown creased her forehead, and her fingers traced a bulge that swooped out from the imprint of the tire. "How strange. Queenie, Chet's wife, had an old Jeep with a bad tire like that. Chet parked it just before she died. No one has driven it since. I wonder if Marley drove it out here." Her voice held a trace of excitement and hope. She looked back toward the strange holes. "I bet those holes are her heels. She never wears anything but heels."

They looked at one another. "Do you think Marley would have taken her?" Haley asked.

"She knows she can't get custody legally," Libby said slowly.

"Could these be from an earlier time when Queenie drove the vehicle out here?" Haley asked.

"The winter would have obliterated any previous traces. The marks are fresh too. Tank has shown me a little about how to track."

"How could she do something like that? Just waltz in and take Brooke?"

"You don't know Marley. Something like this is just what's she'd do. The doll's right here, so I think Brooke might have been out feeding Miki and dropped it," Libby said. "Marley could have driven up and taken her. And Joy."

Haley gasped and put her hand to her throat. "You let Brooke around the bear?"

"Of course not! I have to watch her like a hawk. When he was a cub, and there was no danger, she often helped Tank bottle-feed him. We've kept her away from him since he got larger." Libby looked down at the tracks. "Marley shouldn't be too hard to track down. Let's follow the tracks out."

"I'll drive. You direct me," Haley said. "Call it in first so they know what we suspect."

Libby nodded. "I'll be right back." She ran to the cabin.

Haley got into the truck and started it. Libby came back a few minutes later. "She hasn't been able to raise Tank and Chet yet, but she'll keep trying," Libby said, hopping in. "The search-and-rescue teams are going to be looking for the truck and will stop to help us when they see it." She ran the window down and leaned out to watch the tire tracks. They turned abruptly into what seemed to be a dead end of spruce and brambles. "Stop here," she ordered.

Haley jammed the brake. Libby opened the door. They both

got out and followed the tire tracks into the forest. Thrusting aside a patch of fireweed, Haley pressed through the tangle of vegetation.

A Jeep sat halfway under a tall spruce. Haley hurried to the driver's side and pulled open the door, but the SUV was empty. "Why would Marley abandon the vehicle here?" The keys were still in the ignition. She got in and tried to start it, but it cranked over uselessly. "She must have had engine trouble and ditched it here." She got out and slammed the door, but it did little to vent her frustration.

She and Libby stared at one another. Marley, Joy, and Brooke were wandering the forest with a predatory bear liable to turn up any minute.

Twenty-Two

*T*ank wiped rain from his face and stopped to catch his breath. The dogs seemed hot on the trail, though the rain dampened their excited yips.

Chet put his radio away. "The stupid base radio must be acting up again. I can't get through."

"Everyone is here anyway."

"Yeah, but if there's any emergency in town, I won't be able to be reached." Chet stuck the radio back on his belt.

"It will keep." Tank wanted this to be over.

They plodded on in silence for nearly half an hour. Tank's gaze darted from side to side, knowing the bear could be stalking them even as they were stalking it. As he walked, he prayed for God to keep Miki out of harm's way.

Chet's radio squawked to life. "Finally," he muttered, coming to a halt and holding up his hand to motion Tank to wait. "Gillespie." His shoulders went rigid. "How long ago?" he barked. He listened a few more minutes. "We'll be right there."

He looked at Tank, and he swallowed. "Brooke's gone missing. Joy too."

Tank gripped his father-in-law's arm. "What are you saying? Where? When? She's in town with Libby."

"Libby took Brooke and Joy with her to the cabin to get some things. The girls disappeared when Libby was checking on her garden."

Tank's mind stuttered, unable to grasp the magnitude. His gaze swept the forest shrouded in fog and moisture. Brooke couldn't be out here. "We have to find her." He grabbed Chet's arm and hustled him back toward the truck. Tank tried to quell the flash of anger at his sister. His rational mind knew this could have happened while he—or anyone—was watching Brooke. "How long ago?" he asked again.

"About two hours."

"Two hours." She could be at the bottom of a cliff. Or anywhere. The bush's vastness was numbing. Tank increased his speed. Even he was panting by the time they reached the SUV nearly half an hour later. He threw himself behind the wheel and barely waited for Chet to get inside before he floored the accelerator. The tires spun, then grabbed hold in the rocky dirt and roared off.

13

Haley could hardly sit still. The reality of Brooke and Joy missing in the dark, ominous forest brought back all the hopelessness of listening to her sister's life ebbing away in the dark mine. They had to find the girls. She took her walking stick with her as she traipsed after Libby in the thick underbrush. Her leg ached from the uneven ground, but she pressed on grimly. Her gaze darted from side to side as she scoured the ground for some clue to the missing children and woman. This Marley must be a real nut to have just snatched the girls that way.

Libby had finally stopped crying, but her breath still caught in hiccups. Haley paused to wipe her brow. She brought a package of powdered-sugar donuts out of her pack and handed one to Libby. "You look like you could use some energy."

Libby's touch was hesitant as she reached out and took the treat. "Thanks." She sniffled. "I feel so guilty, Haley. I should have been watching her closer."

"You're a great mother to Brooke," Haley said. "Anyone could see that. It's impossible to watch a child every minute. You'd never get any laundry or housework done. You thought she was sleeping. Every mother does the same thing."

"This is the bush though. One mistake can be deadly." Libby popped a piece of donut into her mouth. A hint of color began to come back to her face.

"We'll find her." Haley put all the confidence she could muster into the statement.

"Would you pray with me?" Libby whispered. "I'm so scared."

Haley couldn't tell her prayer would do no good. Libby needed encouragement now, not derision. "Okay," she said. "I'm not good at praying though." God hadn't listened to her before. She held no hope that he would this time either unless he loved Libby more. And he might. Libby had done nothing wrong. This wasn't her fault.

Libby took her hands. "Can you do the praying? Every time I try to pray, the thoughts jumble in my head."

"I haven't prayed in years," she said.

Tears pooled in Libby's eyes. "Please try," she whispered.

Haley hung onto Libby's hands for dear life. "God, help us find Brooke and Joy. You know where they are. Keep them safe and lead us to them. Amen."

"Amen," Libby said in a choked voice. "Be with them, Jesus." She wiped at her eyes. "Thanks, Haley. I feel like I can tell you anything."

Haley pointed to their right. "Let's go back to the truck. The searchers should be here with their dogs shortly, and we can direct them." Chickadees twittered above her head. Something squealed in the air, and she looked up to see a mouse caught in a peregrine falcon's talons. The bird soared on the thermal currents, then disappeared from sight. Haley shivered. She hoped it wasn't an omen. She turned her gaze back to the ground and moved carefully over the thick carpet of spruce needles. The ground wasn't quite so uneven here, and her gait was more sure and steady.

"I noticed you limping," Libby said. "Are you okay?"

"It's hard for me to walk on uneven ground," Haley said. It had been so long since anyone had noticed she wasn't quite whole, and now the whole state seemed to know. In the city, she wore smart slacks and boots. She walked surely on hard pavement without a limp.

"Do you want to sit and rest?"

"I'm okay. We need to keep moving."

"Want me to carry your camera?"

Haley put a protective hand over her camera. "No, I'll keep it. You can carry my bag if you want." She handed it to Libby.

Libby slung the bag over her shoulder. She paused and put her hand on Haley's arm. "Listen! I hear dogs."

Haley heard a bark, then several more. And voices. "The search teams must be here." She picked up her pace. They thrashed through the brambles and stumbled out onto the narrow lane. Two trucks and an SUV were parked behind the truck, and several people clustered together near the bed. They had dogs on leashes.

The petite young woman with dark red hair and green eyes who she'd met at the wiener-dog race stepped forward to meet them. Her dog, a mix that looked like mostly German shepherd, moved with her. He sniffed the air and looked keenly around. "Bree Matthews," she said. "We met at the race. It's your child that's missing?"

"My sister is one of the children. The other is Libby's five-year-old niece." She introduced Bree to Libby.

"This is Samson," Bree said. She dusted pistachio shells from her hands onto the ground. "What can you tell me about the children?"

"We think they were taken by Brooke's aunt, and now all of them are missing in the bush," Libby said.

A stalwart young man with kind blue eyes moved behind Bree. "I'm Kade Matthews. Do you have an article that belongs to either of the girls? We'll get right to work."

"Any special kind of article?" Libby asked.

"An unwashed sock or something that would be worn close to the body," Kade said. "Don't touch it. Put your hand inside a plastic bag to pick it up, then drop it in a paper bag."

"I'll get it." Libby turned and jumped into the truck then sped off toward the cabin.

"There might be some articles in the Jeep that belong to the woman. Would that work?"

"Do you want the dogs to sniff for the woman or the children?" Bree asked.

"They should be together."

"We could put the other dogs on the woman. Samson can work off the freshest scent with the little girl's clothing. Let them fan out." Bree called the other two searchers to join them. "Would you show them the vehicle?"

"It's this way." Haley led them through the brambles to where the Jeep sat under the trees. She wrenched open the front door. "You look there, and I'll check the back." She took out the keys and went to the rear of the vehicle. It was empty except for a steel whistle. She grabbed it and hung it around her neck. It might come in handy if she got lost. She slammed the hatch back down and went to join the searchers at the front.

"Not much here, but the dogs can sniff the interior," Bree said. She stepped aside and let the dogs nose the seat of the car. Their tails began to wag. "They've got something."

The truck came barreling back down the lane with Libby hunched over the wheel. Bree and Samson stepped out to meet her. The driver's door flew open, and Libby jumped out. "I brought two socks." She held a paper bag in her hand.

Bree took the bag from her and opened it, then held it down for the dog. Samson thrust his nose inside. He sniffed eagerly, then withdrew his nose and turned and strained toward the car. "He's got the scent." She knelt and unsnapped his leash. "Search, Samson." The dog bounded away. He ran off past the car with his tail held high.

For the first time, Haley began to think they might actually find the girls. She started following Bree and the rest of the searchers but soon fell behind. She couldn't run on the rough ground like the rest were doing. Within minutes, she found herself alone. Libby had forgotten she couldn't keep up as well.

Panic flared in her mind as Haley looked around and realized she had no idea where she was or how to get back to the truck. She had no cell phone, even if it would work out here, which it wouldn't.

Stop. Think. She forced herself not to run blindly. Thick spruce trees pressed in on all sides, and she smelled their sharp, pungent odor as she dithered and ground wet needles under her feet. Could she maybe follow her trail back to the truck? Or should she try to find the others? She listened, but all she could hear was the wind in the treetops and the gurgle of the river. The river. Would it take her where she needed to go?

She stepped a few feet to her right. It might not hurt to go there and see if there was any sign of the rest of the group. Following the sound of the rushing water, she pressed through the underbrush. The noise grew louder. She stumbled into a depression in the ground and lost her footing. Her right leg buckled, and she fell face down into the soft spruce needles. She lay there and inhaled the scent.

She smelled something else, something not so pleasant. It brought the taste of fear to her mouth as she remembered the bear standing over her. She shot to her feet and looked around, but she didn't see anything. The hair continued to stand up on the back of her neck, and her throat closed. She stepped to a nearby birch tree. Deep gouges above her head marred the bark. She tried to reach them, to run her fingers over the marks, but they were too high. A big bear had to have made them.

She glanced up. Maybe she could climb the tree. She would feel safer up there, and maybe she could see the rest of the group from higher up. She reached up and grabbed hold of the lowest limb. Hauling herself up, she swung her left leg over the branch. Her grip faltered, and she slipped back to the ground. She wiped her hands on her jeans and tried again. This time she managed to get onto the limb.

She lay there panting for a moment. The ground seemed far away. She edged back toward the trunk and managed to stand. She couldn't see anything. But she heard something. Looking down, she saw the hump on the back of the big bear as it moved toward the tree where she stood. The claw marks were about even with her foot.

She grasped the limb above her and hauled herself up. She managed to get both legs onto the limb, but she couldn't swing to the topside of it. The bear rose on its hind legs and stared straight into her face. She shrieked and struggled to get higher. It opened its mouth and roared, then reached up toward her.

"Go away, go away," she shouted. She finally got on top of the limb and pulled her legs out of reach of the wicked-looking claws. Could grizzlies climb trees? She had read somewhere that they could, but maybe that wasn't true. Frantic, she grabbed the limb above her head. She had to get higher. Her leg throbbed, and her hands burned from being scraped raw by the bark. The bear began to shake the tree. She shrieked and clung to the branch with all her strength. The bear dropped to all fours and moved to the other side of the tree.

She climbed higher until the branches began to thin out and she was afraid they might break. The bear circled the tree beneath her, pausing occasionally to shake the tree. She stared down at its humped back as it lumbered around and around. What would happen if she got too tired? She straddled the limb and hung on as tightly as she could. As she moved, the whistle around her neck swung against her chest, and she grabbed it. She'd forgotten all about it.

She pulled it to her lips and blew on it with all her strength. The piercing shriek hurt her ears. The bear grunted and ran off toward the river. She could only hope one of the searchers heard it.

Twenty-Three

*T*rucks and four-wheel-drive vehicles lined the narrow track and blocked further progress along the lane. Tank pulled up as far as he could go. The vehicles were empty, and trees blocked any view of the people who had to be here somewhere. He jumped out of the SUV and ran to the truck ahead of it. It held a dog crate in the back.

Tank tipped his head to the side and listened. He could hear distant barking. "Search dogs," he told Chet, who matched his steps.

"We're lucky they were still in the area." Chet huffed as he struggled to keep up with Tank.

They followed the sound of voices and dogs. "Libby!" Tank shouted. He heard an answering shout from his sister, and then she came running through the timber.

"Tank!" She launched herself into his arms. Her face was streaked with dirt and tears. "We haven't found her yet."

His chest ached even as he comforted his sister. "We'll find her." He released her, and they hurried toward the searchers.

Dead leaves crunched under his boots, and their decaying aroma filled him with stark fear for his daughter's safety.

He, Libby, and Chet walked silently. They came to a clearing where searchers and dogs milled around. Libby introduced him to the searchers and pointed out the lead search dog, Samson. Tank watched the handsome German shepherd mix meandering aimlessly through the wildflowers. "What's wrong?" Samson looked back at them, then held his head high and sniffed the air.

"They're trying to pick up the scent again," Bree said. "Samson and the others are air-scent dogs. People give off wafts of skin that linger in the air. A good air-scent dog can pick the scent out of the air and follow it to its source. They've lost the scent right now."

"What could cause that?" Chet asked. "Did they ford the river?"

Bree shook her head. "An air-scent dog can track the scent into the water. The most remarkable recovery of a cadaver happened here in Alaska when some dogs found a body three hundred feet under the water." She frowned. "I'm not sure what's wrong. Generally, they only lose the scent if the person travels in an enclosed vehicle. That would be hard to do out here."

"Unless they got picked up by a helicopter or a plane," Tank suggested. He walked to a clearing and scanned the ground for evidence of an air vehicle. "A chopper could land here, or a plane could have landed on a sandbar in the river and picked them up."

"That might be what happened." Regret tinted Bree's words. "Samson isn't getting anything."

Tank's hope began to die. He couldn't see any evidence of a

helicopter having landed here, so he walked to the edge of the water. "Is there any way we can tell where the scent leaves off?"

Bree snapped her fingers, and Samson ran to her. She ran her hand over his curly coat, then held out the bag with the sock again. "Search, Samson." Her tone held urgency. He whined, and his head went up. He ran back and forth across the clearing, then raced to the edge of the water.

"I'd say a seaplane lifted them from here," Bree said, joining Tank at the edge of the river. "The current is pretty slow here, so it should have been able to land safely."

"Yeah." Tank took off his floppy hat and fished a handkerchief out of his pocket, then wiped his brow. "Any other recourse?" He couldn't wait to get his hands on Marley.

"Not unless we get some general idea of the quadrant where they landed. We have to get the dogs close enough to pick up the scent."

Chet dug out his radio. "There's no way of knowing where they went right now. I'll check with air-traffic control in Anchorage and see if a small plane posted a flight plan in this area."

Bree squeezed Tank's hand. "At least you know your daughter isn't wandering alone in the woods. If there's anything else we can do to help, let us know. Kade and I will be here for another two days, but we could delay our departure if you need us to stay."

Libby looked around. "Where's Haley?"

"She was here a few minutes ago," one of the women said.

"She's afraid of the wilderness," Tank said to Libby. "You should have kept a better eye on her. She couldn't find her way out of a paper bag."

"Stay calm," Bree said. "Do you have anything that belongs to her? It will be contaminated with other scents, but Samson is smart enough to figure out what I want him to do."

"I've got her camera bag," Libby said. She slipped it off and handed it to Bree.

"Perfect! Her scent is most likely the only one inside." She unzipped the top and held it out to the dogs. All three crowded around, jockeying for position. "Search, Samson!" He nosed it eagerly, then crisscrossed the meadow. Watching him for several minutes, Bree finally shook her head. "He's not getting it here."

Kade put his hand on her shoulder. "Let's walk back the way we came. We'll have to pick up her scent eventually."

"This way." Tank led them toward the lane. He stopped frequently to check his compass.

"Anchorage is checking into their records," Chet told him. "We'll find them. When I do, Marley is in big trouble."

Samson began to bark, and his tail wagged frantically. "He's found the scent!" Bree called. "Search, Samson." The dog raced off to the east, his tail held high in the air. The other dogs followed.

Tank ran after them. Spruce branches whipped at him and left traces of sap on his face and shirt. The rough, uneven ground slowed him down, but he pressed on. He leaped over a stream that crossed in front him and plowed on. A piercing whistle rose above the rustling of the wind in the spruce boughs. The dogs were moving in the direction of the whistle, and he followed them, his feet kicking up a mixture of needles, wet vegetation, and twigs. He fought his way through blueberry brambles into a small clearing by the river.

The dogs were barking frantically at the base of a white birch tree. He raised his gaze through the leafy branches until he saw a white face peering through the leaves. Haley. She was all right. A weight rolled off his shoulders. He walked to the base of the tree and looked up to find her clinging to a fork in the tree. Both arms wrapped around the smooth bark in front of her, she hugged the tree as if she were afraid the ground would reach up to snatch her.

"Tank, you came. Did you hear the whistle?" Her voice was a croak.

He could still hear terror in her voice, and his conscience smote him again. "That was smart thinking. Libby had your camera case too, so the dogs got your scent and led us here. Can you get down by yourself? What are you doing up there?"

"There was a bear."

"It probably wouldn't have hurt you. Did you remember to make noise?" He held up his hands to help her down. She tumbled into his arms and clutched him with both hands. Her soft breath warmed the skin under his shirt as her panting began to calm. He pulled her closer, and she nestled against him. He rested his chin on the top of her head. The rest would be arriving in a moment, and he'd have to let her go, but he didn't want to release her. It felt right to hold her.

He heard the sound of voices, Libby, Bree, and the rest. Haley wept softly against his chest, and he patted and rubbed her back until she began to calm. "Shh, it's okay," he whispered. "You're safe now. The bear is gone."

She raised her head. Her eyes were red, and her skin blotchy from crying. "I started to climb the tree to see if I could see someone. I'd just gotten to the first limb when the bear came charging toward me. It wanted to eat me and wasn't afraid."

Tank frowned. "It might have had a cub nearby."

"I didn't see one. It had a torn ear. It looked like that predatory bear." She rubbed at her face. "Could I borrow your hanky?"

He shifted uneasily. It could have been the one they were after. A brown bear's home range can be from two hundred to five hundred square miles, and it could cover a lot of territory fast. He pulled out his handkerchief and handed it to her. "It's not the cleanest, but help yourself."

She blew her nose vigorously, then stuck the handkerchief in her pocket. "Thanks. I'll wash it and give it back to you."

The voices grew louder, and the rest of the group broke through the blueberry patch and joined them. Haley stepped away, and Libby rushed to her side. "I'm so sorry, Haley! I should have been watching for you. Are you all right?"

Haley was pale, but she managed a smile and nodded. "I'm fine. Scared, but I'm okay now." Her gaze swept the group, and her smile dimmed. "You didn't find the girls?"

"No." Tank moved toward Chet. "They were evidently picked up in a small plane." He stopped in front of his father-in-law. "Any word from Anchorage?"

"Yeah, a small plane registered to Freemont Wilson flew out this way."

Tank frowned. "The name familiar to you?"

Chet shook his head. "Nope. But maybe she saw him flying overhead and waved him down."

"Maybe." Tank wasn't convinced. It sounded more like a plan. "I guess we'd better get to town and see if we can find this Freemont Wilson. Maybe he knows about my little girl." It comforted him to know Brooke wasn't spending the night in the bush. After Haley's encounter with the bear, the forest he loved and protected felt dangerous and unfamiliar. Tank turned to lead the way back to the vehicles. The rest of the group fell into line behind him.

Haley was silent as they walked through the forest with birds chattering above their heads, and the rustle of small creatures came from all directions. She stayed close to Tank's side, and he could see she was still shaken by her experience.

Chet's radio squawked, and he stopped to answer it. "Gillespie."

Tank stopped to see if there was more news about his daughter. His stomach plummeted when he saw Chet's jaw sag. The trooper blinked his eyes quickly and swallowed hard before clicking off the radio.

"What is it? What's wrong?" Tank demanded.

Chet wet his lips. "That was Anchorage. They say Wilson never reported in, and the last blip on their radar was over the Wrangell Mountains. They think the plane went down there."

Twenty-Four

*T*he wreckage of the plane floated in the swells and eddies of the lake. The fuselage scraped against a rock, the sound as grating as fingernails on a blackboard. The waves tossed pieces of the wings and landing gear onto the deserted beach. The pilot, Freemont Wilson, had been thrown through the windshield on impact, and his body joined the other flotsam in the cold water of the lake.

Marley stared at the desolate scene. Blood trickled from a cut on her head and matted her hair. More blood stained her blouse and slacks. Her shoes were lost somewhere. Joy moaned, and her eyelashes fluttered. Clutching Brooke, Marley assessed their options. At least they were alive. When the plane had answered her frantic wave for help, she'd thought they would soon be away from this wretched place.

How could it have turned out like this? They were miles and miles from nowhere, lost in the wilderness with no idea which way to go to find help. Luckily she and the girls were strapped in. The pilot, a heavy man in his fifties, had complained the belt obstructed his movements while trying to fly and hadn't put his on. Her gaze wandered to his body, floating less than five feet away.

Brooke was sobbing. Her precociousness had dropped away, and she was a normal, scared five-year-old. Marley rocked her back and forth while she tried to decide what to do. The swirling water was beginning to seep into the cockpit. They were going to have to get to shore. The water was deep, but she could swim.

Reaching behind her, she grabbed her backpack. "We're going for a little swim, sweetie," she said, forcing cheerfulness into her voice. She patted Joy's face. "Wake up, Joy," she said. The girl muttered, and her eyes finally opened.

She sat up. "Where are we?" Her eyes widened when she saw the water beginning to pour into what was left of the plane.

"We have to get out of here," Marley told her. "Swim to the shore."

Brooke shrieked and buried her face in Marley's chest. "I want my daddy," she sobbed.

Marley wanted to shake her. Couldn't Brooke see that she was only trying to do what was best? Her mind drifted to the way things would be when they were in the Lower Forty-eight. She would dress Brooke in darling pink and green outfits that made people notice her beauty. It would be the way it was supposed to have been all along. They just had to get through this. She'd find a way.

◇

The radio squawked to life. Tank sprang to turn it up, praying that the connection would hold. It had been all he could do to hold onto his faith that God was looking out for his baby girl. He clenched and unclenched his fists as he listened to Chet speak into the radio. He didn't feel alone, flanked as he was by Libby on one side and Haley on the other.

"Uh-huh," Chet said. He plucked the pencil from behind his ear and jotted down something on a pad of paper. The radio, held together by duct tape, sat on a battered wooden table, and Chet hunched over it as if to keep it from the slightest movement. His knuckles were white where he gripped the receiver. "Thanks, buddy. I owe you!" He hung up and held up the paper. "Got it!"

Tank snatched the paper from his fingers and strode to a map on the wall. The edges were yellow and curled out from the paneling, but the part he needed was more inland. Wrangell-St. Elias National Park. Much of the area had never seen a human footprint. Thinking about the brooding blue mountains, he suppressed a shudder. His baby girl was in there somewhere, and he was going to find her. *Please, God.*

He traced the Kennicott River with his finger. "We can fly in here and land on this lake. Can we get the dogs out there? We'll get choppers scouring the area too."

Chet nodded. "The Matthews team said they were at your disposal. They have a little boy who was lost in the woods, so they know the pain we're going through."

Tank felt like he was wandering a cold, barren glacier. He would have to be very careful, consider every move, if he hoped to get Brooke and Joy out alive. He knew others had gone through this, but right now, he wasn't ready to accept any sympathy. Brooke had to be okay. He wouldn't accept any other outcome.

"What do you want us to do?" Haley asked. Her voice trembled.

He knew she was terrified of going out there again. It was a testament to her courage that she pushed herself on anyway, determined to help find Brooke and Joy. "We need all the searchers we can get. Go door-to-door and see who's willing to help."

Haley nodded. "We'll meet you at the airfield in half an hour. Should we bring supplies to spend the night?"

"I'm not leaving Wrangell without the girls."

She just nodded. "We'll bring tents and food." She limped slightly as she started toward the door, then turned back. "It's pretty rough terrain, right? I think I'd better talk Augusta into staying here with Oscar."

He nodded. "It will be a grueling walk. Are you sure you're up to it?"

"I'll be okay. I'll bring my walking stick." She was still a little pale from her ordeal up the tree, and her scratched face reminded him of all she'd been through. He was probably pushing her too much, but he needed her help. Even with all the area residents he could muster, there wouldn't be more than fifty searchers out there. The state search-and-rescue teams were on their way too, but it would take time to get them all here. They were looking for a spitball in the ocean. He shut his eyes and pressed on his lids. He couldn't think like that. They had to find the girls.

When he opened his eyes, his gaze connected with Haley's.

He turned away from the sympathy he saw there. He couldn't let down his guard. Brooke's life depended on his remaining focused and in control. He turned to Chet. "Where are the searchers assembled?"

"Most of them are at the café. I'll go rustle up all I can find there as soon as I put it out on the radio that we need every able-bodied person to search." Chet hitched up his pants and picked up the radio receiver again.

Tank walked to the door with Libby. "Let's go through town and see if we can find any more volunteers. We need to get supplies for several days too."

Libby nodded. "I threw some stuff in the truck before coming in here. Our things are ready."

"Thanks. I'd better get a rifle. The predatory bear is still out there."

13

"You're not leaving me behind," Augusta said adamantly. "That's my granddaughter out there. I'm perfectly capable of walking in the woods. More so than you, even," she pointed out. "Maybe you should stay behind with Oscar."

Haley would like nothing better. Her experience earlier in the day with the bear had about done her in, but Tank needed her. Brooke and Joy needed her. She realized she was putting Joy in place of Chloe in some ways. "I'll take my walking stick."

"What about Oscar?"

"I guess I'll just take him. I can carry him. Maybe he can learn something from the search dogs and help find the girls."

She smiled at the thought. Oscar was smart, but she didn't know if he would be up to the specialized searching of Samson and his friends. He'd be in good company, though. She stifled a yawn and glanced at her watch. Nearly ten at night, though the sun still hovered high in the sky. She'd fill a thermos with coffee and guzzle it along the way to help keep her alert. The thought of the girls out alone in the night with dangerous creatures made her shudder. Joy would take care of Brooke if she could, but she was only a child herself.

"You're getting very involved with Tank and his family," Augusta observed, her gaze on Haley's face. "Do you think that's wise, darling? You'll soon be back in Phoenix."

"I can't wait!" Haley skirted her grandmother's deeper question. "I hope we find the girls quickly and get this project over and done with. I never want to hear another mosquito buzzing in my ears or smell the stink of another bear. I just want to see the skyscrapers of my city and inhale the exhaust of millions of cars." She grinned and dropped a kiss on Augusta's soft cheek.

Augusta gave her a tiny shove. "You're incorrigible. And don't think you can pull the wool over my eyes with that kind of talk. I see the way you look at big Tank. He's quite a hunk. Even a woman as old as I am can sense his magnetism." Her smile turned to a worried frown. "Just don't get hurt. There's no way to resolve your differences."

"I know." She busied herself with pouring coffee from the room pot into the thermos. She didn't want to talk about Tank anymore. There was no reason to dwell on him. She'd be able to walk away when the time came.

She stuffed their belongings in the bag with the tent and grabbed Oscar. "Ready?" She slung the bag over her shoulder.

"Did you get your walking stick?"

"Thanks for the reminder." She grabbed the long stick that leaned against the wall and opened the door. They headed into the nighttime sunshine that illuminated the people milling around in the muddy street.

Marley lay on the rocky shore of the river. She spit out sand, but she was too spent to move from her prostrate position. Brooke lay curled in the crook of her arm. Her lashes trembled on her pale cheeks, but she was breathing. Marley had made sure her niece's chest still moved; then she fell face forward onto the damp ground. They needed to find a place of safety, but not yet. Joy lay on the other side of her.

Water lapped at her feet. The deep ache of cold dampness invaded her bones. She couldn't feel her feet or legs. If their plane had crashed any farther from shore . . . Marley groaned and rolled to her back. If only her cell phone would work in this horrible place. She sat up and reached for her backpack. Unzipping it, she sorted through the contents and found the first-aid kit. She pulled it out and found an alcohol swab. She dabbed at the cut on Brooke's forehead. The bleeding had stopped, but the little girl flinched at the sting and opened her eyes.

"I want my daddy," she whispered. She began to cry weakly and struggled to sit up. Joy didn't speak, but tears made tracks on her cheeks.

Marley pulled Brooke onto her lap. They were both wet and shivering. They had to find shelter before hypothermia set in—which wouldn't be long. She pulled a solar blanket out of her pack and wrapped it around them. If only she had some dry clothes to put on Brooke. "Let's see if we can find somewhere to sleep," she told the little girl. She stood and shouldered the backpack. "Can you walk?" she asked Brooke.

Brooke shook her head. "Carry me, Aunt Marley. My leg hurts."

She began to cry harder, a dreary sound that made Marley want to scream. It was so out of character for Brooke. She was normally so mature for her age. Marley gritted her teeth to keep from swatting her little behind. "Fine," she said curtly. "I'll carry you. Come on, Joy." She lifted her niece and began to stagger up the bank. Joy followed. They walked uphill in the sparse valley toward a hillside that looked to be about a half an hour's trek. She knew they should stay close to the crash, but they could come back tomorrow. The best shelter would be a cave of some kind. She thought she could see a dark splotch that might be an opening from here. She'd heard this area was pocked with old mines. At least they'd be warm and out of the elements. The temperature was falling fast.

She glanced at her watch and realized they'd been walking for forty-five minutes. The hillside was farther than it looked. Her breath hissed through her open mouth, and her arms ached from Brooke's weight. She pressed on grimly toward the dark area. Fifteen minutes later, she finally reached the base of the mountain and looked up. It was a mine opening. Perfect.

Twenty-Five

The fading light gilded the Wrangell Mountains. The plane swooped low over the Kennicott River valley treetops, and a shimmering body of water appeared. A brilliant blue, it seemed to go on forever and reflected the image of the seaplane as it dived like a giant seabird before gliding onto the smooth surface of the waves.

Tank's gaze went up and up as he looked at the mountains looming in the distance. His daughter was out here somewhere, maybe hurt and needing him. He fidgeted, wanting to fling open the door and hop out into the water. There was no dock here, no good place to leave the planes, but they had to find a spot to do just that.

More planes floated down toward them as the rest of the searchers began to arrive. Seeing the armada of seaplanes, Tank tightened his hold on the hope that had dimmed as he looked at the vastness of the wilderness. They had to find the girls. He jumped out of the plane and helped Libby and Haley down.

Then Chet clambered out of the plane behind the women. "I'm not sure where to start. The tree cover is too heavy to look for wreckage from the sky. They could have flown farther in than the coordinates reported."

"But we have to at least check this place out. We'll see if the dogs pick up their scent anywhere in this area." Tank splashed through the water to the shore and turned to watch the other searchers come ashore as well. The dogs barked excitedly and strained at their leashes.

Bree and Kade organized the search, and the dogs and people were soon combing the woods and tundra for any sign of the downed plane. By midnight, the light became dim enough to hamper the search. "We might as well pitch camp here," Chet said. "The searchers are tired, and we'll need them fresh when full daylight comes."

Tank knew his father-in-law was right. They were all bleary-eyed with fatigue, but he longed to hold his baby girl. She had to be safe. He gave a grudging nod. "We're pitching camp," he called to the searchers. The answering calls of relief were tinged with regret. Half an hour later, the camp fell silent except for the snuffling of dogs and people.

Tank lay in his sleeping bag, but his eyes refused to close. Brooke was depending on him. He tried to pray, but all he could do was whisper, "Please, Jesus, please." Finally he groaned and sat up. This was getting him nowhere. He crawled out of his sleeping bag and slipped out of the tent. A small light glowed in Haley's tent. He stepped past it and approached the fire, then settled down by the dogs. Samson put his head on his knee, and

Tank stroked the dog's curly coat. Having a warm body close brought some comfort. The dog seemed to sense his distress.

He felt rather than heard someone come up behind him. Haley's face was pale in the moonlight. A book tucked under her left arm, she sat beside him.

"I couldn't sleep either," she said softly. Samson transferred his attention to her. She rubbed his ears, and he sprawled onto her lap.

"Traitor dog," he said. Silence stretched as thick as the fog curling over the water. "I'm scared, Haley," he said softly.

Her fingers stilled. "Me too. But we'll find them. Samson will find them." The dog's ears pricked at the mention of his name.

"What are you reading?"

She held it up. "*The Lion, the Witch and the Wardrobe*. I promised Brooke I'd read it to her, and we never got a chance. I'm reading it now so I can tell her I did it."

His eyes burned, and he rubbed them. "Thanks. It will mean a lot to her."

"She's right, it's pretty good." She hesitated. "It sure makes you think about how things may not be like they seem here. Do you really think heaven exists?"

"Don't you, deep down?"

She looked away. "I used to. I had a picture Bible Augusta gave me, and I read it by the hour. Until Chloe died, I thought I was a Christian. My faith sure didn't survive that trial."

"Even Christians get mad at God."

A small shadow came barreling from the direction of Haley's tent. Oscar leaped onto Haley's lap and settled there. He eyed the bigger dog and growled a soft warning. Samson ignored him, and then Oscar edged closer to the search dog. Moments later the two dogs were sniffing noses, then Oscar vacated Haley's lap and the two ran off together.

Haley laced her fingers together on her knees. "Where do we go tomorrow?"

Her dance with God always seemed to be two steps forward, three steps back. He decided to let her change the subject. She'd come to it in her own time. "I've been thinking about that. If I were flying a plane and began to have trouble, I'd look for a water landing. It would be the safest bet even without floats. I want to take Chet's plane upriver and look for wreckage. They're obviously not here, or the dogs would have picked up the scent."

She unclasped her hands and reached over to take his fingers in a firm grip. "How do you stay so strong?"

He laced his fingers with hers. Sitting out here alone, he needed a human touch. "They have to be all right. I'll save my daughter. I've been praying, and I know I can save her."

She tightened her grip. "Don't tempt fate, Tank. You're a strong man, but you can't do everything."

"I mean it. Nothing is going to happen to my little girl. If I'd been home when Leigh—"

"You're the one always talking about God. Are you such a big man that you can dictate to God how things are to be done? I was sitting right beside my sister begging for her life, and God took her anyway. He doesn't always listen."

Was she trying to make him mad? If so, she was doing a good job. He pulled his hand from her grasp. "I thought you came out here to comfort me."

"I did, but you started making stupid statements. If anyone can save the girls, you can. And we're going to do the best we can to find them." She swept her hand toward the forest. "But this land is harsh and unforgiving. And God is the same way. Sometimes he yanks the thing we most love from us. And no one can alter that, not even you, Tank Lassiter."

"I don't want to hear it. I will save her, Haley. You'll see. She's out there waiting for me to find her." He rose and stalked toward his tent. He kicked off his boots, then crawled inside his sleeping bag. Burrowing his head in his arms, he tried to sleep, but her words echoed in his head. *Sometimes he yanks the thing we most love from us.* Not in this case. He rolled over on the hard ground again. *Surrender, my son.* The gentle pressure came, but he resisted it. He curled his knees to his chest and tried to ignore God's insistent impression on his heart. *Surrender.* He rolled to his stomach. For hours he wrestled with God. It was almost time to get up when he finally put Brooke in her Father's hands.

What was that? Marley bolted upright. The blackness of the mine pressed in on her from all sides. She grappled in the darkness for her flashlight. The thin beam pushed back the edges of black, and she breathed easier. Next to her, Brooke enjoyed the sleep of the exhausted. Joy cried out in a nightmare. Marley was beyond exhaustion, but the mine frightened off her ability to sleep. It seemed to echo with the past. Was Leigh here too? She strained to see past the shadows.

She shone the light on the ceiling. It had been shored up with beams that looked half-rotten. It probably wasn't safe in here, but it was even more unsafe outside where animals could get to them. At least in here, the mosquitoes only tasted them instead of devouring their flesh and leaving bare bones behind. She smiled at the macabre thought.

How were they going to get out of this situation? It was up to her to take care of Brooke now. She had to rise to the occasion. Somehow. But people would be looking for them. Surely, someone would find them tomorrow. She shone the light on her diamond wristwatch. The second hand wasn't moving. The swim in the cold water must have ruined it. They should go back to the shore.

She stood and bumped her head on a rafter that was partially detached from the ceiling. It moved several inches, then a rumble started. Marley backed away, her pulse galloping like a grizzly in a full run. Debris began to rain down onto the dirt floor. She scooped up Brooke and shoved Joy back into a side drift. Then the world went dark.

Twenty-Six

Tank leaned over to look down from the window. The sun was already halfway to its zenith, and there was no sign of the plane. Haley sat beside him, watching out the other side. Libby sat between them, which was a good thing, because he could feel the strain and figured Haley could as well.

"Wait, what is that?" Haley said suddenly. She leaned forward and tapped the pilot on the shoulder. "Go down. There's something floating in the water."

Tank could see it now. "This might be it!" He gripped the seat in front of him and watched as the plane swooped lower.

"I see a wing," Haley called. Her voice quivered.

Tank's stomach matched her voice. "Please, God," he whispered.

Libby's hand found his and squeezed. "A water landing might have saved them," she murmured.

"Going in for a landing," Chet said.

The other trooper grabbed the radio and told the other

searchers where to join them. The plane dipped and bounced on the rough ground, then jolted to a stop. Tank exited the plane with Libby and Haley right behind him. Debris floated in the water. He looked frantically around for his daughter. There was no sign of her.

Haley's hand gripped his arm, her nails digging into the flesh of his forearm. "Tank, look." With the other hand she pointed to something floating among the weeds along the bank.

He inhaled sharply. A bloated body floated face down in strands of dead vegetation. *It doesn't mean Brooke is dead.* He lunged toward the woods. He had to find her. Stumbling a little, Haley ran beside him. "Brooke!" he screamed. His boot toe hit a rock, and he sprawled onto the sloping riverbank. Barely aware of his fall, he sprang to his feet and began to run again, shouting his daughter's name until he was hoarse. He ran the length of the sand, too frantic to look for signs or footprints. "Brooke, Brooke, my baby girl." He had to find her. He'd give everything he owned—his job, his home, everything—to feel her small hands gripping his face.

He finally stopped when he was so spent he couldn't run any longer. Hemmed in by trees, he wasn't sure where he was. His face was wet. He wiped it with the back of his sleeve, then turned and realized Haley was still with him. She was crying too. He practically fell into her arms.

She held him tight. "It will be okay. We'll find her. They're not in the water, so they have to have made it."

He pulled away, then pulled her into his arms. He kissed her with the desperation of a drowning man. She was the only solid thing in his life right now. The love that welled up surprised him.

She kissed him back with a strength and passion that made him cling to her all the more. "I love you," he murmured in a broken voice. "I don't want to, but I do. Don't leave me."

"We'll find them," she said again. "Don't say anything you don't mean."

Did she think it was fear talking? He started to explain, but a shout from over by the water stopped the words.

"Tank, the dogs have a scent."

"Thank you, God, thank you," he muttered. Clutching Haley by the hand, he pulled her with him toward the rest of the searchers. The dogs were milling around. Samson woofed and strained at his leash. "Let him go," he said urgently.

Bree nodded and unclipped the leash. "Search, Samson," she said. The dog took off with the rest. Even Oscar was in on the quest. His tiny tail wagging, he stayed on Samson's heels.

Still hanging onto Haley, Tank followed Bree and Kade. The searchers fanned out as the dogs raced over the ground undulating with golden grasses. They seemed to be heading for the closest mountain. The dogs never deviated from their straight course right for the hill. Maybe Brooke, sweet Brooke, would be in his arms before his watch's hands moved to ten o'clock.

He glanced back to see the other searchers dropping behind. Libby was trying to keep up, but Erika and Augusta were at the back of the pack. He faced forward and pressed on to reach his daughter.

13

The topography looked increasingly familiar to Haley. She told herself it couldn't be the site of the old dig. It couldn't. But the panic fluttered more and more madly in her chest as they neared the mountain. She'd come so far in facing her fears, her nightmares. God couldn't be cruel enough to pit her against the one thing she couldn't bear. She looked back at the rest of the group. She wanted her grandmother, but Augusta was back a good quarter of a mile.

Tank still had her fingers gripped tightly. She tried to pull away, but he seemed oblivious to her state of mind. She jerked her fingers free. "Go on, I'll catch up."

He glanced at her leg and nodded. "Hurry." He took off again.

Haley rubbed her knee. The mad run across the uneven ground had taken its toll, but her real reason for lagging behind loomed in front of her. It was the place of her nightmares. She'd vowed never to come here again. Never. She stumbled to her knees and stared. The opening to the mine yawned like the mouth of hell.

Shuddering, she clutched her arms around her. Feeling as old as Augusta, she finally got to her feet. Forcing herself forward, she kept her gaze on the mouth of the mine. She reached the rest of the group in time to see Samson run to the opening. Barking, he dashed inside, but not so far she couldn't still see his tail swishing. Tank ducked inside, but the sunshine still illuminated his broad back.

He uttered a frustrated shout. "It's blocked! There's been a cave-in."

Haley stumbled and nearly fell again. "No," she whispered. She moved forward in a dreamlike trance. Her sister was in there, not Chloe this time, but Joy. Though they'd barely had a chance to get to know one another, she loved the young girl already. Hard and fast, the memories slammed into her.

Tank turned and saw her. "What is it?"

Haley marshaled every ounce of courage she could find. She wasn't the same little girl who had cowered in the dark twenty years ago. She'd learned to walk again with one leg, learned to take the hard knocks that came her way. She could do this. She had to do this. She met Tank's gaze. "I know another way in."

His face changed, and hope glimmered in his eyes. "Show me."

She led the way around the side of the hill. Clambering over rocks and loose shale, she pulled loose shrubs and vegetation away from the opening. "This leads to the main drift." She took off her backpack and stuffed her jacket inside.

"What are you doing?"

She felt frozen inside, terrified, but she continued to move toward the dark hole. "I know the mine. And it takes someone small. You're too big to get through in many places. I might even be too big, but I have to try. Give me a flashlight." He pressed a flashlight into her hands. "If we get stuck, I'll read her book to her. It's in my backpack."

"You're not getting stuck." Tank gripped her shoulders. "I'll never forget this, Haley. You be careful. I don't want to lose you too."

She stared into his face. "Pray, Tank."

"I haven't stopped."

Huffing and puffing, Augusta reached them. Her gaze took in Haley with the flashlight, then wandered to the mine opening. "You're not going in there."

"I have to, Augusta. The other opening has caved in. I have to look for them."

"You're not strong enough to do this, Haley," Augusta said quietly.

"I know, but I have to." Haley closed her eyes and inhaled Augusta's sweet scent. She pulled away. "I'm the only one who knows where the mine goes. It has to be me." Fear contorted Augusta's face. "I'll be okay. Pray."

"I will."

"I can go," Bree said. "Samson will lead me right to them."

Haley wanted to agree, wanted to step back and let someone else do it. Shaking her head was the hardest thing she'd ever done. "I need to do it. I know how it turns and where the floor gives way. But I'll take Samson."

Bree called the dog, and he came toward her. Bree snapped on a leash. "Since it's dangerous, you'd better keep him close. Sound can be distorted in a mine, so you need to let him lead you with the leash rather than rely on his barking."

Haley nodded and wrapped the leash around her wrist. She turned toward the mine again. Her blood thundered in her ears, a roar that made it hard to hear anything other than her own fear. She got on her knees and peered into the inky darkness. She tried to lick her lips, but her mouth was too dry. "I'd better take your canteen along with my water bottle," she said. "They might need water."

Tank handed her the canteen, and she put it in her backpack. "Hand me your camera," he said.

She put a protective hand on it. "No, I'll keep it." She turned back to the gaping wound in the side of the mountain.

"Wait!" Chet stepped past Tank. "Take my radio so we can know where you are."

Her fingers closed around the radio he thrust at her. It was a lifeline to the outside, more than she'd had the first time. At least people knew where she was this time and would be working to get them all out. "Thanks." She stuck it in her backpack, then gave a last glance at the sun. She flipped on the light and let the dog go first, then began to crawl after him.

The light behind her dimmed. The tunnel narrowed, and she pressed past the tight squeeze against her shoulders. She stopped, her breathing too ragged to continue. She could do this. Everything in her wanted to back out the same way she'd come, to take a deep breath of cleansing air instead of this stale oxygen that tasted like dust. Samson tugged at the lead, and she let him pull her forward, even though a ragged cry of despair hovered behind her teeth.

Her knees burned from rubbing along the rough floor, even in her jeans. She came to a place where three drifts branched off. She could stand here. The light probed the recesses of the darkness. Above her head, the ceiling rose to a height of about twelve feet. The drifts were shorter, maybe six feet, but still tall enough that she could walk. She pressed the button on the radio. "Chet, Tank, are you there?"

"Haley, where are you?" Tank's voice was like the sweet, clean air she craved.

"At the convergence of three drifts. I'm just catching my breath. The center one leads out to the main mine entrance. I'm signing off now. I'll call again when I get to the main area." She shut off the radio and stuck it back in her pack. The deeper she pressed into the mine, the more her fear mounted. As long as a few minutes' crawl would get her outside, she'd been able to control it. She was going to have to go right past the drift where she and Chloe were trapped.

She heard something and turned to listen. Something moving fast in the loose rock. She swept her light around and saw Oscar come rushing toward her. "Oh, Oscar," she said. The little dog leaped into her arms. She hugged him close as he licked her chin. "You weren't about to be left behind, were you?" Still carrying him, she walked deeper into the mine. Loose gravel crunched under her boots, and she could hear the sound of water dripping. Her terror rose with every step. Why had she thought she could do this? Whimpering, she stopped. "I can't go any farther," she muttered. She backed away, then whirled to go back the way she'd come.

Coward. Failure. She stopped and told herself to take deep breaths. She pressed her forehead against the cool stone wall. "God, are you there?" She listened, but though she didn't hear anything, she felt a warm wave of comfort wash over her. She'd been furious with God, but she'd never doubted he existed. How would she feel if he failed her at the end of this drift? What if she found Brooke and Joy dead? She slammed her eyes shut. *Please, no, God.*

Did that make him less sovereign? He had the right to do

what he wanted with his creation. Standing in the dark tunnel with only a pinpoint glow to light the way, she remembered hearing her sister's life ebb away. Haley didn't deserve to have a happy life when her sister had none.

God is good, but he's not safe. She remembered Tank's comment. Ever since Chloe died, she'd been looking for safe. But life was never safe. She knew that now. Maybe that's why she'd been attracted to photography. She could freeze life just the way she wanted it, pose it to make it perfect. She'd been frozen behind her camera, just like everyone told her—similar to the perpetual winter of Narnia under the rule of the White Witch. She didn't deserve God's grace though. She tried to remember what the book had said about the deeper magic. Her fingers were stiff as she pulled it from her pack and shone her light on it.

"It means," said Aslan, "that though the Witch knew the Deep Magic, there is a deeper magic still which she did not know. Her knowledge goes back only to the dawn of time. But if she could have looked a little further back, into the stillness and the darkness before Time dawned, she would have read there a different incantation. She would have known that when a willing victim who had committed no treachery was killed in a traitor's stead, the Table would crack and Death itself would start working backward."

Death would start working backward. Death had dropped into her life at age eight and had warped her life. Could God turn it around and restore the lost years? Haley wanted to find out. She dropped to her knees and opened her heart to the healing warmth of God's love.

Twenty-Seven

The suffocating blanket of dust began to lift. Marley coughed and felt around for Brooke. She touched her small body curled next to Joy. Marley laid her hand over Brooke's chest. Her heart still beat. She checked Joy and was relieved to find both girls still alive. She grappled with her backpack and found the zipper in the dark. There was another flashlight in there. Her fingers closed on the cold, hard metal, and she withdrew the light and flipped it on. Nothing.

She shook it and tried again. The blackness was complete. It was like being locked in a closet with no way out. She stuffed her knuckles into her mouth to keep from crying out. They were going to die in here. No one knew where they were. This hateful wilderness. It had taken her sister; now it was going to take her and Brooke. She had to try, though. They couldn't just curl up here and die of starvation and thirst.

She felt in her pack for a bottle of water. There it was. She pulled it out and uncapped it, then ran her hands up Brooke's

body until she found her lips. "Come on, sweet girl, wake up."
She dribbled some water into Brooke's mouth. The little girl
coughed and sputtered.

"I want my daddy," she wailed.

"Shh, shh, we'll see Daddy soon." She hated to lie to the
child. "Let's go for a walk."

"It's dark."

"I know." She patted Joy's face and tried to rouse the girl, but
Joy refused to respond. She was going to have to leave her here.
Marley couldn't risk sitting here and having another cave-in trap
her and Brooke. She stood and took Brooke's hand. "Come
along, Brooke. Let's see if we can find a way out." She slid her
hand along the wall, and they moved a few feet, then her hand
felt emptiness. The tunnel turned here. She felt a draft and wondered if there was more than one tunnel. Shuffling sideways, she
waved her hand in the darkness until she felt the opposing wall.
Another drift led off here. Which way should she go?

In her mind, she flipped a coin and chose the left drift. Then
she heard Joy's voice crying out in panic. She hesitated, not
wanting to go back.

"I want Joy," Brooke said.

Marley shrugged. "Okay." She turned toward the way she'd
come. "Joy, over here."

"I'm scared," Joy sobbed in the darkness. "I can't see anything."

"I'll keep talking. Our flashlight was broken when the ceiling
fell. We're okay though. Just come this way." Marley kept up the
chatter until she felt Joy's hand. "Now we're all together." At
least they'd die together.

Samson strained eagerly at the leash, and Haley knew he'd picked up Brooke's scent. She let him pull her along until they came to a fork. He yanked her toward the drift that led to where Chloe died. "No, Samson, not that way." She tried to tug him toward the front entrance, but he planted his feet and barked. Oscar joined the cacophony. "Traitor," she told him.

Could they have moved from the front? Haley hadn't considered they might be wandering around in the dark. It was a good thing she'd brought the search dog. She radioed Tank and told him what she was doing, then followed Samson.

She so didn't want to go down this drift. Though she understood now that God had forgiven her, the thought of reliving the nightmare made her shudder. Her stump ached, but she pressed on. She couldn't quit now when she was so close.

The dogs stopped and sniffed. Haley swept the ground with the flashlight and saw where the ground had fallen away. Samson stepped cautiously to the edge and looked down. He barked, and Haley gulped. She hoped that didn't mean Brooke and Joy were down there. She edged around the hole, then swept the light down into the recesses. She moved down the drift, and the dog followed without a complaint. She was tempted to start calling for them. If they were down this drift, surely that meant they'd survived the cave-in and were ambulatory.

The dog began to strain harder at the leash. He barked, then half-dragged her. She stumbled and went down on her stump. The pain encased her knee. She rubbed it and staggered back to her feet. "Joy!" she called. "Brooke, can you hear me? It's Haley." She thought she heard something and called again.

Joy's voice answered her. "Haley? Haley, over here."

She didn't need their voices other than for comfort. Samson knew right where he was going. Her wavering light picked up three figures huddled together against the wall. Joy had blood caked on her forehead, and a bruise marred Brooke's left cheek, but Haley had never seen a more beautiful sight than the two children. Her gaze went to Marley. Her slacks were filthy and torn.

Joy stood and ran into Haley's arms while Samson barked with excitement and ran to lick Brooke's face. She put her arms around him. "Nice doggy," she said.

Haley stood with her sister in her arms. She'd failed Chloe, but she'd come through for Joy. And she'd faced down her fears. She clung to her sister in a fierce embrace. "Let's get out of here," she said. Marley said nothing, but she lifted Brooke in her arms and followed Haley out of the mine.

13

Tank couldn't let go of his daughter. She smelled of dirt and dust, but he'd never inhaled a sweeter scent. She held him just as tightly. He opened his other arm and pulled Haley into the circle, then Libby and Joy joined them as well. His family. He'd almost lost them.

Brooke pulled away. "Daddy, you're squeezing me."

"Sorry, baby." He released her, and she wiggled to be let down. "Go play with Samson."

"He and Oscar found me," she said. "And Haley."

"Go thank them." He patted her on the bottom, and she ran off to squat beside Oscar and pull him onto her lap.

"I can never begin to thank you," he said, squeezing Haley around the waist.

"You already did." Her eyes were luminous. "I had to go in there, Tank. I had to face my fears. And I found God was waiting in the darkness."

"Oh Haley, that's wonderful!" Libby embraced her. Joy gave her a shy hug as well.

"I discovered something out here waiting too," Tank said. "I'd trusted in my own strength about so many things. I realized God delights in using the weak and fearful."

Haley poked him in the ribs. "Are you calling me a weakling?"

Her grin told him she wasn't offended. "The people who are the strongest are those who know they can't do anything on their own. You showed your true strength today." He wished he could kiss her right here in front of everyone, but he didn't want to embarrass her. They had a lot to discuss.

"I'm ready to go home," Libby said, yawning hugely. "I don't think I slept at all last night."

"I don't think any of us did." Tank turned with his arm still around Haley. "Let's go home."

The group walked back to the planes. Chet had his daughter in custody, and Tank knew it wasn't easy for him. Marley's face was set in a sullen scowl. She didn't seem to care that she'd nearly gotten them all killed. They all piled into planes and took off for Stalwart. Chet let a trooper from Anchorage take Marley on to the bigger city. He could barely look at her before returning to pilot the plane Tank and Haley rode in. Libby sat in the front with Chet, and Brooke sat on Tank's lap. Joy rode with Augusta in another plane.

Tank could see the side of Chet's face. It looked set and pale. Poor guy. It had to be hard to discover his daughter had nearly killed his granddaughter. The next few months wouldn't be pleasant for Chet.

Tank scooted over beside Haley, and she leaned her head against him and sighed. "I've never been so tired in my life." She pulled her backpack out of the way, then unzipped it. "Want your canteen back?" she asked, raising her voice above the roar of the plane's engines.

"Sure." She pulled it out and handed it to Tank. She frowned, then pulled out the plastic bag of pictures and showed them to him. "I forgot about these." Oscar jumped onto her lap, and she adjusted him so she could see.

"Let's have a look," he murmured in her ear. He settled Brooke against his right shoulder, then took a pack of photos and began to flip through them.

He stopped at the final picture. Two men stood in the moonlight. The fast film had caught both faces. "That's Joe Wooten," he whispered, showing Haley the picture.

Haley's eyes widened. "And Chet's holding a gun on him."

"When did you take this?"

"The night we arrived," she murmured in his ear.

Tank laid the pictures on his leg. "Any more?"

She shook her head.

"This was just two days before we found Joe," Tank said.

"This makes no sense. Why would he arrest Joe and not say anything about it?"

"Is it my imagination, or are we losing altitude?" she whispered in his ear.

His head swiveled. "You're right." He leaned over the front seat. "Hey, Chet, what's wrong? It feels like were going down."

"Something's wrong with the engine. I'm going to have to land her."

There was something in his voice Tank didn't like. A hint of grim determination. He exchanged glances with Haley.

"I think we're in trouble," she whispered. "He saw me take that picture of him. He must be the one trying to get it back. He knows we're back here looking at them."

"My rifle is behind the seat," Tank said in her ear. "I'll try to get to it when we stop."

The plane dipped lower, then settled on top of a lake. Chet cut the engines, then pulled his gun. "Don't go for your rifle, Tank. I'm sorry it's come to this. Everybody out." He opened his door, then yanked open Haley's door and motioned for her to get down. He grabbed a plastic bag by his feet.

Libby was sleeping, but she jerked awake. "What's going on?" she asked, rubbing her eyes. Her gaze went to the gun in Chet's hand.

"Get out of the plane, Libby," Chet snapped. "Tank, put Brooke on the seat."

"She's your own flesh and blood, Chet. You can't want to hurt her." He'd jump Chet if he had to, gun or no gun. He wasn't going to meekly let him kill them all.

"I'm not going to. Let her sleep on the seat. This won't take long." He gestured with the gun again. "Don't make me shoot you in front of her."

Tank laid her down on the seat and pressed a kiss on her forehead. She murmured but didn't awaken. He climbed down from the plane to join the women. The cold water took his breath away and came nearly to his thighs. Haley and Libby were on shore, but Chet stood close by to make sure Tank did as he was told. Tank slogged through the water. He heard a splash behind him and looked back to see Oscar swimming toward them.

"You tried to get the pictures before we found them, didn't you?" Haley asked. She picked up her wet dog.

"I never wanted to hurt anyone." Chet pulled out handcuffs and cuffed Tank. "I don't think the women will give me too much trouble."

Tank's mind raced, trying to make sense of it. Nothing clicked into place. He couldn't get his mind around the fact that his own father-in-law would want to kill him. And Libby and Haley. Why?

"Joe Wooten was helping my mother smuggle artifacts from the dig, wasn't he?" Haley asked, her voice neutral. "And you looked the other way. Or were you on the take too?" She stopped.

"Move," Chet ordered. He gestured with the gun, and the small troop walked toward the woods.

It clicked into place for Tank. "Did Leigh see you and Joe hauling out artifacts? You killed your own daughter?"

"I loved my daughter!" Chet said, raising his voice. "I wouldn't hurt a hair on her head. But Joe . . ." he broke off.

Tank's mind raced. "She came to you, didn't she? Leigh told you what she'd seen Joe doing." He stopped. "She saw Joe set fire to the Walsh house, didn't she? She was so upset the night after the fire. She changed then too, grew quieter and more discontented. I thought it was the fire. She didn't know how to handle it. You told Joe, and he killed her, didn't he? Did he drug her so she couldn't swim?" He wasn't sure if any of this was right, but when Chet's face changed, he knew he'd hit paydirt.

"He killed my baby girl. He had to die for that. I didn't know it, not at first. When you asked me about the pills you found at the house, I knew then that he'd drugged her. She would have had no reason to have her mother's sleeping pills." Chet shrugged. "When I confronted him that night, he admitted it. He wrote a fake prescription for you, Tank, to cover himself. He was afraid she was going to turn us in. I told him I'd handle her, but he took it into his own hands. She saw me set fire to the cabin, but she would never have turned me in. I hated that she had to see that. It hurt me to see her cry." He wiped his eyes on his sleeve, but his gun never wavered.

"You killed my parents?" Haley asked, her voice quiet and strained. "Wait, you're the man my father was blackmailing, right? What did he have on you?"

"I think I know," Tank said slowly. "You killed Queenie, didn't you? It always seemed odd she would have a heart attack and drown in the bathtub. She'd never had any heart trouble."

Chet scowled. "You think you're clever, don't you? Queenie was going to leave me. I couldn't let that happen."

"My father saw you?"

Chet's nod was reluctant. "He stopped by the house to talk about the next shipment of artifacts. He saw us through the bathroom window. It was fine at first, but then he got greedy. He wanted more and more of the take. Joe said he'd take care of it."

"There's no need to kill us. It's going to come out, Chet."

"How?" He grinned, a humorless grimace. "I'm the law in these parts. I'm not going down." Chet sighed and rubbed his forehead. "You were like a son to me, Tank. Why did you have to get involved in this?" He held out his hand. "I'll take those pictures now, Haley. The negatives too."

She handed them over. "What are you going to do to us?"

"Why, nothing." Chet glanced around. "The predatory bear should be around here somewhere. This is near where Kipp was killed. He should take care of all of you." He opened the plastic bag and upended the contents on the ground. Reeking garbage: old hamburger and french fries, a half-eaten bag of potato chips, and donuts.

Libby stared at him. "I don't know you, Chet," she said in a stunned voice.

"Sorry, Libby. I hate this more than you know."

"I hope there's a lot of money in those artifacts that makes it worth this," Tank said.

"Oh there is," Chet assured him. "I have a collector who will buy the whole lot for two million dollars. I don't have to share it now either. I'll go back to Stalwart with the story of how the plane went down, and how we were attacked by the bear. We camped out, and the bear ravaged the camp. Only Brooke and

I escaped alive. If I'm lucky, there won't be much found of your bodies."

Tank had to figure out a way to get free. He strained at the cuffs, but even his muscles couldn't move the steel that encased his wrists. He sent a pleading look toward Haley and Libby.

Something crashed in the trees, and Haley jumped. Her face went white. She looked around for a weapon. All Haley had was her walking stick. That would do little to deter a bear bent on finding its next meal.

Chet began to back away. "I think I'll watch from the safety of the plane. Besides, I want to make sure Brooke doesn't see it."

The crashing came again, then a grunt Tank recognized as a bear's. Adrenaline surged. He couldn't die here, not like this. He sent a prayer up for help.

The brush parted, and a big brown bear wandered out. Tank recognized the jagged ear with a feeling of despair. "Move away slowly," he told the girls. "See if you can find a tree, or back into the water." Browns liked water, but maybe this big guy would back off. Looking at the gaunt animal, he knew his hope for the foolishness it was. This bear was desperate, the most dangerous kind.

The bear dropped to all fours and popped its jaws. It huffed and laid back its ears. "Get ready," Tank said. "It's about to charge." He backed away slowly. "Cluster around me so we look bigger to it." The women moved to either side of him. Oscar began to bark ferociously.

Chet still stood behind the women and had not yet made the safety of the plane. Tank knew the trooper was afraid to move quickly for fear of inviting an attack. Bears sensed weakness as well as they did carrion.

"Do you have your bear spray?" he asked Haley.

"I took it off when I went into the mine," she whispered. Terror made her voice tremble.

The bear popped its jaws again and charged. "Don't run, it might be a test charge," Tank said urgently. Then he saw the way the bear looked directly at them. This was one bruin that wasn't going to veer away. "Run!" he shouted. He wheeled and shoved Libby and Haley with his chest. He expected to feel claws shredding his back at any moment. He spared a glance over his shoulder and saw another bear charge from the brush. It ran directly at the predatory bear. Miki!

Tank wanted to cheer, but instead he turned and raced toward the plane with the women. If one of them could get to his rifle, they might pull this out yet.

Zing! A bullet buzzed by his head. He ducked and dived into the water and moved around the tail wing of the plane. The women moved around the nose and joined him. "Get my gun. It's behind the seat."

Libby nodded and clambered into the plane. She slid feet first back into the water with the rifle in her hand. "Is it loaded with shot or drugs?"

"Drugs. But they'll drop a man even quicker than they will a bear." He peered out the end of the plane and saw Chet approaching. "Don't miss your first shot, Libby," he said.

"I won't." She took aim and pressed the trigger. A dart popped from the rifle and dug into Chet's thigh.

He swore and grabbed at it. Chet was trying to move through the water, but his motions slowed. He listed to one side, then crashed to the water. Behind him, the battle of the bears continued. Miki was smaller, but better fed and stronger.

"Get him before he drowns," Tank said. "And get the key to these cuffs. I need to help Miki."

Haley ran forward and managed to flip Chet over onto his back. She supported his head above the water. Libby laid the gun on the floor of the plane and ran to help her.

She fished out the key and handed it to Haley. "Get Tank unlocked. I'll hold up Chet."

Haley took the key and rushed to Tank. He turned so his hands faced her, and she unlocked the cuffs. Once free, he grabbed the rifle and ran to the shore. Oscar was going nuts—running in circles, he was barking like they were in a circus act and he was giving them orders. "Call your dog," he yelled back to Haley. He didn't want the dachshund to get hurt.

The bears' ferocity was enough to frighten the most stoic man. He tried to aim at the big bear, but Miki kept getting in the way. With a last growl, Miki lunged, and the predator turned tail and ran. Tank aimed a dart into its disappearing flank, and the shot traveled true. The bear disappeared from sight, but he knew he'd find the bear a few feet into the forest.

Miki and Oscar sniffed noses, and then Miki ambled off into the forest. Tank cautiously followed. "I've got to secure the bear while I can," he said. "You two get back in the plane and radio in for help. Call Anchorage and get some troopers out here."

Haley hesitated. "Don't go alone, Tank."

He turned back to her and took her in his arms. "I'll be okay, Haley. And we have a lot to talk about." He kissed her quickly, then hurried after the bears. When he reached the forest, he moved cautiously. The old bear was a large mound of reddish brown fur. The drugs had taken it down. He knelt and checked the animal. Dead. The battle with Miki combined with the drugs and its poor condition had finished it off. A kinder end than Chet had planned for them.

Twenty-Eight

Stalwart buzzed with the news of Trooper Chet Gillespie and his daughter both being taken into custody. Within hours, troopers from Anchorage arrived and began hauling out crates of artifacts from the dig. The Walshes' bodies were going to be exhumed for autopsy. All the tentacles of the plot would be exposed.

Bixby wandered around the scene barking orders. He stopped Tank when no one was looking. "Looks like I owe you an apology," he said gruffly. He looked at the ground, and his cheeks were flushed. He finally looked up. "I'm never going to like you, Lassiter."

"I know. But regardless of what you think, I loved Leigh."

"Not enough to give up anything for her."

"I thought you said you owed me an apology. This hardly sounds like one."

Bixby's face reddened. "You like rubbing it in, don't you? You like making me look like a fool. Don't think I don't know people are snickering at me. But at least I cared enough about Leigh to try to find out the truth."

"Yeah, you cared about her. And I can thank you for that."

Bixby regarded him with a suspicious tilt to his eyebrows. "Are you making fun of me?"

"Nope." Tank thrust his hands in his pockets. "I'd better let you get back to work." A soft answer might turn away wrath, but it was hard to do when he wanted to tell Bixby what he really thought. A small part of him wondered if the trooper was right.

&

Haley sat in Tank's cabin and looked out the window into the yard. Oscar was curled up on top of Miki's back. She grabbed her camera and stepped to the door. Easing it open, she snapped some pictures, then went back to her seat at the table. Libby handed her a cup of coffee, and she took it with an absent-minded nod.

Libby sat in the chair beside her. "You seem deep in thought. Are you okay?"

"I guess."

"Want to talk about it?"

Now might be a good time. The film team had gone off to produce a TV special of the last days of bear activist Kipp Nowak, Augusta had flown to Anchorage with Joy to buy the girl some new clothes, and Brooke was down for a nap. This time, nothing could keep the girl awake. Haley could use some woman-to-woman advice before Tank came back from town. "Tank told me he loved me. Do you think he means it?"

A smile began to play around Libby's mouth. "I knew it," she said with a triumphant clench of her fist. "Why on earth would you even doubt it?"

"He told me during an emotionally charged moment. I thought he might be reacting that way because of Brooke's disappearance." She ran her hand over the blue and white gingham tablecloth to avoid looking at Libby.

"Tank doesn't say things he doesn't mean. Have you two talked since?"

Haley shook her head. "There's been no time. He had to document the kill and turn over the carcass to the State, give a statement to the troopers. It's just as well. I don't know what to do." She raised her gaze and directed it at Libby. "I love him, but I don't know if I can live here, Libby."

"I thought you got over your fear when you went into the mine."

"I did, but I'm still a city girl." She pulled on her shirt. "Rebecca Beeson silk tees. Joe's jeans. I love shopping and dining out. I like going to plays and museums. There's nothing like that here."

"You'd have Tank and Brooke."

"I know, and that's a strong draw, but is it enough for a lifetime? I've been praying about it, but I'm not getting any clear direction. I would hate for him to end up being unhappy with me because I'm so different from him. I'd be giving up who I am inside. I'm afraid I'd resent Tank after a while."

"I see what you mean, but I've never seen two people more right for one another. I'm sure you can work it out."

"I just don't see how."

"Talk to Tank about it. Here he comes now."

Haley heard the rumble of the truck, and her heart slammed against her ribs. Would she always react this way when Tank appeared? She stood and rubbed damp palms against her jeans. Oscar began to bark, and she saw Tank scoop him up as Miki lumbered away.

"I'll be in the garden," Libby said with a wink. She crossed the wood floor and exited the back door.

The way Tank's face lit up when he saw Haley made her feel even more nervous. "Hi," she said.

"Hi yourself." He dropped Oscar to the floor and approached her with a confident grin. He put his hands on her shoulders and leaned down to kiss her.

She leaned into him and kissed him back. He smelled like the wilderness—fresh air, sunshine, and spruce. Leaving him would be the hardest thing she ever did. She broke the embrace and stepped back. "We need to talk," she said.

"Somehow I don't like the sound of that." His gaze searched hers, but he dropped his hands and stepped back. He folded his arms across his chest. "I'm listening."

"Can we sit down?" Without waiting for an answer, she walked to the sofa and sat on it with her good leg tucked under her. She patted the spot beside her.

He approached slowly. "Before you start, let me say that I love you, Haley. I love your spirit that surges up no matter what the adversity, I love the way you tilt your head when you're listening, I love the color of your hair when the sun strikes it and it shines like a new penny. I love everything about you. And if you think having only one leg bothers me, you're mistaken."

A glow started somewhere inside at his words. She wet her lips. "It's not that, Tank. I love you too."

He straightened and slipped his arm around her. "You do? I was afraid you were about to tell me to buzz off." He nuzzled her neck. "I know I'm rushing you. We can take it slow. I can wait. We could get married in October maybe."

She laughed and pushed him away. "That's slow? And how can we have a serious conversation when I can't think?"

"Thinking is highly overrated." He sat back and laced his fingers together over his crossed legs. "Okay, spill it."

"We're so different, Tank. I don't think I can live here forever. I've only been here a month, and I'm already missing the malls and the theaters."

He regarded her with a sober expression. "I'm a bear biologist, Haley. I have to work where the bears are. I guess I could work in a zoo or something, but I'd sure stagnate in a place like that after all my work with wild bears."

"I know. And I'd stagnate here. I don't think there's an answer. If you gave up your life for me, you'd grow to resent me, and if I gave up everything for you, I'm afraid I'd grow to resent you."

He rubbed his forehead silently. "I don't want to lose you, Haley."

"I don't know what the answer is, Tank. I think I should go back to Phoenix."

His smile was wry when it finally came. "What a blow to my ego. If you can forget me by going back home, then we didn't have much."

"I don't think I can forget you," she said softly. "But I think I have to try." Her vision blurred, and pressure filled her sinuses. She sniffled, and he handed her his handkerchief. "Thanks."

"You're afraid of really living, Haley." He flicked his finger at her camera. "You hide behind your camera instead of stepping out and engaging life. You're so afraid you'll fail at something that you won't even try."

"Maybe. I've failed at plenty of things, Tank, and I'd hate to fail at the most important thing."

"I think we have something special, Haley. Will you agree to pray with me about it for a month? I believe God will show us the way if we ask him."

"Okay. I'm still learning about this praying stuff, but I'm willing to listen to what he has to say."

He took her in his arms. "Just for a little while, let's forget that you're a city girl and I'm a country boy."

His lips found hers, and she found she was very willing to forget all their differences, at least for now.

13

Haley leaned against the headrest of the car. The parking lot, otherwise known as I-10, stretched as far as she could see. The bright Arizona sunshine beat through the windshield of her Mazda Tribute in a blinding curtain of light. She fanned her face, still hot though she had the air-conditioning going full blast.

"I've never seen so many cars," Joy said in awe. She squinted. "I should have brought my sunglasses." Joy had been with them for two months now. She'd agreed to move in with Augusta and see how she adjusted to Arizona. She hated the heat but loved the sunshine.

Haley missed Tank with an ache that dogged her every minute of the day. She kept telling herself it would get easier, but even taking Joy to the Scottsdale ArtWalk failed to lift her out of the doldrums, even though she'd gotten some great pictures. She sighed and fingered the camera around her neck.

"I miss Alaska," Joy said, unconsciously echoing Haley's thoughts.

"So do I." What was she doing here? Haley's gaze swept her beloved Valley of the Sun. This was a place, not her life. She glanced at the visor where she'd jotted a verse from Psalm 56:3. *Whenever I am afraid, I will trust in You.* Fear of making another mistake had ruled her life for so long. The thought of change terrified her. Stepping out to a new life was like looking down into a pit of black water. It was easier to go through life one day at a time on the bank without stirring the waters.

The thought struck her in a way she'd never considered. If she did that long enough, she might forget she was alive. Was she going to let her fear of living ruin her chance for happiness with Tank? Her life was what she allowed God to make of it, the path she chose to follow. She could stay here in Phoenix with her life in a nice, controlled, linear path, or she could step through a doorway that led to hills and valleys, joy and despair. Was the joy worth the threat of pain?

She edged onto the shoulder and drove to the exit. Hope began to spring up in her chest like a plant reaching for the sunshine. She'd watched the plants do that in the Alaskan springtime. Maybe spring had finally come to her heart.

"What are you doing?"

"I'm going to quit plodding on a familiar path. I'm going to go home and pack."

"Pack for what?"

"I'm going to Alaska to tell Tank I'll marry him."

"Yahoo!" Joy bolted upright in the seat. "Can I come too?"

"I thought you loved the sunshine."

"I do." Her smile dimmed. "I wish I could live there in the summer and here in the winter."

"Don't we all?" Haley turned onto Estrella Parkway toward her subdivision. Fear still slicked her palms, but she would always regret it if she didn't at least try. She parked in the concrete driveway and ran toward the front door. Joy followed her. Oscar met them at the door.

"Call the airline and get me a ticket while I pack," Haley told her.

"What about Augusta?"

"She'll be home from shopping soon. I'll tell her then. The two of you can join me for the wedding." Haley hurried across the tiled floor to her bedroom. She dragged the biggest suitcase she owned down from the shelf and began to pack. The doorbell rang, but she ignored it. Joy could get rid of whoever it was.

Oscar nosed among the clothes and grabbed a pair of socks in his mouth. He crouched over it as if it were his personal toy. She turned at the sound of heavy feet on the tile. Tank stood in the doorway, his massive shoulders nearly spanning the doorjamb.

"Hi," he said. He shuffled and stared at her as if he'd like to gobble her up.

Haley started to tremble. She wet her lips. "I've never seen you without a flannel shirt." He didn't look like Paul Bunyan today. His pale but muscular legs stretched out impossibly long from under denim shorts. "And I've never seen legs that white. I think I'd better get my sunglasses before they blind me."

He grinned. "Woman, the things I go through for you. I might even get a suntan if you give me time." He took a step closer to her. "What would you say if I told you I figured out a way for us to live in Alaska part of the year and here part of the year?"

"How? Your job requires you to be on call." It was enough to see him and know she was right to make the sacrifice. She didn't want to hope for more.

"I took a seasonal job in the park, and I got another job with the Phoenix Zoo. I'll be in charge of constructing a new bear habitat. It will be the first one of its kind in the world. They're excited to let me continue my research in Alaska in the summer. I think it's the perfect compromise." His gaze went to her suitcase. "You're packing." His voice held a trace of disappointment.

She took a step toward him. "I had a yen to see Paul Bunyon."

His eyes widened, and his gaze went to the book on home canning that lay on top of her warm clothing. "Me?"

She nodded, and the words she wanted to say caught in her throat. Instead, she reached up and slipped her camera from her neck, then held it out to him.

Tank's eyes widened, and he began to smile. He took the camera and laid it on top of her suitcase. "Step out from behind that camera, Haley, and experience life with me. You won't be sorry."

"I could never be sorry for loving you." He opened his arms, and she stepped into them. "I'll marry you on one condition."

"Anything," he murmured, his lips in her hair.

"Tell me your real name."

He raised his eyebrows and grinned. "After the wedding. I don't want you to back out."

"Nothing could make me back out. Give."

Amusement lit his eyes. "It's Elmer."

"Come on, your real name."

"I'm telling you, it's Elmer. You still want to marry me and be Mrs. Elmer Lassiter?"

Her jaw dropped. "You're serious."

"As a heart attack. If we're blessed with a son, you have to promise me you won't ask to name him after me."

"Can I name a girl after Augusta?"

"You can have whatever you want," he said, pulling her closer. "I'm going to spoil you so rotten no one else would ever have you. I'm not like your parents, Haley. I'll love you unconditionally as long as I live."

His lips touched hers, and Haley wrapped her arms around his neck. She didn't need her camera or her books. God had given her a second chance, and she was going to seize it with both hands.

Acknowledgments

Alaska is such a vast and wondrous place that the research was even more daunting than usual. I put out a plea on my writers' loop at American Christian Fiction Writers (www.americanchristianfictionwriters.com) to ask if anyone lived in Alaska, and two super writers were quick to offer to read the manuscript and offer suggestions. Any errors are mine of course! My special thanks to Kristen Blincoe and Amy Bang.

I'm blessed beyond all measure to work with my Thomas Nelson family: editor Ami McConnell, who has taught me so much with every book; Amanda Bostic, who keeps us all on schedule and smiling while we do it; visionary publisher Allen Arnold; his assistant and my fellow Hoosier and friend Lisa Young; publicist extraordinaire Caroline Craddock; creative marketing genius Jennifer Deshler; and amazing cover designers Mark Ross and Belinda Bass. I've grown to love and appreciate the Thomas Nelson sales staff more and more. You all are the greatest, and I wish I could give you all a big box of DeBrand truffles!

I'm also fortunate to work with Erin Healy as editor. Writers who think all they have to do is write a book and it's done have never worked with a good editor and realized how much better it can be after a topnotch editor gets through with it. Ami and Erin both bring so much to the finished product. I'm a revision junkie now. If you like my books, thank my editors!

Thanks to my agent, Karen Solem, who has held my hand through more than one panic attack this year. You're the best, Karen!

To my critique partners—Kristin Billerbeck, Diann Hunt, and Denise Hunter—who took time out of their own writing days to go over my manuscript and make sure I got this right, thanks a bunch, friends! And thanks to friend Robin Miller who read the manuscript for me as well.

And as always, my heartfelt thanks to my wonderful family. My husband, Dave; my son, David; and my daughter, Kara, have been my cheering section from the first day I sat at the computer to write, even during those long first seven years when no one wanted to buy anything. I love you!

And devoted thanks to my Constant Companion, the Lord Jesus Christ, who has put me in my "sweet spot" and allowed me to write the stories of my heart.

ESCAPE TO
BLUEBIRD RANCH

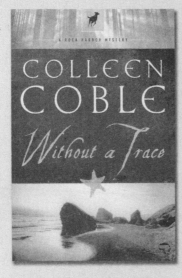

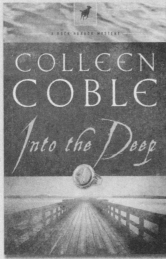
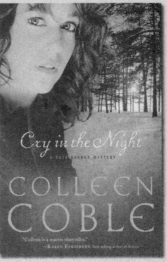